Kathryn Pinas

Long Hill Home
by Kathryn Pincus

Published by

köehlerbooks™

210 60th Street
Virginia Beach, VA 23451
212-574-7939
www.koehlerbooks.com

 **bitlit**

A **free** eBook edition is available
with the purchase of this print book.

CLEARLY PRINT YOUR NAME ABOVE IN UPPER CASE

Instructions to claim your free eBook edition:
1. Download the BitLit app for Android or iOS
2. Write your name in **UPPER CASE** on the line
3. Use the BitLit app to submit a photo
4. Download your eBook to any device

To Bob, my home.

LONG HILL
HOME

KATHRYN PINCUS

VIRGINIA BEACH
CAPE CHARLES

CHAPTER 1

KELLY: SEPTEMBER 23, 2011

KELLY MALLOY GAZED through her eighteenth-floor window to distract herself from her uncomfortable conversation with Jack Barnard. His booming voice rattled the speakerphone on her desk.

"Come on, Kelly, you have to withdraw your motion to dismiss the appeal. It was only late by one day."

She turned in her chair away from the window to face the speakerphone, taking a deep breath to calm herself. "Jack, the law clearly says it is a matter of jurisdiction, and the court has no discretion."

"Think about it, Kelly." His incessant arguing became a dull buzz in Kelly's ears as she turned in her chair again toward the window. She tuned out the bombastic attorney on the line and tuned in the remnants of the autumn sunset and the colorful treetop fringe that lay just beyond the city. Her eyes followed the snaking dark line of the Brandywine River as it trailed away from the office buildings of Wilmington's business district and into Trolley Square, a neighborhood of densely packed town homes and apartment buildings, quaint shops, restaurants and bars. The Highlands neighborhood came next, with its towering oak trees, meticulous green lawns and grand homes. Kelly's eyes rested on the spot in the Highlands where her home stood, and she imagined herself there, ensconced in its solid walls and warmth.

The voice from the speakerphone suddenly grew louder, abruptly transporting Kelly back to her office. *"Come on, Kelly, cut me a break! How about for old times' sake?"* Kelly pictured Jack Barnard, all six feet of him, dressed in his usual pressed grey suit, black cowboy boots, and his crocodile belt straining over a mid-life spread. She imagined his face turning red as he leaned over his speakerphone to yell at her while standing in an office only two blocks away from her office. "Mr. Johnson will lose his appeal rights! That's not fair to him!"

Kelly had recently learned that Barnard had just returned from a weeklong fly-fishing trip in Idaho. She pictured him calmly standing knee-deep in a wide river framed by beautiful mountains at the very moment that his client's appeal period lapsed. She spoke carefully—trying to quell her adversary. "You are asking me to do the impossible. The court has no jurisdiction. It cannot take the appeal, and there's nothing I can do about it even if I wanted to."

The voice from the speakerphone became inflamed. "You think you are so fucking high and mighty, with your big law firm practice. You are going to regret this for a long, long time. Mark my words!"

Kelly felt the knot in her stomach tighten. Barnard was known for his harassing and intimidating tactics, which often brought lucrative settlements from corporate defendants lacking fortitude to fight. These tactics were rewarded with tremendous commission checks which paid for his new Jaguar, his tailored suits and his penthouse on the Brandywine River. But this time his venom sounded personal. His menacing tone and his threatening words made her flinch, her stomach tighten, and she was left almost breathless. She looked out the window at her refuge down the road, took a long deep breath, and attempted to sound like she was calm and in control. "Jack, there is no reason to be uncivil or to threaten me. I am going to end this conversation now." She pressed a button on her phone. Her office was silent.

Kelly's secretary, Margaret, poked her blonde curly head through Kelly's doorway. "Tough one, huh?" She offered Kelly the usual pick-me-up: a dish of jellybeans.

Kelly let out a sigh as she grabbed a handful of the colorful treats. "You have no idea. Jack Barnard is such an asshole. That bully thinks he can intimidate me."

"I know, honey, I heard him all the way out here in the hallway. That man is scary. He was in the class ahead of me at Concord High School. I remember one night he beat up some poor kid in the parking lot of the Charcoal Pit, just because the kid was talking trash about Concord's football team. That poor boy left in an ambulance, unconscious. As I recall, Barnard was arrested and everything, but his big lawyer-daddy intervened... he was back in school the next day as if nothing had happened." After a pause, she added, "He goes through secretaries and wives like they're disposable. Supposedly, in his last divorce his ex-wife accused him of abuse. I bet he threw money at her to make her go away quietly."

Kelly popped some more jellybeans and chewed for a moment. "I remember he harassed me once, years ago. I was at O'Malley's Tavern with a bunch of new lawyers celebrating the day that the bar exam results came out. Some of us were dancing to the jukebox. Barnard asked me to dance, and when I declined he grabbed my arm and literally dragged me onto the dance floor. So I screamed over the music that I'd had one too many shots of tequila and was going to be sick, and he let go of me really fast. He had the gall to come back to my table that night and brag that he had been a football player at Texas Tech and that he had all the cheerleaders he wanted. I guess that cowboy swagger doesn't have the same effect on the women of the Delaware bar."

"Well, at least you don't have to see him outside of the occasional case where you unfortunately cross paths." Margaret laughed. "And then I've got your back, girl."

Kelly smiled. "Actually, I sometimes see him fly-fishing when I run along the river in the morning. I always try to slip by quietly, so he doesn't even notice me."

Margaret touched Kelly's elbow gently. "Well, it's Friday and it is quitting time, so let's get out of here and forget about the Jack Barnards of the world until Monday." Margaret walked to her cubicle outside of Kelly's office door, turned off her desk light and pushed a button sending all of her phone calls to voicemail.

She took a cardigan sweater off of her chair, and turned toward Kelly's office. "You coming?"

Kelly sat back in her chair. "You go ahead without me." The knot in her stomach relaxed as she gazed at framed photos on her desk of her daughters, Anna and Grace, and her husband, Dan. Kelly picked up and studied a photograph that captured a moment at the Jersey Shore. Anna, with her long, wavy auburn hair and blue eyes, and little Grace, with her dark brown curls and freckles, peeked up at the camera. They crouched in front of a lopsided sandcastle, smiling in matching pink bathing suits. Dan, wearing blue boarder shorts and black Ray-Bans, stood behind the girls. Kelly admired his tall, lean body, his curly black hair and wide smile. As she rose from her chair she smiled and briefly thought about pressing herself against the skin of Dan's chest on that beach, of feeling its warmth and smelling the salt on his skin.

*****

In the elevator as it descended to the parking garage, Kelly looked at her reflection in the mirrored wall. She was relieved to see that she did not look as tired as she felt. Her oval blue eyes flashed back at her and her chestnut hair fell in waves below her shoulders, framing her fair skin and prominent cheekbones. Her dark blue suit was a little wrinkled after a long day, but it fit nicely over her small frame. Shapely runner's legs extended from her skirt hem to her black pumps. She hurried out of the elevator and walked toward the last car in the parking lot, her blue Volvo.

Within five minutes of pulling out of the downtown parking lot, Kelly was in a different world. Stately homes of brick and stone stood facing each other along narrow roads enveloped by ancient oak trees and green lawns. The neighborhood was flanked by an enormous span of green space known as Rockford Park. Miles of protected woodlands surrounding the park extended to the banks of the Brandywine River. Rockford Tower, a hundred-year-old stone tower, stood sentry at the highest point of the park.

Kelly and Dan had stretched to buy their home in the Highlands. It was a turn-of-the-century Georgian colonial.

Dan had been the architect on a large addition and renovation to the house five years before. After the renovation, he had requested that the owners notify him if they ever decided to sell. His background in historic renovation helped him appreciate its special qualities: a staircase of hand-carved spindles, three working fireplaces, a butler pantry with leaded glass cabinets, a slate-floored mudroom and wide-planked white oak floors. Kelly shared his enthusiasm when she saw the new open kitchen and the light-filled family room leading to a stone patio, a small green lawn and a rectangular swimming pool.

Kelly turned off the radio and pulled into her driveway.

"Mama, you're home!" Anna flung herself into Kelly, wrapping her slim arms tightly around her mother's waist. Anna's football jersey hung from her slight frame and her long auburn hair seemed to rebel against a ponytail holder.

Kelly put her hand around her daughter's ponytail and gave it a playful tug. "I'm so happy to be home with you. What do you say we liberate that hair of yours and find your sister?"

"She's probably up in her room playing with those dumb dolls again," Anna said, as she tried to tuck a renegade hank of hair behind her ear.

"Anna, that is not nice. You know better." Kelly spoke as she removed the hairband and let Anna's hair fly. "I'm going to go upstairs and change into my shorts. I'll get Gracie while I'm up there." She turned to walk out of the mudroom.

"Put your bathing suit on too, Mom, because Dad set up for dinner outside and he said we can swim after."

"That sounds like exactly what I need," Kelly said just as Dan entered the mudroom. He extended one hand holding a glass of white wine and wrapped his other arm around Kelly's waist as he kissed her cheek. "I almost didn't recognize you without a briefcase attached to your hand."

"I know, isn't it great?" Kelly kissed Dan on his lips. "The Johnson appeal went away today, so I have no work this weekend."

Kelly walked upstairs to Gracie's bedroom. Her six-year-old daughter sat on the floor with her back to the door, oblivious to her mother watching. Her hands moved Barbie and Ken around the dollhouse and her sweet little-girl voice created conversations between the figures. Kelly felt overwhelmed by her desire to go wrap her arms around her young daughter, to bury her nose in her hair and to brush her lips against her chubby little-girl cheeks. Loving her children so completely made her feel like the luckiest person alive, but scared her to death at the same time. "Mama!" Grace said, as she finally noticed her there. She sprang to her feet and wrapped her arms around her mother's waist, her head against Kelly's stomach. Kelly touched her nose to Grace's dark curls and inhaled the wonderful scent of her daughter.

"Hey, kiddo. How about dinner by the pool and swimming after?"

"Oh, yeah!" Grace yelped as she ran to get her bathing suit.

Two hours later, in cut-off shorts, Birkenstocks and a faded cotton T-shirt, Kelly lingered at the backyard table with the remnants of dinner spread out around her. As she sipped her second glass of Pinot Grigio, thoughts of Barnard's threats and the now-dead Johnson appeal dissipated into the warm September night. She felt content, watching Anna and Grace splash in the pool and holding Dan's hand across the table.

CHAPTER 2

KELLY: SEPTEMBER 24, 2011

THE SOFT, RHYTHMIC sound of her running shoes and her own steady breathing were the only sounds Kelly heard as she ran along the wooded banks of the Brandywine River. It was a spectacular September morning as the chill began yielding to the sun's warmth. Slices of sunlight pierced the low morning clouds and collided into the river, creating millions of tiny white diamonds on the river's surface. Thick green-and-brown vegetation covered the steep riverbanks. The foliage opened up several hundred feet ahead revealing the historic Breck's Mill, with its solid grey stone exterior and a large wooden wheel spinning quietly in the water.

Kelly slowed as she approached the last and most strenuous part of her run, a long steep ascent from the river's banks, past Rockford Tower and to her home in the Highlands. She had run up this hill hundreds of times and she knew its every rise and bump. It was a formidable foe and a familiar friend. She loved pushing herself when her thighs started to fatigue and her hamstrings complained, because she was running toward her home and her family. She inhaled slowly as she ran through a thicket of trees between the mill and the river and prepared to conquer the long hill home.

Suddenly a searing pain shot through the back of her right leg. *Shit! Did I tear a hamstring?* As she twisted around to grab her injured leg, she saw something small—a dart?—sticking in the back of her thigh. Kelly quickly pulled the piercing object out of her flesh. Her heart raced. *Someone just shot me!*

Staggered by immediate dizziness and nausea, Kelly tried to get to the Breck's Mill parking lot. She could see a few cars and hoped someone would be nearby to help her. Bile rose up in her throat and she retched the sour remnants of her morning coffee. Her legs grew wooden and heavy, and then numb. She could no longer move. "Help!" she yelped weakly to no one in particular as her knees buckled. Then her legs crumpled under her, her vision blurred and little spots of black filled up her head until there was nothing but darkness.

She drifted in an endless black slumber marred only by white-hot flashes of pain. She tried to rouse herself from her horrible nightmare. When she finally regained consciousness, terror flooded her as she realized that she was still entombed in darkness and pain, and her nightmare was only beginning. A rough cloth covered her eyes, allowing only slivers of light where the blindfold tented over her nose. Her eyelashes brushed against the coarse cloth as she blinked furiously, desperate to see anything. A sticky tape covered her mouth and wrapped around her aching head, pressing against her hair. She tried to lift her right hand to uncover her eyes and mouth, but she could not lift her arm. Her wrists were tightly bound behind her back, and they felt lifeless now except for the sensation of pins and needles as the circulation in her arms slowly ceased.

She kicked her legs furiously against what felt like a cold bumpy floor. *A floor? How? Where am I?* She flailed frantically, twisting and arching her back and pushing with her feet, only to fall in a heap back to the cold surface, sobbing into her blindfold. Her mind raced back to her morning run—the sudden, searing pain and nausea and then the blackness. She imagined Dan coming to her rescue. *He must know I'm in danger, and he must be searching for me.*

Kelly's heart raced as she recalled Dan that morning, quietly drinking his coffee and reading the sports section while she had laced up her running shoes. She wished desperately that she could go back to that exact moment and choose differently. If only she had taken their daughters to soccer practice, or

answered an emergency phone call from a client—or had chosen
to do anything but run alone through the woods. Kelly's teeth
chattered uncontrollably and her body shook against the cold
floor. The only sounds were geese calling and the river flowing
nearby.

Suddenly the stillness was broken by the sound of a door
opening, and then footsteps approaching heavily on the hard
floor. Kelly startled as she felt two hands touch her just above
the waist. She began kicking her legs as she tried to scream
through the tape over her lips. Through the dim light that seeped
through her blindfold, she could see the shadow of a large man
kneeling down on the floor and leaning over her. To her horror,
she heard a metal belt buckle hit the hard floor and then she felt
her running shorts and underwear yanked down her legs, over
her running shoes and off of her flailing feet.

A pair of strong hands grabbed her ankles and pulled her legs
apart. Kelly tried to pull and kick, but the unbearable pain and
pressure on her thighs was too much to resist. The naked skin
of a stranger brushed her thighs as his body violently banged up
between her legs, and then....the unthinkable. Pain, humiliation,
shame, anger and nausea all filled her at once. Tears welled up in
her eyes, soaking through the rough blindfold and spilling down
her cheeks. She felt the searing pain of his violent, rhythmic
thrusting. He made soft grunting noises for what seemed like
an eternity, and then, one final shudder. He slumped on top of
her after he finished, breathing heavily and smelling of sweat.

Kelly could barely breathe with her mouth taped shut and
the heavy weight of his spent body lying on her chest. But finally
she felt the weight get up quickly and a shadow passed by her
blindfold. She heard a case open and shut, and then the shadow
approached her again. She braced herself. Her blindfold had
loosened during the attack, and she could see the man's hands
as they passed near her face. They were large, with thick white
fingers and dark knuckle hair. One hand pulled her T-shirt sleeve
up over her shoulder and the other hand held a large needle. The
hand with the needle had a small crescent-shaped scar near the
wrist and a thick gold ring on the ring finger.

Kelly moaned as the needle pierced her shoulder muscle.
Instinctively, she kicked her legs and flailed about for a moment,

but then she felt her muscles shutting down again. Her eyes grew heavy against the rough blindfold and total darkness consumed her for the second time.

*****

Solid black became black dots, which morphed into a thick grey haze. Shouting exploded above Kelly's head, piercing her dark and drowsy state.

"Oh, my God! Michael, come here quick! *Michael! MICHAEL!*"

Kelly braced herself as she felt hands touch her sore head, but this time the hands were gentle. Her head was lifted gingerly and her blindfold was removed carefully. Kelly opened her eyes to see a woman leaning over her. The woman's eyes were wide with alarm, and she kept turning her head and screaming for someone named Michael. The woman's skin was a smooth caramel color, and long black braids fell across her face as she leaned over Kelly to untie her wrists.

"My name is Jen," she said, in a voice that strained to sound soothing and calm. "Don't worry, dear. We're going to help you. You're safe now. I'm just moving you a little to untie your wrists." Kelly had never seen the woman before, and yet she felt an immediate and overwhelming love for her. The woman called Jen stood and unzipped her Nike sweatshirt, exposing a T-shirt with the words *One Love* and the smiling face of Bob Marley. She carefully wrapped her sweatshirt around Kelly's legs, talking to her the whole time. Kelly then noticed a blue plaid blanket tucked around her chest and shoulders. She raised her right hand and tried to touch her mouth where the tape had been. Her fingers were still numb and clumsy.

"*Michael!*" Jen yelled again, looking up the trail. Kelly heard the rapid and high-pitched barking of a small dog and then a man's voice.

"I'm coming, I'm coming. Quit your yelling!"

"It's an emergency!" Jen yelled, as the barking got closer.

A white-and-brown Jack Russell terrier danced around Kelly excitedly and then jumped on her chest. "Ziggy, down!" Jen yelled to the dog. She turned to the tall man jogging down the trail toward them. His jog turned into a sprint when he saw Jen leaning over a body.

"Oh, shit!" he said, as he stopped and bent down next to Kelly. He pulled a cell phone out of his sweatshirt pocket with alarming intensity. Kelly observed their fearful and urgent actions with a dazed detachment. The man dialed the phone and tapped his foot nervously on the ground, waiting for the call to connect. Gold lettering across the front of his sweatshirt read *Temple University School of Medicine.* "Come on, come on," he said repeatedly, and finally, "Hello. We have an emergency and we need an ambulance right away! Oh, and we need the police, too."

Still shivering, Kelly took the sweatshirt off her legs and wrapped it also around her shoulders and chest.

"We found a woman who was tied up and hurt pretty badly. We're in the woods on the north hiking trail of Rockford Park, about one hundred and fifty yards from Rockford Tower. I'll come out in a few minutes so I can flag them down in the parking lot by the tower, and my girlfriend will stay with the injured woman." Kelly saw the man glance down at Kelly's newly exposed legs with a look of alarm. As he was about to hang up the phone, he changed his mind and added, "I'm an ER resident and I have not examined her or anything, but she may be in shock. I think, uhm, it looks like she may have been sexually assaulted." A moment later he said, "I don't know. We just found her a minute ago, about nine-fifteen or so. I don't know how long she's been here."

The man pressed his cellphone against his sweatshirt to speak to Kelly. "The police and ambulance are on their way." He continued to alternately speak and listen to the phone as Kelly watched. The woman sat in the dirt next to her now, holding the small dog and trying to quiet him. Kelly noticed a stray tear rolling out of her left eye and down her cheek. She wondered why this stranger would cry here in the woods.

The man squatted next to Kelly and spoke softly. "Hi. I'm Michael. You're safe now and help is on the way. We're going to wait here with you for an ambulance and the police."

Kelly tried to respond but only yielded a whimper. Michael quieted her.

"Rest now. You can explain things later."

Sirens started getting louder.

Michael looked directly at Jen. "Stay with her. "I'm going to flag them down. I'll be right back." Then he turned and sprinted up the trail toward Rockford Tower.

Kelly started to shudder violently and then sob. The fog obscuring what happened began to clear. She remembered being bound on a cold, hard floor on her back, completely exposed and defenseless to her attacker. Her crying turned to loud sobs, as Jen gently stroked her head and said, "Shhhhh, it's okay, now. It is going to be okay now. You're safe."

CHAPTER 3

CHAD: MAY-JUNE 2011

CHAD WATCHED WITH disgust as his father plucked a drumstick out of the Kentucky Fried Chicken bucket between them and started to tear at the greasy meat. At a mere thirty-nine years old he looked like an old man, with deep grooves in his face from endless hours in the sun, sunken eyes, and a mouth filled with teeth stained dark by chewing tobacco. Unruly tufts of graying hair sprang out from under a dirty baseball cap that had the words *Charlie McCloskey Landscaping* embroidered across its brim. Chad saw bitterness and defeat in his father's eyes.

"You know, your mother used to say, 'Chadbourne is so handsome,' and 'Chadbourne is so smart'." He used a high-pitched voice and a mocking tone to imitate Chad's mother. He stabbed the air between them with the drumstick bone for emphasis as he spoke. "Now look at you. What the hell are you doing with your life? Here you are, eighteen years old and still living with your old man, pushing a lawnmower all day and taking long walks alone in the woods."

"Enough!" Chad said, abruptly pushing back his chair and standing up. He strode through the tiny cluttered kitchen and down the back hall to his bedroom where he collapsed onto his unmade bed. He looked at the large world map on his wall and remembered how his mother had pointed to the places they would explore while describing the adventures that they would share. There were vast blue oceans and wide rivers to sail on, snow-capped Alps, Rockies and Tetons to ski down, remote islands where they would bask in the sun and bathe in waterfalls, and foreign cities filled with museums, cafés and cobblestone piazzas where they would meander.

Chad's gaze moved to the top of his dresser which held numerous treasures that he had collected on the banks of the Brandywine River. Shoeboxes and clear plastic bags contained bird feathers, dried wildflowers, colorful stones, bird nests, eggs, and even a few skeletal remains of small woodland creatures. He wasn't sure why he still felt compelled to pick up these items and bring them home. His mother had brought him with her on "treasure hunts" in the woods when he was a child, but he knew that he should abandon that silly practice now.

Chad tried to drown out his father's words as they echoed in his head. He breathed deeply and listened to the sound of the gurgling river outside his room as he retrieved a worn photograph from his dresser drawer. His mother's gaze seemed to go beyond the photographer, as if she was trying to look past her sad little life in that house in the woods. Long, wavy black hair framed a petite face with a delicate little nose, large almond-shaped eyes and full lips that set firmly against each other in an expression of perpetual sadness. Chad realized now that she had always carried this deep sadness, even when he was a young boy. He did not understand it then, but he could still feel it. Chad put the photograph of his mother down, reclined on his bed, suddenly exhausted, and remembered.

When Chad was thirteen, he started rising from his bed in the morning only after he heard his father's truck driving away down the gravel driveway. His mother always wrapped him in her arms and clung to him when she greeted him in the morning, as if she were clinging to a tree in a windstorm. When he walked to his school-bus stop, he fought the urge to look back at her. He could not bear to carry the image of his mother standing alone on the sagging front porch in her bathrobe and waving her hand, looking so forlorn.

On the way to the bus stop by Breck's Mill, Chad would peer in a small gardener's shed and wish that he could climb inside and hide while the bus rolled by. He used to watch the mallard ducks on the river and envy them: they had the ability to fly away on a whim. This longing filled him as he eventually climbed aboard the school bus with its rows of middle-school students, each one mocking or shunning him. Almost daily, the leader of the seventh grade started a chant as Chad tried to find an empty seat: *"Chad, Chad, he's so sad. His father's a drunk and his mother is mad."*

Chad recalled how his face turned hot with humiliation as he felt the stares and heard the giggles of the other kids on the bus. He remembered how he sat quietly in school, trying merely to be avoided, to be invisible, and how he began to relax as the classroom clock clicked toward dismissal because his mother would be waiting. Chad remembered how he would go to her surely, silently: she was the one person who made him feel whole. They would walk along the sidewalks of the Highlands neighborhood, past large brick homes with the stylishly dressed moms, and nannies unloading groceries and children from expensive SUVs. He and his mother would stop at the base of Rockford Tower and have a drink at a cool water fountain. When the tower was open to visitors, they climbed its circular stairway to an observation deck. From that perch they could see thick green woods to the north and west, tall grey office buildings to the southeast, and the expanse of Rockford Park and the Highlands neighborhood at their feet. Chad remembered the regret and longing as he stood at the top of the tower and watched smiling teenagers throwing Frisbees, young couples kissing as they lay on blankets in the sun, and fathers playing with their children. He recalled looking at the big homes below and imagining that inside their walls, children had normal dinners with parents who spoke lovingly to each other.

Chad realized now that their walks together were not just their shared oasis from their turbulent home life. They were also the times his mother tried her best to give Chad some hope and guidance. He sighed as he remembered one particular day in March of his seventh grade year, as they walked home through the woods counting the early spring flowers emerging from the ground.

"Mom, why did you name me Chad?" he asked as he crouched down to inspect a purple crocus head popping through the soil.

"Chadbourne was my family name," Louisa said.

"What does that mean?" Chad asked, squinting up at his mother.

"Well, as I told you before, I was raised in an orphanage. You know, I had no mother or father to take care of me. So, the only thing I really had to connect me to my family was the name I carried, Louisa Chadbourne." Louisa noticed Chad's eyebrows knit together as he contemplated this explanation. "What's the matter, honey?" Her voice was so filled with love that Chad's heart hurt.

"It's just... uhm, I mean..." Chad stammered. "Oh, Mom!" Chad caught his breath with a loud shudder. "The kids at school make fun of me every day. They call me *Sad Chad* and they laugh at me."

"Oh, baby." Louisa wrapped Chad in her arms. "People can be mean. That's just a fact of life. God knows we have our share of meanness in our family. You can let it make you feel bad about yourself, or you can realize that they are the ones who are wrong and are acting small. Keep being the kind and smart person you are and you'll find good friends with good hearts like you. When we get home you should look at your world map and just think of the possibilities." His mother had hugged him harder then. "And Chad, nothing would be different for you if you had a different name. It's in here that matters," she said, tapping him on his chest.

That was five years ago, and Chad still had no friends. His eyes became moist as he looked at the world map on his wall, and he wondered where his mother was at that moment. He remembered the day she left.

*****

One humid afternoon in late May, Chad ran into his house, eager to tell his mother that he had earned an A on his final History exam and was going to graduate from high school with honors. The house was empty and his mother's station wagon was gone. Chad assumed she had taken a trip to the supermarket, since she rarely went anywhere else in her car. He went to the kitchen to get a Coke and to see if there was anything worth eating in the refrigerator. His hand froze in midair as he reached to open the refrigerator door. An envelope was taped to the door, with red cursive writing on it saying, *My Dearest Chad*. He tore the envelope off the refrigerator, ripped it open and began reading the delicate script written on pale lavender notepaper:

My dearest, sweetest Chad:

You are the best thing that has ever happened to me. Any joy or true love I have experienced in this life was because I had you, my beautiful child.

You are old enough now to understand that I am deeply unhappy. Every day I feel as if I am drowning, and most of the time I just want to give up struggling for air and for light. I cannot continue suffering here like this and I fear that I am dragging you too, my sweet boy, down into the black depths with me.

I need to go somewhere right now and I must go alone. But I carry you always in my thoughts and in my heart. I hope that one day you can understand my choice and my actions. I am doing the only thing that I can think of to help us each find peace, lightness and happiness. Go out and find your happiness. I know you have it in you. My dearest Chad, be strong and follow your sharp mind and your beautiful heart.

I love you more than life itself,

Mom

Chad's eyes burned with tears as he bounded from the house that afternoon. He ran into the woods in a blind rage, crashing through tree boughs and rocks until he fell exhausted on the mossy banks of the river. He was alone now; she had left him. Her warmth, her comfort, her belief in him—gone. He curled his legs up toward his trunk and wrapped his arms around himself like a fetus.

As the woods grew dark and a chill settled on his skin, Chad rose stiffly. He moved with heavy feet toward the dilapidated farmhouse, which no longer felt like home.

He walked up the sagging porch steps, swung open the door, and saw his father sitting at the kitchen table, his head in his hands. An open bottle of Jack Daniels sat on the otherwise empty table.

"Dad!" Rage and pity welled up in him and burned his throat.

"Is she coming back? How can she just leave me?"

Charlie raised his head out of his hands and fury shone from his eyes. "How the hell should I know? She didn't even leave *me* a note." He pointed at the note that Chad had dropped on the kitchen floor. "That woman has been crazy for years. The only reason she stayed on here was because of you. I could never make her happy." His chin quivered as he spoke.

"Jesus Christ!" Chad shouted at his father. "You never even *tried* to make her happy. You criticized her and mocked her and made her cry. You drove her away!"

After his outburst, Chad ran to his bedroom, slammed the door and fell onto his bed. For the first time in his life, he did not care if he angered his father and he did not fear him. Chad peeled off his clothes and climbed into his bed in his boxer shorts. The clock on his nightstand showed it was almost eight-thirty, about three hours before he normally went to bed. He lay motionless, numb, listening to the sounds of the river through his open window. A few minutes later he heard his father's heavy footsteps shuffling down the hallway to what had been the couple's bedroom.

CHAPTER 4

CHAD: JUNE 2011

FOR SEVERAL WEEKS after his mother left, Chad waited for the telephone to ring, or for the sound of his mother's station wagon in the driveway. Every day he ran down the path to the mailbox eager to see her letter, but instead he found only junk mail and an occasional magazine. One afternoon he opened up a large envelope and found his high school diploma inside. He had skipped the graduation ceremony, figuring it would be pointless to attend. He traced his index finger over the words distinguishing him as a graduate with *high honors,* knowing that he had no one to share his accomplishment with.

He went to work with his father every day. Together they drove silently to the job sites and spoke to each other only when necessary.

"Gather up those leaves over there, bag 'em up and put the bags in the truck," or "cut the grass on the north side a little longer today, it's burning out a bit." Chad kept his head down and did his work. Loneliness gnawed at him as he tried to go about his life without her.

One warm June evening, as Chad carried steaming cartons of Chinese food and a six-pack of Miller Lite into the house, the sound of the telephone ringing in the kitchen made him jump. He ran into the kitchen and deposited the bags quickly, but his father beat him to the phone.

"Hello? Yes, I'm Charlie McCloskey."

"What is it, Dad? Is it about Mom?" Chad asked, impatiently.

His father waved him off. "How long do you think it's been parked there?" Charlie said into the phone. After listening for a moment, he added, "We don't know where she is, she just up and left. She left a note for my son saying she was going away. We didn't do nothin' funny with her, if that's what you're thinking."

For once, Chad didn't wince in embarrassment at his father's manner of speech. His urgency to find out about his mother silenced every other emotion. After what seemed like an eternity, he heard his father say, "That's fine officer, we'll be here," and he hung up.

"What? Please tell me!" Chad begged his father.

"The Wilmington police got a call from an attendant at the bus station. Your mother's car has been parked there for over a month now, since May twentieth. After a month they tow it if they can't find the owner, and they call the police as a precaution in case the car was stolen or involved in a crime."

Chad was exasperated. His questions were not being answered. "Where did she go? Did they say? Have they found anything out about her?"

"I just told you all I know. The police are bringing the car back to us. They don't consider it evidence of a crime or nothin'. I had to agree to pay her parking, which is adding insult to injury. But I guess you can drive her car now. The police do have some questions for us, and you can bug them with all of your questions, I guess." Charlie drained a beer and started rummaging through the bag of takeout. Chad stared at the back of his father's head with disgust.

Chad sat on the porch until he saw his mother's station wagon finally coming home. It was not the comforting sight he had hoped for, with a black-and-white police cruiser following close behind the blue station wagon as it came up the driveway. A police officer parked his mother's car and climbed out of the driver's seat while another officer exited the cruiser. Chad walked down the steps to greet them. "Hello, officers," he said, as he walked toward them extending his hand. "I'm Chad McCloskey, Louisa McCloskey's son." A lump caught his throat as he heard himself say these words. "Please come in." He led them up the steps and into the kitchen. "This is my father, Charlie McCloskey." He pointed reluctantly toward his father as Charlie drained his second Miller Lite and wiped his mouth with the back of his hand.

"I'm Officer Stevens and this is Officer Morgan." Stevens handed Charlie the keys to the wagon. "Fortunately, the bus company's long-term parking requires that you leave your car key with the parking attendant. Oh, and this needs to be paid as soon as you can get around to it," he said, handing Charlie a document.

As the four men sat around the kitchen table, Officer Stevens took a pad and pen out of a leather briefcase and started asking questions. After the usual questions about the missing woman's name and date of birth, Stevens looked squarely at Charlie to begin the real questioning. Chad wondered if they suspected foul play. "So, when did you last see her?"

"I don't know, I guess about a month ago," Charlie said, with disgust filling his mouth as he spoke. "I went to work. You know, somebody has to pay the bills. And my wife up and left me without even so much as a goodbye note. Why don't you write that down?" he asked angrily, glowering at the officer with the pen and pad.

"May twentieth was the last time we saw her, officer. I had breakfast with her before I left for school," Chad spoke quickly, in an attempt to defuse his father's escalating anger. Both officers looked up at Chad, seemingly surprised by the fact that he spoke up.

"Was there anything unusual that morning, Chad, when you had breakfast with her? Did she say or do anything to suggest she was going away?"

Chad felt that old ache in his chest as he remembered the last time he saw his mother. It seemed like a normal morning then; she brought him a plate of toaster waffles with syrup, and she sat across from him as he ate. But as he thought about it now, there *was* something different.

"Yes," he said, surprising his father, who lifted his head suddenly and squinted at Chad. "She seemed much happier than usual, in a way. I mean, instead of moping around in her bathrobe, she had showered and was dressed, and she looked nice. She smiled a lot more than usual and she asked me a lot of questions about the end of my school year." Chad fought the urge to cry as he felt his throat constricting with the memory. "She always kissed me before I left for school, but that morning she hugged me real hard and told me she loved me, too. I didn't think anything of it then, but now I can see that she was getting ready to leave." Chad dug his fingernails deep into the palm of his hand to distract himself from his painful realization.

Officer Stevens stopped writing notes to look up at Chad. "Why do you think she would be happy to leave, Chad?"

Chad swallowed hard and looked at his father. He wanted to tell them about his father's verbal abuse and his drunken rages. "I'm not sure, Officer. I know she was very unhappy here for a long time. She saw a therapist at the clinic downtown, and she had a prescription for something that was supposed to help her with depression."

After a pause, Officer Stevens resumed. "Is there anything else you want to tell us about her leaving?"

Chad thought for a minute. "Excuse me for a second, I have a few things I think might help." He walked quickly to his bedroom and returned holding two items. "This is the note she left for me while I was at school the day she left, and this is a recent photo of her," Chad handed both to Officer Stevens. "Those items are pretty important to me."

"Yes, we understand. We'll keep them safe and return them when we no longer need them." He carefully wrapped them in plastic and clipped them to his notepad.

"Thank you," Chad said.

"Mr. McCloskey. Can you tell me about her family or friends? Anyone she might have gone to stay with?"

"Sherry." Charlie sneered a little as he spoke her name. "She was her only family that I ever met and her only friend."

Chad winced to hear his mother described as "friendless." He realized he would be described the same way if he ever went missing. He listened intently as his father continued.

"Louisa and her sister Sherry were put in a Catholic orphanage when they were very young. I think it was St. Mary's or St. Joseph's…Saint something. Sherry was only about two years older than Louisa and they were real close. The nuns there didn't want to split them up, so they had trouble getting them adopted."

Chad noticed that Officer Stevens jotted, *St. Mary's or St. Joseph's—check records.*

"Okay, so the sister would be about forty years old, and her maiden name is Sherry Chadbourne. Is there anything more you know about her?"

"Sherry was a little louder, a little freer. I thought she was too close to Louisa and a bad influence. She was always filling her head with crazy ideas of traveling or saving some cause."

Chad glared at his father. He had never known he had an aunt, and he had never known his mother had someone else who loved her and made her happy. And now he knew why. His father had run his Aunt Sherry out of his mother's life because she threatened his ability to keep her.

"Do you know where she lives?"

"One day she just stopped by and told us that she had her van loaded up and she was heading to the Southwest to find the sun. She had a certificate from some beauty school and thought she'd make a living at that. That's all I remember, except Louisa took it real hard; she cried for days. It was a good thing she had Chad to take care of. It helped her to have a reason to get out of bed in the morning."

Chad sorted through the information swirling in his head. For the first time he realized why his mother had stayed with them despite her suffering, and why she left when she did. She stayed for him. She had endured for him. She could not be a free spirit and *find the sun* like her sister. Even her leaving was a selfless act. Chad knew that he would not move on and out of the small, miserable house along the Brandywine River, and into a real life of his own, if she was still there, needing his comfort.

The two policemen rose from the table and shook his father's hand as they concluded their interview. They told Charlie they would keep in touch. Chad felt empowered, energized and even dared to feel happy for the first time in a very long time.

She loves me. She left because she loves me, he repeated to himself. Chad's heart leapt, as he began to put together his plan.

*****

After Charlie left for his nightly visit to the local tavern, Chad quickly pulled down the attic door and climbed up its stairs. He pointed a flashlight around the warm and dusty space. He saw gardening tools, a pile of discarded drapes and an old trunk. He opened the lid of the trunk, started rifling through his mother's keepsakes, and found a small worn photo album. After he rummaged through the remainder of the trunk, Chad retreated to his room and sat on his bed, pausing to study each snapshot of his mother's life. First, a yellowing photograph of two little girls holding hands in front of a Christmas tree. One girl, his mother, had dark hair, while the other girl had lighter hair. "Sherry," Chad whispered, just to hear someone acknowledge her out loud.

The next several pages had photos of the two girls in various settings, as they got progressively older and taller. They were always alone in the photos, except occasionally a nun in her black-and-white habit appeared in the background. At the end of the album, Chad turned the page to find a photograph of his parents' wedding day. An impossibly young woman, a teenager really, embraced a thin, smiling version of his father, and they both looked at the photographer with expressions suggesting hope and promise. The last page of the album contained a faded color photograph of his mother wearing a long flowered dress and a wide smile as she held her baby boy in her arms.

Chad's heart leapt when he found a postcard in the last page with the words, *Greetings from sunny Scottsdale!* floating over a fiery red sunset sky and an endless canyon. He flipped it over and read the faded blue handwriting. *"Hi Sis: Scottsdale is warm and welcoming. I got a great gig at a beauty parlor and I found me a nice man. Come out here with that beautiful boy of yours for some rest and recreation. Love, Sherry."*

There was no date written on the card, but the post office had processed it on April 10, 1995. The return address read, *"Sherry Chadbourne, P. O. Box 3012, Scottsdale, Arizona, 85254."* Chad stared at the address, trying to magically glean more information from its printed words. There was no street address, and possibly the sister had a different last name now. But he knew he was going to find her. *Aunt Sherry exists and she lived in Scottsdale, and maybe she's still there.*

Chad got ready for bed and turned out the lights, exhausted. He wanted desperately to call a telephone operator in Scottsdale and try to find his aunt, and in turn, his mother. He ached to hear her voice and to make sure that she was safe.

But he knew he had to be careful. His plan had evolved as he looked at photos in the attic. He would surprise her in person, and wrap his arms around her and reassure her that he would not lead her back to darkness and oppression. His father would not, under any circumstances, be allowed to follow. He drifted off to a sound sleep for the first time since his mother had left.

CHAPTER 5

MARIA: SEPTEMBER 24, 2011

MARIA HERNANDEZ BENT carefully to dust an antique table. Bending and stretching had become increasingly difficult as her pregnancy progressed. But she needed her weekly paycheck from the Cleaning Angels Maid Service, so she kept cleaning a seemingly endless supply of homes and workplaces. She was relieved that it was Saturday because Sunday was her only day off.

She was working alone in her favorite job site—an artist's studio and gallery in a historic mill. The job required an early start because the gallery opened to the public at ten. Maria disliked walking to the city bus stop in the dark, but she always felt rewarded with the sunrise through the mill's large windows. She looked up from her work occasionally to watch the wash of a pink and orange sky replace the blackness. Later, as the sun ascended, she watched the river and its inhabitants come alive.

The light on the river reminded Maria of her childhood home where the color of the cliffs, the ocean, and the sky changed with the strength and position of the sun. Her family's dusty farm in the Baja Peninsula was a world away from her spot that morning on the Brandywine River, and yet, in both places she had gazed at the water with hope for her future.

Maria polished and dusted stone floors and brick walls while imagining that the builders and craftsmen who constructed the mill two hundred years earlier probably had come to this country from their motherlands, believing that they would work hard and build things, including a better life. Maria sighed when she thought about how times had changed, even if people's circumstances and their dreams had not.

It was just after seven-thirty when Maria finished two of the three floors of the mill. She decided that she had time to rest her body briefly and eat a quick breakfast. She sat on a window seat on the third floor and in quick gulps ate a banana and a granola bar. She was perusing the river scene below her when something stopped her eyes. Far down to her left, in a wooded section near the riverbank, she saw a large man crouched down behind a pine tree. He looked as if he was hiding from something, and Maria was sure she saw him raise a gun to his eye as if he were aiming. A large black bag rested at his feet.

Maria gasped, fearing that this man was preparing to shoot one of those beautiful geese or ducks that glided so peacefully on the river. She watched intently as the man put the gun down for a moment and pulled his sleeve up to check his watch. Horrified, Maria saw him raise the gun to his shoulder and take aim just as a woman came running into view. The man moved his body to follow the woman as she jogged past, oblivious to her stalker. Then Maria saw the unthinkable. The man fired and the woman stopped. The woman reached around to the back of her thigh, took a few steps and then collapsed. Maria cried out loud as she saw the man strap the black bag onto his back and quickly scoop up the woman into his arms before disappearing deeper into the woods.

As Maria grabbed her cell phone, goose bumps rose up on her skin and a lump developed in her throat. She started to dial 9-1-1, but she quickly hit the end button before the call connected. She had to do something, but she knew that she could not call the police. She couldn't even call her boyfriend, Juan, because she knew that he would admonish her and tell her not to call the police.

Maria tried in vain to replace the image of the woman falling to the ground and being carried away with a picture of Juan holding their newborn in his arms. She had to try to forget the woman and her plight to ensure her own child would grow up in America. They were so close.

"Focus," she whispered to herself over and over as she continued with her vacuuming, dusting and polishing. Her fingers continued to shake and her legs felt weak. When she finished her cleaning, she carefully looked around and then stepped out into the parking lot. As she was putting a bag of trash into a garbage can behind the mill she heard her ride approaching. But as she rounded the corner, she was surprised to see a blue station wagon and not the pink Cleaning Angels van that she was expecting.

Maria retreated quickly and hid against the corner of the building. She watched as the station wagon came to an abrupt halt on the edge of the parking lot farthest away from the mill, and closest to the woods below Rockford Park. A young man in jeans, a T-shirt and a zippered sweatshirt got out of the car and nervously looked around. He hurried to the back door of the station wagon and leaned in. Maria watched him pull out a large bundle that looked like a rug or blanket. With great effort, he pulled the bundle out of the car and hoisted it over his shoulder. He staggered under its weight as he moved toward the woods. Maria's hand covered her mouth when she saw two pale legs and running shoes dangling from the bundle.

This was not the same man who she had seen shoot the woman earlier, but Maria knew that the incidents were related. Her heart pounded and her stomach heaved. As she bent over and retched, she heard the sound of the Cleaning Angels van pulling into the mill's parking lot. An older woman with bleached hair climbed out of the van looking alarmed as Maria trudged toward her, wiping her mouth with her hand. "Are you okay, hon? You look white as a sheet."

Maria glanced quickly and saw that the man carrying the bundle had disappeared into the woods. "Yes, I'm okay. I am just tired," she said, holding her stomach. "Baby coming. I'll rest here in the car and drink some water and I'll be fine. Thank you."

As Maria walked around the van to get in, she looked at the back of the blue station wagon parked at the other end of the lot. There were no distinguishing marks or stickers and it had a regular blue Delaware license plate. She tried to appear casual as she squinted to read the first four numbers of the plate, *8266*.

As the van pulled out of the driveway the older woman said, "Are you sure you are up for this? You look pretty wiped out."

"Oh, yes," Maria said, flustered. "I am just a little tired. I'll be fine, thank you." When the woman turned her attention to the van driver and a discussion about her preferred radio station, Maria quietly took an old receipt out of her wallet and wrote down "8-2-6-6."

*****

At four o'clock that same afternoon, Maria finally climbed the stairs to the one-bedroom apartment over busy King Street that she shared with Juan. She was exhausted, hungry and had to urinate so badly that she thought she might wet her pants. She pushed the door open and rushed to the toilet. Her swollen face and red eyes looked back at her from the mirror. She had cried the entire trip home, oblivious to the curiosity or alarm on the faces of strangers along the way.

She kicked off her shoes and reclined on their worn sofa. Images of the morning's horror replayed in her head. She closed her eyes, concentrated on her breathing, and fell asleep within minutes.

Maria woke to the sound of Juan coming through their front door. He had on dusty Levis and a navy blue T-shirt that fit his body perfectly. He flashed his beautiful smile to greet her. He clutched a plastic bag that said Boston Chicken. "Hi, baby," he said, as she wiped sleep from her eyes. She got up from the couch and walked to him.

"Juan, we need to talk. I saw something today, something bad."

After Maria finished telling Juan her story she began to shake. "I was gonna call you, but I was scared. I didn't know what to do. I was afraid to call the police."

"You definitely cannot call the police. You know that." Juan's tone frightened Maria and she started crying again.

Shhhhhh." Juan gently placed his fingers to Maria's mouth. "I'm sorry, baby. Let's relax a little first, and then we'll talk more, okay?" He led her back to the sofa and helped her sit. He bent over and took her socks off carefully, slowly rolled up her jeans and started to rub her bare feet.

"I know you're upset, Maria. But maybe the whole thing is over, one way or the other, and you can't help. We'll get a newspaper in the morning, okay?" Juan stopped rubbing her feet and looked into her eyes, to see her response.

"No Juan, that's not enough. There may be a woman out there right now who needs rescuing. I may be the only one who knows." Maria caught another sob in her throat.

"Okay, look, we can't call from our phones because maybe the police can trace it to us. We'll go down to the pay phone by Herman's Liquor Store and call the police right now. But, you *cannot* tell them your name or where we live or why you saw this or anything about you okay?"

"Yes," Maria nodded, wiping a tear off her cheek. "Let's do that, please."

"Man, oh, man," Juan shook his head as he handed Maria back her shoe. "You are a stubborn woman. I hope our little one gets your strong will." He tried to get Maria to smile. He took her hand and together they left the apartment.

A police siren screeched a few blocks away as they stepped onto the sidewalk. Maria held Juan's hand firmly as they walked around the corner to the phone booth in front of the liquor store. The glass was dirty and the booth smelled of urine, and the black receiver hung by its cord inside the phone box. Juan stepped in, put the receiver to his ear and then clicked the bracket and pushed buttons in vain, trying to get a dial tone.

"It's broken, baby. No surprise, though—no one uses these things anymore."

Maria looked at him, her eyes pleading with him to let her do what she knew was right. She felt compelled to aid the woman who was carried into the woods. She could not shake the constant feeling that a person's fate was in her hands.

"I know what you're thinking, baby," Juan said, reading her thoughts. "But if you call them on your phone about this, you'll be an eyewitness. You'll be on the list for police and lawyers who prosecute criminals—and who enforce the law. What then? They will track you down and talk to you as they investigate this thing and maybe even expect you to testify. They will find out that you are here illegally."

Juan continued pleading, "Come on, baby, we have a lot of great things about to happen here. The lawyer we got from the Latin American Community Center is working on our papers. My citizenship will come through any day now and, soon after that, you will be here legally. Then we can do a lot of things. Then you can call the police whenever you want. And I can move up a lot quicker in the building business, maybe even have our own business someday. We'll get much better pay and benefits, and we'll be able to get a real home for our family."

Juan flashed a broad smile that assured Maria that they were capable of anything together, even as they stood in a dirty phone booth on a street corner between a rundown liquor store and a vacant building with boarded-up windows.

"Come on, I still have that dinner waiting for you."

Moments later, Maria sat on her bed smelling the strong aroma of chicken heating in the microwave. The aroma of dinner and the sound of Juan singing softly in the kitchen normally made her feel so safe and content. But tonight she could not sit still. Her stomach churned and her hands trembled. Quietly she picked up her cell phone next to their bed and dialed 9-1-1.

"Police. What is your emergency?" the emergency dispatcher's answer came quickly.

"Um, this morning I saw a kidnapping, or maybe even a murder," Maria whispered.

"Ma'am? I don't understand you, ma'am. Are you in immediate danger?"

"No. I saw something today and I think someone else is in danger."

Frustration came through in the dispatcher's voice. "Please speak louder, ma'am."

"I was at Breck's Mill, on the Brandywine River. I saw a woman get shot and then carried away by a man who had been hiding behind a tree. And later, I saw a different man pull up in a car and carry a woman's body in a blanket into the woods that lead up toward Rockford Park." Maria started to sob again as she finished her sentence.

"I'm not following you, ma'am. Let's take it step-by step. Can I have your name and address please?"

Maria pictured the dispatcher poised to record Maria's name

and address. A wave of panic overcame her as she realized that the dispatcher did not ask for her cell phone number, because that information was probably automatically recorded when her call was connected! She pushed the power button on her phone and slammed it shut.

"Dinner's on!" Juan called to her.

Maria entered the family room in time to see Juan placing a tray piled with food in the center of their rickety dining table. But tonight, he had transformed the table into something beautiful, with a clean, white sheet as a tablecloth, set with their only matching dishes and a single candle burning softly. Maria tried to regain her composure as she saw Juan's big brown eyes watch her with adoration as she walked toward him.

CHAPTER 6

CHAD: SEPTEMBER 24, 2011

Chad rose quietly and went to his closet to retrieve a blue shoebox that held his savings. It had been almost three months since he made his plan, and in that time he had saved every dollar he got from his father. He had started saving some of his allowance when he turned sixteen, foolishly thinking he could buy a cool car—or worse, that a car could make him happy. Now he could not wait any longer. Whatever he had in the box had to be enough. He was leaving; he could bear it no longer.

After counting the dollar bills and estimating the value of a bulging bag of coins, he figured that he had about eight hundred and fifty dollars. He carefully put the cash back into the blue shoebox and hid it back in his closet. He decided he would go to a travel agent after work and buy a ticket on the first plane that would take him to his mother. Then Chad heard his father leave his bedroom and shuffle to the kitchen.

"Hey Dad, I'm heading out for a little walk." Chad knew he could not bear to sit with him this morning.

"All right, but we're leaving for work at nine sharp, so don't lose track of time out there looking for your little treasures."

Chad felt unsettled as he strode toward the waterfall near Breck's Mill. As he neared the gardener's shed, something had caught his eye. The shed's door was wide open and it looked like a red-and-blue clad body was lying inside. He ran to get a closer look. His heart raced and his throat tightened as he realized he was looking at the body of a woman, in light blue running shorts and a bright red T-shirt, lying on the stone floor. Her wrists were bound behind her back and a wide cloth was wrapped around her head and over her eyes. Long reddish-brown hair spilled out of a ponytail holder and matted under her head. A piece of duct tape was stretched tight across her mouth and her cheeks.

"Oh my God, oh my God, oh my God!" Chad muttered as he leaned over her limp body. Terror seized him. He was afraid to touch her and yet he felt compelled to do something. He got down on his knees next to the woman and saw goose bumps on her slim forearm. He was relieved to see her chest rising and falling softly and rhythmically. He gently pulled at the tape over her mouth, exhaling as he pulled it away from her lips and skin. He braced himself for the woman's reaction, but there was none. He noticed that her lips parted slightly and she started breathing through her mouth.

She looked almost peaceful, except she had been bound and gagged in a way that conveyed violent and criminal activity. He looked around the woods for someone who could help him, someone who could call for help. But a moment later, the thought of someone seeing him with this woman, in this condition, terrified him. *What if they thought I did this?* He was alone in the woods, with a woman who had obviously been the victim of some horrific crime. Despite the chill in the air, he wiped off a thin layer of perspiration that was forming on his forehead. He shook all over.

He could not walk away and leave her here. But he was sure he did not want to be implicated in this terrible crime, either. Just then Chad heard the distant sound of joggers coming through another trail farther up the river and closer to Rockford Park. Chad ducked down for a minute until he no longer heard their voices. But then he had an idea. *People use that trail in the morning, jogging and walking their dogs. Someone else could find her. She'll be safe and I won't get stuck in this at all.*

Chad removed his sweatshirt and spread it across the woman's torso. Then he got up, looked around to make sure there was no one watching, and started running toward his house. He slipped quietly back into the kitchen and listened for his father. He heard the shower, so he grabbed the keys to his mother's station wagon from the kitchen counter. When he got to the car, he was relieved to see that his mother's old plaid picnic blanket was still in the back seat. He drove to the shoulder of the road near the gardener's shed, parked the car, and looked quickly in every direction. He ran to the shed with the picnic blanket bundled loosely under his arm.

As he got closer and could see the woman still on the ground, the sound of blood pumping in his head drowned out every other sound. His heart raced as he spread the blanket next to her. He squatted down and put his arms under her back and lifted her just enough to get her onto the blanket. Her body was still limp, and this time Chad noticed some bruising on her thighs when he put her down on the blanket. The stench of vomit, urine, and other nauseating smells filled his nostrils as he worked furiously. He wrapped the blanket around her, concealing her face and torso. He bent his knees, put his hands and forearms under her shoulders and buttocks and lifted. She weighed little more than the hundred-pound bags of fertilizer he routinely lifted. He awkwardly slung the whole load over his right shoulder and moved as quickly as he could toward the station wagon.

Chad put his bundle down on the grass briefly to open the station wagon's back door. He squatted down, and then lifted the bundle again with a groan. As he slid the woman into the car, he pulled the blanket away from her face to make sure she could breathe. The dashboard clock read 9:04 when he turned the key in the ignition. "Shit!" Chad said loudly, picturing his father's wrath as he waited for him in the driveway. Chad drove up the road and turned in to the parking lot for Breck's Mill. He drove fast through the empty lot to its outer edge, bordering the woods below Rockford Park.

He heaved the woman in the plaid blanket over his shoulder one more time and took a deep breath. Her running shoes dangled out of the blanket and bumped his back as he walked quickly into the woods. He hid behind an evergreen, waiting for a group of four runners to come through. Once they were gone, he quickly carried his bundle to the exact spot where the runners had been, a sun-splashed section of trail under an oak tree. He lay her down as quickly as he could, gently rolling her body out of the blanket and placing her face up. He grabbed his sweatshirt, which had become entangled in the whole bundle, and dropped it next to him on the trail. Then he placed the blanket over the woman's torso and quickly tucked it under her back and shoulders. He was afraid to remove her blindfold.

Chad grabbed his sweatshirt off of the ground and started running back toward his car. He stopped and hid at a point where he could still see the plaid blanket with what appeared from his vantage to be a small lump beneath it. He was panicking about being late for his father and the certain storm of rage and reprisal when he returned. But he was even more frightened for this vulnerable woman who he watched over from afar. Chad waited for about eight minutes, which seemed like an eternity, before he heard voices.

"Oh, my God! Come quick, Michael! Michael.....*MICHAEL!*"

Chad heard a woman's urgent screams. He saw a young woman unzipping her sweatshirt and then crouching next to the woman lying on the ground. He watched as the young woman quickly removed the blindfold and untied the ropes on the woman's wrists. Chad saw the young woman use one hand to elevate the woman's head while she stroked her cheek with the other. With great relief, he saw the woman on the ground move her head and emit a loud cry as she regained consciousness.

As he turned to escape to his car, Chad heard another person coming down the path toward the woman. A tall man ran down the trail with a little dog. Chad saw the man pull a cell phone out of his pocket and make a call. While they were absorbed in the woman's rescue, Chad slowly and silently walked backwards, until he was sure they would not see or hear him. Then he turned and ran as fast as he could to his mother's station wagon.

CHAPTER 7

KELLY: SEPTEMBER 24, 2011

Kelly lay on an examination table with her feet in cold iron stirrups while a young woman with round glasses swabbed her in tender areas deep inside her body. "This will only take a minute. I am really sorry for any discomfort I am causing you. I know you have been through enough."

The woman's words seemed rote as she continued to work methodically, collecting evidence as if she were swabbing a petri dish. Kelly stared at the ceiling and tried not to cry. She was exhausted, bruised, and her head throbbed with pain.

"There. I am finished." The woman put the last of three long swabs into a plastic bag marked *Medical Evidence* and peeled off her latex gloves. "I know it's awful. I am so sorry. They'll move you to a bed in a minute so you can finally rest, but I needed to do this now. My job is to help them catch the animal that did this." The woman gently took Kelly's legs out of the stirrups and awkwardly pulled down Kelly's thin hospital robe.

Kelly rolled onto her side and pulled her legs up against her chest. The woman's attempt at compassion made Kelly cry again. Sobs wracked her body, her mouth opened and remained slack as shrieks and sobs came out in waves. *Animal.* Kelly heard the woman's words echo in her head as she was pushed in a wheelchair to a hospital room. The same questions kept cycling through her mind. *Who would hurt her like this? Why would someone hurt her like this?* As Kelly eased into her bed, she heard Dan's voice in the hallway. "Dan!" Kelly tried to call out, but her throat was dry from the sobbing.

Dan poked his head in to the room hesitantly, with a look of anguish and fear on his face. His beautiful, strong, confident and happy wife had been replaced with a battered and vulnerable body curled into the fetal position. He stood with his fists clenched in the front pocket of his sweatshirt, his eyes locked on his wife's pale, frightened face.

"Dan?" Kelly asked, softly. "Please." That was all Kelly could muster before her voice cracked and she started sobbing again.

Dan rushed over to her side. Without looking into her eyes, he quietly took the cold, pale hand that peeked from under the hospital sheet and enveloped it in both of his hands. He bit his lip in his attempt to be strong.

"Hi, baby, I'm here. I am so sorry. It's going to be okay. I'm here. You're safe."

"It's... not.... going to.... be okay." Kelly responded as she sobbed and tried to catch her breath. Kelly turned her face toward his and stared into his eyes. "I need to know what happened. Tell me everything you know, Dan, please!"

He began hesitantly, "Well... this morning I knew something was wrong when you weren't home in time for the girls' soccer practice. So I dropped them off at practice and I started driving around all of the places that you run. I guess... about eight-thirty... I called your mom and asked her what she thought. Of course, she told me that if I did not call the police, she would. And then she said she was coming... right away. So I called the Wilmington Police and told them everything."

"What did the police say?" Kelly thought of herself bound and gagged on that cold hard floor while the police discussed her whereabouts with Dan over the phone.

"They took some information, but they did not tell me if they were going to go out right away or not. So I called the Delaware State Police and the New Castle County Police, but I was told it was a matter for the Wilmington Police. Finally, an officer called and said he was going to come by the house to talk to me within the hour. It was, like, nine-fifteen or so and I was frantic at that point."

Kelly felt herself growing angry with her husband as he told her the details. *He* was frantic? Suddenly, she spat out, "Sorry to have frightened you so, Dan," and then she turned her face away from him.

"Oh, Kel," Dan said as he stroked her hair. "It wasn't like that. I mean, I was so scared because I love you so much and I felt helpless. I wanted to run and run and comb every inch of Wilmington to find you but I knew that wasn't going to work either. I am so sorry." Dan made a sudden gurgling noise, and then the sounds of muffled crying.

Kelly had never heard Dan cry before, so she listened first with alarm, and then with a detached curiosity. She felt completely separate from him, as she lay with her arms wrapped tightly around herself. "Dan," Kelly said impatiently, "Okay, okay! Please keep going. What happened next? The police guy on the phone was coming to the house....Then what happened?"

Dan took a few breaths, steadying himself. Then he began speaking slowly, carefully.

"Your mother showed up about nine-thirty or so, and just a few minutes after she arrived, the phone rang. Someone from the Wilmington Police Department told me they had found you in the woods and that you were on your way to the hospital." Dan paused for a moment and swallowed. "When I got here they told me that you had been assaulted."

Kelly felt her stomach tighten at Dan's words. Then she snorted. "Assaulted? They said *raped,* didn't they?" Dan was silent. Sounds of hospital staff being called in the hallway slipped into her room. "So, where is my mom?" Kelly sounded hostile.

"She's home with the girls. She's a little bit of a wreck too, but she does want to come see you. She just wants you to know she's here in case you need her."

"I don't have the flu, or a broken arm, Dan. It's not that simple." Kelly surprised herself with her bitter tone.

Dan looked like he had been slapped. "Kel, I am doing my best. I really don't know how to deal with my wife's rape, okay?" Kelly was almost relieved to hear anger in Dan's voice. It sounded much more natural under the circumstances. "I mean, you go out for a run and then you don't return. The next thing I know, I'm in the hospital and my wife is a bruised and battered rape victim. I'm trying to process this and react to it, but I have no idea what to do. I have no idea what even happened. How did we get here?" Dan's voice cracked again as he tried hard not to cry. He waited a few moments before he spoke again. "I love you, baby. I hate that you were hurt so much. I don't know what to do. Tell me what I can do... I'll do anything." Dan's voice grew desperate and he finally gave in to full sobbing. His big strong right hand softly caressed the back of Kelly's head.

Kelly grabbed Dan's hand with her hand and pulled it away from her head. "My head hurts. Please stop."

Dan took a step back.

With her head turned away from Dan, Kelly spoke to him in a tired and quiet voice. "I can't do it. I can't do it." Kelly started to cry again. Dan just stood there dumbfounded, afraid to talk or touch her. He looked up as a knock sounded and the door to the room opened suddenly. A tall, bearded man in a white jacket entered. Kelly didn't turn or in any way acknowledge his presence.

"Hello... I am Doctor Kamali." He and Dan shook hands.

"Dan Malloy, Kelly's husband."

The doctor cleared his throat. "Kelly, I have some findings about your injuries and instructions about your care after today. I'm talking about your CAT scan, X-rays, that sort of thing. I do not know anything about the rape kit, though." He looked at Kelly directly. "Do you want me to talk to you with your husband here, or would you rather I talk to Dan outside while you get some rest?" The doctor's question was met with silence. Kelly didn't acknowledge him. She felt an overwhelming sense of fatigue and detachment. Dr. Kamali shrugged his shoulders at Dan and then motioned with his head toward the door of the room.

"I'm so terribly sorry about what has happened here to Kelly. It's awful what people are capable of. The good news is, her scans showed no major damage. She has a mild concussion, so her head will be sore and she may be nauseous for a few days. She has also suffered some bad bruising on her back, her buttocks, her inner thighs and her pubic area, and she has rope burns and abrasions. The nurse will give you printed discharge instructions and a few prescriptions that you will need to fill right away. One is to be applied to her rope burns and scrapes a few times a day—just follow the directions on the label. There is also a medication to help her get some much needed rest in the aftermath of such a trauma."

"Do you mean a sleeping pill?"

"No. It's actually more for anxiety. I consulted with a staff psychiatrist here at the hospital, Dr. Scott, who has an appointment to follow up with Kelly in a week or two. Dr. Scott also advised that Kelly meet with and talk to a counselor who specializes in this sort of thing."

"Who?" Dan looked confused.

"The state or the city—I am not sure which—provides this resource whenever there has been a sexual assault. A licensed and certified counselor who specializes in sexual abuse victims is available to meet with Kelly and help her try to work through the emotional and psychological injuries that she has sustained."

Dr. Kamali put his hand on Dan's shoulder, as if to fortify him for his next words. "Your wife was kidnapped and brutally raped. Her physical injuries fortunately will heal soon. It's her other injuries—her pain, her fear, her self-esteem, her anger and a host of other emotions and psychological impacts—that will be with her for a long, long time. You are going to have to be very patient with her."

"I will, of course," Dan said, quickly, sounding defensive. Then the impact of Dr. Kamali's words hit him. *Brutally raped.*

Dr. Kamali looked at his watch. "I am sorry, but I have to run to my next patient."

"Of course. Thank you, Doctor." Dan shook his hand and then watched him walk quickly down the hallway to his next patient.

Dan stood silently in the hallway of the hospital for what seemed an eternity, hearing sirens outside the building and urgent calls for doctors and nurses over the intercom. People donning green scrubs and white lab coats hurried by him, oblivious to his anguish. In the midst of this chaos, Dan was unable to move his feet, to take those steps that led him back to his wife and to what came next. He felt his hands clenching and unclenching into fists as he tried to block out the images that kept flashing through his head. A picture of another man, large then small, white, black, brown, in a sweatshirt, in a denim jacket, with black hair, curly hair, long hair, no hair, climbing on top of her, brutalizing and defiling her—his wife and the mother of his children. He couldn't make out a face, but the ever-changing man attacked, assaulted and tried to destroy everything that Dan held dear.

Dan simultaneously struggled with feelings of rage, disgust, hurt, and the most uncomfortable one of all—fear. He was terrified at the thought that he did not protect his wife—that he could not protect her. He was also terrified at the thought of what could have been. If her attacker had wanted to kill Kelly, there had been nothing to stop him. Dan feared for his beautiful daughters, knowing now that there are dangerous and deranged men out there who could harm them for their own sadistic pleasure. And, he realized, as he turned to force himself to walk back into Kelly's hospital room, he was most fearful of the broken person lying under the sheets on the hospital bed ten feet away.

Dan had always known who Kelly was, and he had always been certain about their life together. But now, as he re-entered her hospital room and approached her bed, he placed his feet slowly and carefully as if he were stepping onto thin ice. He felt a colossal shift in what he thought was their life together. He silently resolved to be brave and strong and patient, and so he kept moving forward into the room and toward his wife.

CHAPTER 8

CHAD: SEPTEMBER 24, 2011

AS CHAD APPROACHED his driveway he felt sick with dread. The events of the morning had left him physically spent, and he still had to face his father's rage. As he turned into the driveway, he was surprised and relieved to see that his father's truck was gone. Chad quickly ran into the house. His hands were shaking as he poured himself a glass of water and stood leaning against the kitchen sink. He took a deep breath and tried to calm himself down. "Mom," he called out, "where are you when I need you?" A deep and painful pang of longing hit him. She would have known what to do. Chad pictured her soothing the woman on the ground while Chad ran to call the police. Chad's panic transitioned to deep regret, as he realized that was how the ordeal should have been handled.

To make matters worse, Chad spotted an empty bottle of Jack Daniels on the counter. He retrieved his father's coffee mug from the sink and smelled the strong odor of Tennessee whiskey. He had seen the clues before and he knew what followed. His father became angry and belligerent when he was drunk.

Chad made his decision at that very moment. It was already nine-thirty and he was very late for work. His father would be too difficult to contend with, and Chad was already unable to cope with the range of emotions that gripped him.

Someone had tied up a woman, attacked her and left her for dead…. in his woods.

He pulled the yellow pages phone book out and flipped to "Travel Agencies." He ran his index finger down the column of listings, looking for the one that was closest to him and had Saturday hours. He circled in ink two agencies within five miles from his house, ripped the page out of the book and stuffed it into the front pocket of his Levi's. Then he went to get his money out of his closet.

*****

Chad's first stop was the local Wilmington Trust Bank branch. He did not have an account there, but he had been there with his mother on numerous occasions when she came in for deposits and withdrawals.

"Hello, son. Can I help you?" A heavy woman in a yellow dress asked Chad as he stood, looking a little lost, in front of the counter.

"Um, I just want to exchange coins and small bills for bigger bills. Can I do that here?"

"Sure," the woman said. "Normally I would send you to a teller, but I'm not doing anything at the moment, so I'll get you started. What are we talking about here in the coin category?"

Chad felt his cheeks flush in embarrassment as he pulled three bulging Ziploc bags out of his backpack.

"Wow!" The woman chuckled. "That's a lot of coins. Fortunately, we have a machine for that!"

"Thank you, Ma'am." Chad followed her to a large machine and watched the woman dump the coins into it. After a few minutes, it spit out a receipt for $213. As he walked out of the bank, Chad tucked his $847 worth of savings, now crisp new bills, carefully into his wallet and threw his shoebox and empty Ziploc bags into a garbage can.

Ten minutes later, bells jingled on the door of Adventure Travel Agency, and a bearded man looked up from a computer screen as Chad entered. "Hey, man, what's your adventure?"

"Excuse me?" Chad muttered.

"Where are you going, dude?" The man looked at Chad with curiosity.

Chad noticed colorful posters depicting surfers skimming tall blue waves, climbers rappelling down steep rocky cliffs and skiers crashing through waist-deep powder. "Um, I want to go to Arizona," he said quietly.

"Awesome," the man said extending his hand. "I'm Ken. What are you planning out there? Camping? Rock climbing? Rafting maybe?"

"I'm not sure. I really just want an airplane ticket." Chad said.

"Oh, I see. You'll kind of just figure it out when you get there, huh?" The man looked back at his computer screen.

"Yes. Can I get an airplane ticket here?" Chad asked, again feeling self-conscious by his lack of experience and worldliness.

"Sure, man," Ken said. "The Internet has sort of made us obsolete in the air travel category. People usually come to us for the whole adventure ticket—we have connections to get you the best services and equipment for adventure travel. But, hey, we still deal with the airlines, too. So, sit down," he said, gesturing toward a grey plastic chair opposite his chair and desk, "and I'll hook you up."

"Okay," Chad said sitting down.

"Where in Arizona do you want to go?" Ken asked.

"Scottsdale," Chad said.

"Okay. Then you'll be flying into Phoenix and then just get a local bus to Scottsdale. You'll be leaving out of Philadelphia, right?" Ken asked.

"Um, yeah," Chad replied.

"Round trip, right?"

"Uh, no, I'm moving out there," Chad replied, this time sounding certain about where he was going and what he was doing.

"Oh, cool. People don't realize it, but Arizona is very diverse in its geography and its climate. It can be snowing in a canyon up north and you can be swimming in the southern part of the state, all at the same time." Ken rambled on as he typed into his computer, pulling up various options and screens and occasionally jotting notes.

For a moment Chad followed Ken's words, imagining fiery red sunsets and giant canyon walls. But then he found himself drowning out Ken's words, and instead picturing his mother's face. He didn't care where his mother was; he just knew that she was his home.

"When were you planning on going?" Ken asked, still looking at his computer screen.

"Today or tomorrow," Chad said.

The travel agent looked up at Chad's face, with surprise. "Wow! Man, you're a bit spontaneous, aren't you? What are you doing, running from a girlfriend or something?" Ken chuckled.

"Yeah, something like that." Chad replied, shrugging his shoulders as he spoke.

"Let's see what we got. You know the fares are cheaper when you don't book them last minute. But at least this is not a holiday or anything. Can you travel late at night?"

"Yeah, I'm flexible."

"Are you okay with a stop or two along the way?"

"It's my first time on a plane," Chad said. "So I'd really like to just take off and land once. But that depends on how much the different options cost."

"Okay," the agent said as he finished up the typing, comparing and jotting. "Here are your options. There's a flight out in an hour that you would never make. There is also one tonight that is nonstop but completely booked. Tomorrow, we have a one-stop in Chicago then on to Phoenix. That costs four thirty-five, or, what I think is your better deal, there's a nonstop that costs four seventy-five."

Chad swallowed hard. His savings would be more than cut in half instantly. "I want the one that leaves tomorrow, nonstop." Chad said. He knew without hesitation that he could not wait a minute longer to get away.

"Okay, then," Ken spoke as he started typing again on his computer keyboard. "Flight 138 out of Philadelphia P-A to Phoenix, A-Z, leaving at four on September 25th." A printer next to his desk started noisily churning out a page. Ken stood up and pulled the printed page from the machine. "Here's the confirmation and details. If that is what you want, I can book it and print your boarding pass even. Of course, you'll have to pay me first."

"Okay," Chad said as he pulled a roll of bills out of his wallet.

"Wow!" Ken said. "Real money. No one uses paper money anymore."

"Well, I don't have a credit card yet," Chad said, embarrassed.

"I'll have to see some I.D., though, man." Ken said.

Ken took Chad's driver's license and made a photocopy on the same machine that had printed his confirmation a moment earlier.

"You're all set," Ken said, handing Chad his boarding pass, his license and his change. "Have a good one and good luck in Arizona."

Chad carefully put his license and his boarding pass into his wallet. He exited Adventure Travel with his hands tightly clutching the wallet, knowing its contents would lead him to his mother and away from the loneliness and the feeling of certain doom that engulfed him here.

CHAPTER 9

KELLY: SEPTEMBER 24, 2011

KELLY AWOKE TO find herself looking up into the face of a tall woman with very short blond hair. The woman looked down at Kelly with kind eyes, and she rested her hands lightly on the metal rail of Kelly's hospital bed.

"Hi Kelly. I'm Detective Helen Becker, with the Delaware State Police. I specialize in sexual assault cases, so the Wilmington police have me helping out with your case."

Kelly continued to gaze into the woman's eyes but said nothing. She was exhausted and her whole body ached, but she found herself somehow comforted by this woman's presence.

"I'd like to ask you some questions about what happened this morning, for the purposes of the investigation. Are you up for that?"

Kelly slowly nodded her head "yes" without opening her mouth.

"Okay, then." Detective Becker retrieved a notebook and a pen. "Your husband already confirmed some background information for me, so let's get right to what happened this morning, okay?"

Kelly sat up and pulled her knees against her chest. "May my husband come in for this?" Her head throbbed, her entire backside ached and she shuddered as she realized her inner thighs and her vaginal area felt bruised. She put her face against her knees and sobbed.

"Sure. Let me go get him." Detective Becker replied quickly, relieved to leave the room as Kelly cried. A moment later, Dan followed her back through the doorway to Kelly's room. He strained to mask the pain that he felt at the sound of his wife's sobbing. He looked at Detective Becker, who shrugged as if she had no words for the situation.

Kelly wiped her eyes and took a deep breath. "I feel safer with you here."

Dan took her hand in his and squeezed. In a few short hours he had been transformed from family protector to feckless bystander.

Detective Becker spoke up. "Kelly, can you tell me when you left the house this morning to go running?"

Kelly took a sip of water and started slowly. "I, um, I left the house about seven. I ran a route that I often run, which is about five miles and takes me about forty minutes."

"Do you normally leave your house at that time?"

Kelly was quiet for a moment, with her eyes gazing straight ahead. Dan, desperately wanting to help, answered for his wife. "She usually leaves around seven a.m. We are both morning people."

"Does that sound about right, Kelly?" Detective Becker would have liked to hear the facts directly from the victim, but she realized here she would have to be satisfied with this approach.

"Un-hum," Kelly murmured to show she agreed with Dan's account.

"Are you pretty regular about your running times, though?"

Dan waited a moment to see if Kelly would answer. Then he looked from Kelly's face to Detective Becker and started to answer for his wife again. "Yes, I guess so, except you know, when work schedules or kids' stuff changes it."

Detective Becker looked at Kelly for corroboration. Kelly nodded her head to show her assent. "Got it," Detective Becker said as she kept scribbling. "What about your route?" Detective Becker sounded as if she were growing impatient. "Do you run past Breck's Mill every time?"

Kelly continued to sit silently, holding her knees to her chest. Dan jumped in again, "She runs a few routes, but mostly one that takes her down by the river near Breck's Mill." Then he looked at Kelly. "Kel, is that right?"

Detective Becker tried to hide her frustration. "Kelly, I know this is very difficult for you and that you have been traumatized. I also know that you are feeling pretty banged up and exhausted right now. But please, try real hard to answer my questions, because it is the best chance we have at catching the guy who did this to you. He is still out there and we want to put him behind bars as quickly as possible."

Exhausted, Kelly slid onto her back and looked up at the ceiling. She spoke slowly, licking her dry lips in between her words. "I'm a creature of habit. Most of the time I run that route." Kelly sighed heavily, almost sleepily, before continuing, "I like the river and the woods, especially right by the falls and the mill." Suddenly, Kelly put her hand up to her mouth and started crying again. "Oh, my God!"

Then Detective Becker's questioning became urgent. "That's where it happened, right, Kelly? It is really important that you tell me everything you remember!"

The room fell quiet for a moment as Kelly's sobbing became softer and then subsided. Several agonizing minutes ticked off on the clock on the wall as Kelly lay in the bed, mute.

Dan realized his fists were clenched at his sides. He felt anger, like bile, rising up in him and he summoned all of his strength to suppress a scream. He could not stand it another minute. He was murderously angry at the brute that had done this to his wife. He had to know who this monster was—what he had done. He wanted all of the details! But Dan realized there was something else causing rage to boil up inside of him. He was angry with Kelly. He could not stand that she put herself in a position to get attacked in the first place. He resented how she always acted like she was immune to risk—a little too confident and a little too brazen. And now, his resentment boiled up in a tangled mass of emotions at his wife as she refused to cooperate with the police.

"I'm outta here!" Dan blurted out, startling Kelly. He immediately regretted his outburst when he saw the look on his wife's face. He pulled his cell phone out of his pocket and waved it in the air. In a softer tone he said, "I mean, I am going to step out to call the girls. Okay?"

After Dan left the room, Detective Becker put her hand on the bed next to Kelly and spoke quietly. "Kelly, I need you to dig deep and do this for me. This is critical information we need so we can find your attacker, okay?"

Kelly thought of the smelly, grunting man who had hurt her, violated her and shattered her world. She put her hand up, signaling to Detective Becker that she needed her attention. "Yes."

The detective took a little device out of her bag. "Then... I am going to record this if you don't mind, so I get everything." She placed a small tape recorder on the bed and turned it on.

Kelly started speaking quickly. "I was running along the river and feeling great. And all of a sudden, I felt this painful, sharp sting. It was like a piercing and then a burning, in the back of my right thigh."

Becker interjected. "Where exactly were you when you got shot in the thigh?"

"I was just coming out of the woods and I was approaching Breck's Mill, with the river on my left."

"Did you see anyone before this happened?"

"Not that I recall. Sometimes I see people running or walking dogs in the woods. Sometimes I see people fishing in the river. But I don't really remember seeing anyone there this morning."

"Did you get a look at the object that caused the sharp piercing pain you described?"

Kelly nodded her head slowly. "I stopped and reached around. I saw a little dart sticking right out of the back of my right leg, just under my running shorts. It was metal, I think, but real thin—not like a dart you throw at a board."

"Then what did you do?"

"I grabbed it and pulled it out. I looked around and didn't see anyone, but I knew someone had shot me. I was really scared then, so I tried to run out toward the road. I just took a few steps and I felt really weak and dizzy... and then everything went black."

Detective Becker paused for a moment. "That sounds pretty awful. You must have been terrified." She put her pen down for a moment and looked at Kelly to register her empathy. "What is the next thing that you remember?"

Kelly paused for a moment before responding. "I woke up lying flat on my back on a very hard and uneven surface. I think it was a stone floor, because it was bumpy and cold. My hands were tied together behind my back, and maybe they were also tied to something... I'm not sure about that. I tried to get up but I couldn't, even though my feet seemed free. I had a rough, scratchy blindfold over my eyes. I was shaking. I couldn't stop shaking."

"Did you know where you were?"

"No. I couldn't see much, except for a little slit of light coming in where the blindfold gapped over my nose. So, if I moved a certain way, I could just see down toward my chest a little. I couldn't figure out where I was, except I could hear a river moving nearby and I could smell earthy smells, like mulch or fertilizer or something like that." Kelly stopped for a moment and closed her eyes, trying to remember the terrifying dark place where everything changed forever for her.

"Did you yell for help?" Detective Becker asked.

"No, I couldn't, I had tape over my mouth. I remember being so scared because my nose was sort of stuffed up—I had this sour taste, like vomit, and I think that was making it difficult for me to breathe through my nose, too. I was terrified that I was going to suffocate there, and all I could think of was the fact that breathing through my mouth wasn't an option. I was shaking all over and completely freaking out."

"Now, this is going to get difficult, Kelly. I know it's really painful to remember. But it is so important for our investigation. A clue might come from anything you remember, so please, bear with me." Detective Becker looked at Kelly with her eyes practically begging.

"Okay." Kelly wiped a tear that was slowly trailing down her cheek.

Detective Becker got her started again. "Did you hear anything other than the river?"

"No, except when he came in." Kelly shuddered and caught her breath after she finished the sentence.

"How long do you think you were there before he came in?"

"I don't know. Maybe a few minutes after I woke up, but I

was pretty out of it."

"Tell me about him. What can you tell me about him and about what he did?" Detective Becker tried to keep Kelly's recollections flowing while she had a chance.

Kelly took a few gulps of water while she prepared herself for this part. "I heard what sounded like a nearby door open, and then, for a moment, the sound of the river got louder. Next I heard the door close and then footsteps coming slowly, like the person was unsure. The footsteps got louder as he approached. They sounded like real shoes—you know, with real soles, maybe even a heel?"

"Good! Those are very good details." Detective Becker encouraged her.

Kelly took another deep breath. She sat up a little in her bed again and Detective Becker hoped what she saw in her eyes was a look of determination.

"I heard what sounded like a metal belt buckle hitting the floor. Then my shorts and underwear were being grabbed at the waistband and yanked off. I started to wriggle and kick, but he was too strong, too heavy."

"Did he say anything while you were kicking?"

"No, he never said a word."

Detective Becker knew this was a critical juncture. She had to keep Kelly talking. "Kelly. Did he violate you then? Did he penetrate you?"

Kelly's chin began to tremble and then she started to cry again. "Yes!" she sobbed loudly. "Oh, my God! He pulled me along the floor violently and then I felt him shove himself into me, between my legs. It was so awful! I just remember this whiteness coming through my head. I can't explain it. It was like fear and rage and revulsion all blanketing my brain with static, or fog. Maybe my brain tried to take me somewhere else, but I had nowhere to go." Kelly stopped speaking. She dabbed at her eyes with a wrinkled wet tissue.

"I am so sorry, Kelly. And I am so sorry that you have to re-live it here for me. You're doing great, though." Detective Becker gave Kelly a minute to collect herself and then she spoke softly. "Kelly, as an attorney, you can appreciate that everything I ask you has a purpose here. It is really tough stuff we are talking about, I know. It's painful and terrifying to remember and it is awkward personal stuff. I hope you know I get that." After a moment she began her questioning again. "Did he touch you anywhere else?" the detective asked.

"He was rough with me, you know, pinning me down, pulling me across the floor and he pushed so hard on my thighs, and it hurt so much. But that's all I remember as far as the touching... other than his entering me."

"Are you able to tell me about that part? Could you tell if he had a condom on?"

"I don't know. I was just trying to hang on, to block it out. But the police and doctors have done exams, so they probably have an idea about whether he wore a condom or not."

Detective Becker spoke softly, trying not to upset Kelly. "I can tell you that the initial gynecological exam and evidence collection led the doctors to believe there was a condom used. This means he probably was careful to not leave....uhm.... evidence behind."

Kelly digested this fact. "Well, I guess that's better for me, right?"

"Yes, better health-wise." Detective Becker hesitated, "But unfortunately, it is helpful to us to have DNA evidence. There are other possible sources for that, and we are still analyzing your clothing, the ropes and tape, and anything else that might contain a clue to this guy's identity." Detective Becker gently refocused the conversation. "I have a few more questions about what you remember, okay?"

Kelly nodded.

"Did you ever hear his voice?"

"No. Except I did hear him grunting when he was, you know, attacking me."

"And you could not see any part of him at all, correct?"

Kelly propped herself up in the bed so quickly it startled Detective Becker. "I did! I caught a glimpse of his hands when gave me a shot in my shoulder."

The detective paused, trying not to sound excited. "Okay. This could be important. I want to know about everything you saw and then I want to hear about the shot."

Kelly closed her eyes as she responded, as if she thought she could recall the memory more vividly without any distractions. "His skin was white and he had dark hair on his knuckles and on the back of his hand. And his hand was large, long and thick, like a big man's hand."

"Did you see anything else, a tattoo, a birthmark, jewelry?"

"Oh yes! He wore a big gold ring with a colored stone, the kind you get when you graduate from a school, or win a sports championship."

"Did you see a sleeve or anything else?"

Kelly waited a moment to think. "No. I saw the hands go by under my nose and then I felt a sharp piercing again, like a shot, in my upper arm near my shoulder. I instantly felt very funny again. I just started shutting down. I was scared that I was dying. I really thought I'd never see my girls again, or Dan. Then everything went black." Kelly caught a sob in her throat. She stopped for a moment and took a sip of water.

"I'm sorry to keep pushing you Kelly, but we're almost done. What do you remember next?"

"I woke up in what felt like a different place. The ground under me wasn't as hard and the river sounded much farther away. My wrists were still tied and I had the blindfold on, but the tape had been removed from my mouth." Kelly closed her eyes for a moment and murmured, "Then I heard a woman's voice. God, it made me feel safer immediately to hear a woman's voice. She took off my blindfold and then I was looking up at tree branches and sky. I was lying in the middle of a path just past the bottom of Rockford Park."

"Where, exactly?"

"Near the lawn where the dog park is. A woman was bent over me, trying to untie my hands and my legs and telling me over and over it was going to be okay."

"Tell me about the woman."

"She was a slender African-American woman, probably mid-twenties. She had long braids and an accent, like she was from the islands. She said her name was Jen. Then, after a few minutes, a man in a hoodie and a little dog came running toward us. He shouted something to us about not moving, and then he took a cell phone out of his pocket and called 9-1-1."

"Can you describe the man?"

"He was average-to-tall with an athletic build, probably in his mid-twenties or so too. His sweatshirt had the name of a medical school on it. He was African-American, I think, or maybe bi-racial. He had short dark hair, his face was clean-shaven and he had no noticeable accent."

"Had you ever seen these people before?"

"No, but I was sure glad to see them then. Soon after that, there were policemen and emergency medical technicians swarming around and I was being strapped onto a board and carried through the woods." Kelly paused to rest and to take another sip of water. "I would like to see those people again and thank them."

"They both came to the hospital after you arrived to see how you were doing. You were busy with doctors and evidence collection, but they answered my questions and they did get a chance to talk to your husband."

"Where's Dan? Where is my husband? He's been gone a while."

"He's been standing right outside your door, and he's looking worried. I shooed him away a few times, because it seemed like you were much more willing to talk when he wasn't here." Detective Becker attempted a smile.

Kelly looked away. "It is really hard to imagine that some man did this to me. He tied me up and just fucked me, violently, like he had a right to use my body for his deranged pleasure." Kelly glanced at Detective Becker's face to gauge her reaction. "And now it's hard to even look at Dan. How can I talk about this in front of him?"

Detective Becker patted Kelly's hand. "It's very common for a rape victim to feel anger and guilt afterward. It's so unfair though, since you were the victim. I hear that often in my work. I am not really equipped to help you cope with it though, unfortunately. But, victims that I have worked with have told me that the rape crisis counselor helped them tremendously with these feelings. Call her when you are ready, and let her help you. But right now, I am going to bring your husband in."

Detective Becker left the room as Dan walked back in. "She'll be okay, she's a fighter," the detective said. It was intended more to shore up Dan than to reveal Detective Becker's true feelings about Kelly's state. She knew from experience that Kelly's healing process was going to be long and gradual, with twists and turns that no one could anticipate.

Dan strode over to Kelly with his hands in his jeans pockets, projecting a false sense of assurance. "Hey, babe," he said as he arrived at her bedside. He bent down and kissed her gently on the forehead. "Is there anything I can get you? Do you want something to read? Something to eat?"

"Dan, I need to know what you told the girls? How are they doing?"

"Right now they are with your mom at home, getting pizza delivered and watching a movie. I told them that you got injured when you were running and that you hit your head pretty bad. Of course they want to come see you, but I told them they can't come to the hospital." Dan spoke the next words carefully, dreading her reaction. "I'll go home for dinner with the girls and your mother can come visit you then. The doctors told me that you have to stay here tonight, because of the head injury. But you'll probably be home tomorrow."

"Oh, no," Kelly started to cry again. "I want to go home."

CHAPTER 10

MARIA: SEPTEMBER 25, 2011

A LOUD CONTINUOUS shrieking shattered Maria's deep sleep. "No. It can't be time to wake up," she groaned. "The baby kicked and wiggled and had me up most of the night."

Juan quickly reached to turn off the alarm clock, knocking the lamp off the night table. "It's Sunday, baby. You can go back to sleep. I'm the one who has to work today." He leaned over and kissed her on the cheek. "Once that sweet baby comes, you will stay home in your pajamas and nap when he naps."

Maria closed her eyes and tried to picture their baby sleeping peacefully beside her. Suddenly, the horror of the images from the day before flooded her thoughts. "Oh, my God!" She sat up suddenly.

"What is it?" Juan said, in alarm.

"The lady. Yesterday." Maria turned to Juan. "I need to see the newspaper!" She tugged at Juan's elbow.

"Okay, okay. I'll get it. You are going nowhere today. You start the coffee and I'll run down and get a *News Journal* at the corner," Juan mumbled sleepily as he put on jeans and a white T-shirt.

Maria got out of bed after she heard Juan close the front door. She pulled off the sweaty T-shirt she had slept in and tried to wrap her old bathrobe around her lopsided figure. Even though Juan kept telling her that she looked beautiful with her swollen belly, she was embarrassed by it. She shuffled out to the kitchen counter to start the coffeemaker, listening to its wheezing sound and inhaling its scented steam.

Suddenly, Juan rushed back through their door. "It's in here!" He held the newspaper in front of his face, with his elbows pointed outward, and began reading. *"Woman Assaulted, Found in Park."* He stopped to look at Maria's face. She stood up straight and looked Juan in the eyes.

"Keep reading, please," she begged.

"The Wilmington Police Department reported that yesterday morning, at approximately 9:15 a.m., a woman was discovered tied up and blindfolded on a popular walking trail in the Rockford Park woods. A couple walking their dog found her and called the police. The victim reported that she had been running near Breck's Mill when she was first attacked, but that she did not see her attacker. The victim was admitted to Wilmington Hospital and was reported to be in stable condition. Her name is being withheld because she was the victim of a sexual assault. There is no suspect at present, but the police are following several leads. Anyone with information should call the Wilmington Police Tip Line at (302) 555-TIPS."

Juan finished reading the article and looked up at Maria. "She is okay, baby. She will be fine. She's safe now."

"But I saw the men who did this." Maria said. She raised her hand to her mouth, horrified. "They asked people with information to call the police."

"The paper says the police are already following leads. Most importantly, she is safe now. I am going to ask you once and for all, please leave it alone." He put the paper down and pleaded with her with his large brown eyes.

"Okay, okay, I understand," Maria assured him.

Ten minutes later, Maria poured her second bowl of cornflakes, milk and sugar. Now that she knew the woman from the jogging trail was safe, she realized she was famished.

Juan hurried by, showered and dressed for work in clean tan chinos and a blue polo shirt. Even his steel-toed construction boots were tidy. His wet hair was short and neat and his face was clean-shaven. Juan once told Maria that he would never give anyone a reason to call him a *Dirty Mexican*. He had said it to her as if he was joking, but Maria knew what he meant. She often observed people looking at her with disdain or fear. She noticed old women on the bus gripped their bags tighter when she sat next to them, and she heard other blue-collar workers complaining about Mexicans stealing U.S. jobs.

"That baby is eating me out of house and home—and he or she is not even here yet." Juan joked as he hustled by. "I've got to get down to the corner or I'll miss my ride." He kissed her on the head and strode quickly out the door.

Maria's relief and her fatigue overwhelmed her, so she climbed back into bed. Her thoughts lingered on Juan. From the moment she had met him, she felt compelled to share everything with him and to follow him anywhere. She closed her eyes with a deep sigh, and let her thoughts travel back in time to her home in the Baja and the first time that she met Juan.

*****

Maria was restless after turning eighteen and graduating from high school, and her unrelenting desire was to leave her family's farm in Todos Santos. Her father had purchased the land very cheaply, after drought and market forces brought the former landowner to financial ruin. Through his hard work and with modern irrigation, the land became productive again, yielding tomatoes, Poblano chili peppers and mangos. It was beautiful also, its verdant fields against the backdrop of the Sierra Laguna Mountains. But its natural beauty did not deter Maria in her pursuit of America and its endless possibilities. She had studied hard in school and her English was impeccable. She remembered how she had argued with her parents about it, and her parents' constant refrain that she was "too young, too poor and lacking a plan."

On one fateful afternoon, as Maria hung laundry on a clothesline, she saw a handsome young man climb out of the cab of a large fruit truck in their driveway. She was instantly attracted to his muscular arms as he lifted large boxes of produce, his quiet confidence as he greeted Maria's father with a smile and a handshake, and his generosity as she watched him feed half of his sandwich to one of their farm dogs.

She had summoned up the courage to speak to him, and

their connection formed immediately as they learned that they both shared the dream of building a life in America. Juan had explained that his parents had mastered English in order to advance their careers in the hotel industry, and that their dream was for their son to go to university, travel abroad, and maybe even live in America someday.

Maria remembered how horrified she had been when Juan explained that his parents were killed by a drunk driver when he was sixteen, and that he moved in with his father's only relative, his Uncle Miguel. She recalled this moment with perfect clarity because of the emotions it evoked and the colossal impact that it had on her life. Juan had continued to explain that he was moving to the U.S. with his Uncle Miguel and his Aunt Sabrina who had already secured their visas and employment in Delaware with his Aunt Sabrina's family. But he also confessed that he was drawn to her and needed to see her again.

She smiled as she recalled how, for almost two months after their first meeting, they had spent every free moment together watching the sunset from the edge of the Pacific Ocean or lying together on a blanket in a mango orchard. They held each other and talked for hours, and Juan repeatedly reminded her to be patient and wait until they were both where they needed to be, settled together in America, before they went any further.

When Juan came to say goodbye to Maria, he gave her an envelope containing instructions on how she would join him. Two weeks later, Maria started her journey. She had left her goodbye in a note and slipped out of her house before dawn, because her family would have stopped her. When she sprinted to the end of their driveway and climbed into a large tractor-trailer, she was filled with terror and joy. A friend of Juan's uncle who regularly exported Mexican textiles through the border crossing at Tijuana hid Maria in a large box in the cargo compartment of his truck. After they were safely over the California line, she moved to the cab of the truck and saw America for the first time.

Maria remembered so clearly the hardship of the journey. She slept in the cab of the truck, ate food out of vending machines and washed in highway rest stops, as the truck made its way across the country. She was hungry, tired and frightened in the big cities and in the lonely stretches of highway, with the company of only a stranger. But the ordeal led her to her necessary and euphoric reunion with Juan. On the fifth day, Maria's heart leapt as the truck bounced into an industrial park in Wilmington, and she saw Juan running toward her. When Juan wrapped his arms around her she had known that she was home.

*****

The shrill ring of Maria's cell phone brought her abruptly back to the present, and to the little apartment that she shared with Juan.

"Hello?"

"Hi Maria, it's Gloria. Boss says he knows it's Sunday, but we have to be at a new job by eight o'clock. He is bringing the van to get us. So, the good news is, you will get paid time and a half since it is Sunday, and you don't have to catch the bus. The bad news is, there goes your day off. We'll be by to get you around seven forty-five in front of your place on King Street."

Maria sighed and rubbed her left temple, which throbbed with pain. She briefly fantasized about refusing to go to work. Her exhaustion overwhelmed her and her ankles were swollen with fluid. She was desperate to climb back into her bed and close her eyes. But she knew that she could not lose her job yet. With the baby came new expenses—and loss of her income.

After she showered and dressed, Maria hurried to the kitchen to pack her food for the day. A photograph taped to the refrigerator door caught her eye. Her parents smiled at her against the backdrop of the Pacific Ocean. Maria studied her father's face and felt as if his eyes were looking into her soul. She could almost hear her father's voice say the words that he had spoken to her many times as a child.

"Maria, always treat others as you would like them to treat you. That is known as the Golden Rule, and you should always try to live your life according to that rule."

Maria looked away from her father's gaze in shame, as she thought about the woman she had seen carried into the park. She peeked at her watch to check the time and then she reached for her cell phone. Maria pushed the numbers on her phone, exhaling and inhaling slowly to give herself courage.

"Hello, Wilmington Police Tip Line." Maria was relieved to hear it was a woman on the other end of the line. "Are you calling with a tip?"

"Yes. I'm calling about the lady attacked and then found near Rockford Park yesterday."

"Okay, ma'am, I am going to transfer you to a detective for this. Please hold...."

Before Maria could object, she heard a man speaking. "Hello, Detective Johnson here. May I have your name please?"

"Um, I'd rather not say."

"You don't want to give me your name?"

"No." Maria said, feeling a little ridiculous as she continued. "Look, I want to tell you what I saw because it might be helpful—can we just start there?"

"Yes, ma'am," the man said. "We can start there. What did you see?"

Maria chose her words carefully. "Yesterday morning I was in the Breck's Mill Art Gallery, next to the Brandywine River. I saw a woman who was jogging along the river get shot or something, and then she was carried away by a man. A man with a gun shot something that hit the lady in the back of her leg as she ran by. He was hiding behind a tree, and after she ran by, it looked like he hit her with a dart or something." Maria paused for a moment to accurately reconstruct her memory of the events. "The woman stopped immediately and reached around like she was in pain. She pulled the dart—or whatever it was—out of her leg. She took a few steps and then she just went down and like, collapsed."

"Okay, this is all very helpful. What did you see next, ma'am?"

"The man came out from behind the tree and picked her up in his arms and walked into an area that was heavily wooded. I couldn't see them anymore."

"What did the man look like?"

"He was white and very tall, maybe over six feet tall." Maria vividly recalled the memory of the hulking figure carrying away the small seemingly lifeless woman. The image made her shudder suddenly.

"What was he wearing?"

"I don't remember the details, really. I think he was dressed casually, in some sort of pants, like corduroys or jeans. He had a tan jacket on, cut kind of like a jean jacket, but bigger."

"Take your time, ma'am. Is there anything else about the man you can remember, like the color of his hair, or if he had facial hair?"

Maria closed her eyes as if that would help her remember. "I don't remember facial hair, I don't think he had any. I am almost certain that his hair was dark, maybe dark brown or black but maybe graying. It was pretty short, too."

"Okay, ma'am. That's helpful. Is there anything else you can think of regarding this man?"

Maria paused, again with her eyes closed. Then she shook her head to no one in particular and said, "No, that is all."

"What did the woman look like?"

Maria thought for a moment. "She was petite. She had on running clothing; shorts and a T-shirt, and running shoes."

"Was she fighting or screaming or anything?"

"No. After she got hit with that dart she seemed to just fall over and go limp."

"What time did you see these events unfold?"

"It was a little after seven-thirty in the morning."

"Do you think we've covered everything you can remember seeing?"

Maria envisioned the detective marking boxes on a police investigative report. She pictured the lines next to *Name* and *Address* left blank.

"Well, that's the weird thing." Maria replied. "I saw more than that. About nine I saw another man involved. But I am pretty sure it was the same woman."

"Excuse me?" The detective sounded truly puzzled.

"I was still at the Breck's Mill site, and I saw a man pull up in a car, unload a woman wrapped in a rug or a blanket, and carry her into the woods." Maria looked at her watch. She would be late for work if she did not finish this conversation quickly. But she could not bring herself to abandon the effort. She felt lighter and better able to breathe all of a sudden, just from unburdening herself of this information.

"What can you remember about the car?"

"It was a station wagon. It was blue, I think."

"Did you see the license plate?"

Maria glanced at the crumpled piece of paper she had retrieved from her wallet. "It was a Delaware license plate, and the first four numbers are 8-2-6-6."

"What about the man? You said you saw a man, right?"

"Yes. He was a white man, with a medium to tall build and dark hair. He was thinner and a little shorter than the man with the gun. Also, he was wearing blue jeans and a dark T-shirt." Maria added, "Oh, and he looked pretty young. Maybe in his late teens or early twenties."

"Okay, then what did you see specifically after he pulled up in the station wagon?"

"He pulled out a large bundle in a blanket and slung part of it over his shoulder and walked quickly into the woods below Rockford Park. I saw a pair of feet dangling out of the bottom of the blanket and then I knew there was a body in there."

"Ma'am, why didn't you call the police when you were witnessing these events?"

Maria bit her thumbnail as she spoke. "I, um, I was really scared. At first I wasn't sure what I had seen and I was afraid to get involved. I am still scared, but I read in the paper this morning that the police need information to catch these guys. I realized I might be the only one who saw this."

Maria pictured the expression on the face of the detective as he listened to Maria with growing cynicism or disgust. Maria suddenly became very self-conscious of her Mexican accent and her obvious fear of the police. She felt her face grow warm, and she gripped the phone with white knuckles.

"Ma'am, can you tell me what you were doing at Breck's Mill?"

"Um, I really don't want to talk about myself, okay?" Maria started to panic, worrying that she had already gone too far. She thought about Juan and his desire to always play it safe.

The detective spoke softly and casually, trying to keep his reluctant witness on the line.

"I am going to forward this information to the detectives assigned to this case. These are important details. Can you come to our building on Walnut Street today? Or we can send a detective to your home."

"I'm late for work, I have to go now. I am sorry."

Maria grabbed her lunch box and locked her apartment door behind her.

*****

Maria stood on the sidewalk in front of her apartment. Newspapers blew by and empty bottles rattled around on the ground. A loud city bus rumbled past and a homeless man pushed a shopping cart across the street. Maria felt lost and frightened. She was not sure where the nice homes with the big green lawns were, or if they were ever going to live that dream. She adored Juan, and she believed in him, but she was losing her faith in the dream that their home was here.

CHAPTER 11

CHAD: SEPTEMBER 25, 2011

CHAD PULLED A duffel bag and a knapsack out of his closet and began packing everything he was taking. He tightly rolled his clothing in order to cram them into the duffel. He left behind his heavy down parka, snow boots, and anything else that he would not need in Arizona. When the duffel bag was stretched taut with his clothing and belongings, he turned to his knapsack. He packed toiletries, a handful of Power Bars, sunglasses, and two guidebooks on Arizona. In the front zippered pocket he put his airplane ticket and the remainder of his cash. Then he carefully enclosed an envelope containing two old photographs of his mother with her sister, as well as the postcard from his aunt. He had everything packed and stored in his closet when he heard his father stir for breakfast. Chad had hoped that his father would sleep late, since it was Sunday and because he had heard him stumble into the house drunk after closing time at the tavern. He walked casually into the kitchen. "Hey, Dad. Good morning."

"Good morning, yourself. How about you make the coffee and I'll get the Cheerios?"

"Deal." Chad said as he started to pull a can of ground coffee from the pantry. "Hey Dad, I was wondering if you're working today?"

"Yeah, how come?" Charlie McCloskey asked as he pulled a

giant box of Cheerios out of the closet.

"I sort of have an engagement."

"Hey, hey," Charlie chuckled. "A date, you mean? An actual date with a live girl?"

Chad bristled at his father's sarcasm. "Yeah, I guess you could say that," he awkwardly responded.

"Who is she?" Charlie asked with a smirk of amusement on his face.

"No one you know. I met her at the library the other day."

"When do you need to leave?" Charlie asked.

"I'd like to take her to Philadelphia. We're going to the Art Museum and then to dinner. But I'd like to run a few errands first, maybe get a haircut and things like that." Chad had already devised his explanation, hoping it would sound plausible. "And it's already nine o'clock and I'd need to be home by noon, so I was hoping I could just skip today."

"Wow, sounds like a lot of work for a girl you don't even know." Charlie scratched the rubble on his chin. "Whatever happened to a burger and a movie? You trying to impress some spoiled college girl or something?"

Chad pretended not to feel the hurt and humiliation that his father's comments intended. He could play the game a little longer, knowing what his father wanted to hear. "Come on, Dad. She is really cute."

"Well son, I have never so much as heard you mention a girl, so I guess.I should just be relieved you're not a fag."

"Dad! Geez, why do you have to make everything so hard?"

"Okay, okay, I am just pulling your leg, son. I don't have much to do today anyway, so I guess I don't really need you."

"Thanks." Chad thought for a second, wondering if he should be bold. "I was also wondering Dad, could I maybe get my allowance for the week?"

"Hell, now you are pushing it." Charlie shuffled across the linoleum floor and retrieved a coffee can out of a drawer. He pulled out a roll of bills and started to peel them off. "Here's your allowance for the week." He stopped for a moment and then waved two twenty-dollar bills in the air. "In fact, I think I'll give myself a little allowance too, because I got me a little date tonight too, at the tavern at five." He laughed a little at his own joke.

Chad took the money and, without counting it, shoved it into his wallet. Charlie surprised him by snatching the wallet out of his hand. "Tell me this pretty girl's name if you want your wallet back."

Chad felt his face flush with rage at his father's typical demeaning behavior.

"Oh, look, your face is getting all red. Are you embarrassed?" Charlie sneered.

"Dammit, Dad! Why do you have to be so mean all the time?" Chad surprised himself with his own honesty. He saw the smirk on his father's face quickly disappear.

"Oh, come on son." Charlie said. "Here's your wallet. Here, I'll give you another forty," he said as he shoved two more twenty dollar bills into Chad's wallet and held it out to his son.

Chad swallowed his pride and took the wallet and the extra forty dollars without another word. He had earned them anyway. More importantly, he needed them now to get out of there and find his mother. "I'll see you later, Dad."

For a brief moment Chad felt sorry for his father, realizing that he would soon be left all alone in the sad house by the river, with his brown liquor bottles and his bitterness and rage. But Chad could not bear to stay with him for one more minute. When Charlie took the newspaper into the bathroom, Chad ran to his closet and grabbed the duffel bag and knapsack. He slipped quietly through the front door and ran to his mother's car. He stuffed the bags in the back of the station wagon. He reached for the old picnic blanket to cover them, only to realize that he had left it with the woman on the ground. A shudder ran down his spine as he thought about his ordeal the day before. He bit his lip and thought about how he would put this all in his past for good, in just a few more hours.

After breakfast and a quick shower, Chad walked calmly to his mother's station wagon with the car keys in his hand. His father finished loading a leaf blower onto the back of his pickup truck and climbed into his driver's seat. Just as they started to back both vehicles down the driveway a black-and-white police cruiser pulled up. Chad's heart began to race as two officers got out of their car.

Those guys again. Now what? Chad thought.

Charlie heard them pull up and got out of his truck.

Chad reluctantly climbed out of the station wagon and approached the officers, fearful that this time they were there to arrest him. "Good morning," Officer Stevens greeted them both.

Charlie called to them, "Have you found my wife?"

"No, sir. I am sorry to say that we have not. We are here today because we are looking into a matter involving the same car—her station wagon, the one that was abandoned at the bus station." Officer Stevens spoke as his eyes rested on the station wagon that Chad had just climbed out of. "Who was driving that car yesterday, sir?"

Chad started to sweat. He wiped a drop as it came down his forehead.

"Well, I guess my son here is the only one who has been driving it since last June when you returned it to us. Chad, have you been lending that damn car to anyone?"

Chad had no time to think of a safe answer and he did not want to look suspicious, so he just answered quickly with the truth. "No, sir. Unless, of course, if someone took it without my knowledge," he added, hoping to confuse matters a little.

Officer Stevens produced a piece of paper and stepped forward as he spoke. "I have a search warrant here for that car. We are going to impound it down in the Wilmington City Police lot and have it searched. May I have the key?" Officer Stevens looked at Charlie and then at Chad.

Chad reached into his jeans pocket and handed over a key chain with two keys. He started to extend his hand toward the officer, when Charlie's voice stopped him. "Wait! What the hell for?"

Chad stood dumbfounded. He silently extended his arm and dropped his keys in Officer Stevens's upturned palm. He felt his face heat up and tried to swallow a lump in his throat.

Officer Stevens was blunt. "Chad, I know you're not going to like this. I have orders to take you in for questioning as a person of interest in an assault that occurred yesterday. Will you come now, peacefully, or do I have to wait on the arrest warrant that will be available very soon?"

"No fucking way!" Charlie raised his voice. "My kid would

not harm a flea. You're not taking him anywhere. What the hell is going on"? He spit as he talked, and his face became scarlet.

"It's okay, Dad," Chad said. "I'll go."

"This is crazy!" Charlie continued to rant, as Chad followed the officers to their car. Chad walked with an officer on each side of him. They got to the patrol car and he slid into the back seat without uttering a word. "I'm following you over. This is bullshit!" Charlie ran to his truck and started its engine.

A flatbed tow truck arrived and idled at the end of the driveway, waiting for the patrol car to clear the path to the blue station wagon. Chad rode in silence, with his heart pounding and his knees shaking. Desperately he pictured the carefully packed duffel bag and the knapsack with his plane ticket in the station wagon that was about to be impounded and searched. Instead of flying to reunite with his mother, to her love and to the warmth of Arizona, he was being taken to the police station for questioning.

Chad took a deep breath, trying to control his fear. He shuddered at the realization that the truthful account of his last twenty-four hours would lead most people to think the worst. He desperately wanted to turn back the clock so he could do the right thing this time. He pictured himself calling 9-1-1 and describing to the police exactly where he saw the woman. But he was confused and terrified. Chad nervously twisted his hands. *I should have minded my own business,* he thought. But he knew he would not have been capable of leaving even a stranger to suffer and possibly die.

"Christ!" he moaned out loud, as he ran his hands through his hair and exhaled loudly.

"Are you okay back there, son?" Officer Morgan turned and asked him from the front passenger seat.

"Yes, sir," Chad lied.

*****

The patrol car parked next to a one-story brick building with a blue and white "Wilmington Police" flag fluttering in front of the building.

"Okay Chad, this is where we get out," Officer Stevens said as he opened Chad's door.

Chad followed the officers into the building. They took him straight to a small room, containing only a square table and two chairs. The room had no windows, except for a glass pane on the door. Chad sat in the chair that Officer Stevens motioned to which faced an empty seat on the other side of the table. Beyond the empty chair he saw his reflection in a large mirror, which no doubt was a window through which he was being observed and possibly recorded.

The officers left the room and a man in a grey suit entered. He looked trim and athletic, with salt-and-pepper grey hair and steel-blue eyes that looked animated as he paced back and forth beyond the table. He stopped mid-stride and looked at Chad. "I'm sorry, I don't know where my manners are. Sometimes my mind gets working on something, and then my feet get moving and I sort of lose the ability to be polite. I'm Tim Hahn, Wilmington police detective."

Chad tried to look as calm as possible, but when he glanced at the mirror opposite him he saw a pale face with dark stubble on his chin and frightened eyes. He saw the face of a criminal. "I....um, I am Chad McCloskey." Chad said awkwardly.

"Well, Chad, we have a few things to talk about here." Detective Hahn sat down and looked almost gently at Chad as he leaned forward over the table. "Do you want a Coke or a bottle of water or something?"

"No thanks, Mr. Hahn," Chad replied, trying in vain to appear casual and unconcerned as he avoided his reflection in the mirror beyond his interrogator.

"Please, call me Tim," the detective said, trying to relax Chad and free him up to speak. Chad ran his hand through his hair, trying to smooth it down. "Look, sir. Uhm, I mean, Tim, I think there's been some mistake. I have not hurt anyone. I would never hurt anyone. I have never committed a crime in my life... if you would just check, you'd see."

"Let me stop you there, Chad. We've already run the check on you, and I know that you have never had a conviction or arrest or any contact with the law. Your old man is another story, though. It seems he is no stranger to a bottle or a fistfight, and so he's got a little rap sheet."

Chad swallowed hard and tried to take a long slow breath

to calm himself. He focused his eyes on his sneakers under the table, trying to stop the panic welling up inside of him.

"But," the detective continued, "early this morning we received a call from an eyewitness who placed someone looking just like you, and driving your car, at the scene of a crime committed yesterday." He looked right into Chad's eyes and held his gaze. "So maybe you can answer a few questions for us."

Chad looked at the scared pale stranger in the mirror as he heard himself say, "I'd like a lawyer before I speak to you, sir."

"There you go, calling me 'sir' again." The detective shook his head as if to make light of the situation. "Why do you think you need a lawyer?"

Chad sat quietly, choosing not to answer the last question.

"Did you hear me, Chad?" Detective Hahn's voice rose as he started to grow frustrated.

"Yes, I heard you, sir." Chad looked down again at his feet crossed under the table. He summoned all of his courage, cleared his throat and said, "I am innocent and yet I was told that a warrant for my arrest is about to arrive. So yes, I'd like a lawyer."

"Do you have a lawyer you want to call?" Tim Hahn asked Chad.

"No, sir, I don't know who to call. I've never had a lawyer. I don't even know a lawyer." Chad studied the stitching and the Nike swoop on his running shoes under the table.

After a moment passed, Detective Hahn rose from his chair. He slowly walked to the door, opened it and leaned out into the hallway. "The kid wants a lawyer. Call the public defender and get somebody over here. I know it's a Sunday, but we need someone right away. I don't want any delay. Oh, and let's get him before the Magistrate while we are at it, we might as well make it official and execute the arrest warrant." He poked his head back into the room where Chad sat. "This might take a while. Someone is coming from the public defender's office. Do you need a bathroom or anything?"

Chad nodded his head. He had been fighting the urge to urinate since he had been placed into the patrol car that morning. An officer in a dark uniform came into the room and escorted him down the hall to the restroom. Right before he went in he saw his father sitting out in the waiting area, nervously rubbing his chin. His father's eyes met his with a glare of contempt. Chad wondered if the police had told his father what they thought he had done.

Chad was brought before a Magistrate Court housed in the police station. He was told what he already knew; that he was being charged with rape and kidnapping. He had a right to counsel and he should not say anything because it could be used against him if he did. Chad felt like he was watching this on television, because *it could not be happening to him.*

After his appearance before the Magistrate, Chad waited in the interrogation room for what seemed like hours. Finally a tall, thin young man in an ill-fitting suit came in and extended his hand to Chad. "I'm Stuart Harlan, from the public defender's office," he said nervously. "I am your lawyer in this matter."

"I'm Chad McCloskey," Chad shook his hand, but did not look him in the eye.

Stuart spoke up. "I know you were a person of interest when you came in this morning, but I was told on the way in that now you are officially under arrest, and you had your initial appearance. So from here on out, you do not talk to anyone but me, and you are going to have to be real straight with me if I'm going to help you, okay?"

Chad looked up at him to answer. "Yes."

"And," Stuart added, "whatever you tell me is between you and me only. It is the law and my professional responsibility to keep our conversations protected. So you really have no reason whatsoever to be less than completely honest with me."

Chad nodded.

After a moment, Chad said, "Can I ask you a question first?"

"Sure," Stuart said.

"How many cases have you had? I mean how long have you been doing this?"

"Well, I am pretty new at it, I guess. I just graduated from law school and passed the bar last year, but I worked for the public defender's office when I was in law school and I have had a few cases already. This is my first felony, though."

"Great." Chad said with sarcasm and despair.

"Let's get started." Stuart took a legal pad out of his shiny new briefcase. Next to it he placed a set of stapled documents.

"I just got assigned to this matter, so I don't have much yet. But, I do have the affidavits in support of the arrest warrant, and the search warrant itself. I am going to ask you to tell me your version of events before I share these with you." Stuart pushed a photo of a woman's face toward him. "Do you know Kelly Malloy?"

Chad examined the photo. "No. I don't know that name and I don't think I have ever seen her before." Chad replied. Then he thought for a moment. "I mean, I had never seen her before yesterday."

Stuart suddenly sat up straight. "So you did see her yesterday?"

Chad was quiet. He was unsure of what to say. It all sounded so unbelievable.

"Did you pick up her body and carry it somewhere in the woods?" Stuart asked.

"What did they tell you? Did they tell you I was seen carrying her?" Chad asked.

"Listen, Chad," Stuart said slowly "you are going to just have to tell me everything, from the beginning, and be honest. It's the only way I am going to do my job."

Chad looked down at his hands in his lap and heard the clock in the room tick off the minutes. He clearly recalled the previous day's events, but he was terrified to say them out loud. His discovery and his actions would seem implausible to any reasonable person.

"Yesterday morning I was walking in the woods near my home, near the Brandywine River." Chad started. "I glanced at this gardener's shed that I walk by all the time, and its door was open. Something big and colorful in the shed caught my eye. I walked closer and saw it was a woman. Her hands and legs were tied, and she had tape over her mouth and a blindfold over her eyes. She was breathing though, so I knew she was alive." Chad stared off into the distance, as he replayed the memory.

"Why didn't you get help?" Stuart asked the obvious question.

"I was really scared. I mean, this woman was bound and gagged. I knew she had been assaulted in some way, and now I am alone with her in the woods. I was sure I looked guilty just being there. I mean, I was terrified and I didn't think straight."

"So what did you do next?" Stuart asked.

"I put my sweatshirt over her to keep her warm, while I ran home and got my car and a few other things to help her."

"What do you mean, 'help her'?" Stuart asked.

"I moved her to a place where other people would find her and get her help."

"How did you do that?" Stuart asked, again with his eyebrows arched.

"I wrapped her up in a blanket, put her in my car and drove her close to where the trail is heavily used. Then I moved her to a spot on the trail and I hid out where I could keep an eye on her until she was rescued." Chad looked straight at Stuart when he said this.

"Where exactly was this?" Stuart kept scribbling on his pad as he asked questions.

"The loop of the path that is just below Rockford Tower, near the dog park area. Lots of people come through there, jogging and walking dogs. I put her down on the trail and then I ran to a hiding spot to watch until she was rescued."

"Who did you see rescue her? Give me every detail, this is important." Stuart said.

"A tall African-American woman with long black hair and a small dog came first. A minute after them a man she called Michael—I guess her husband or boyfriend. He was tall and he wore a sweatshirt."

"Hmmm," Stuart rubbed his chin. "Those are good details, Chad, because they jibe with the details I already have. I don't have a description of the couple, and they don't give me the names of witnesses, but the other details match."

Stuart rubbed his temples and Chad was certain he saw Stuart's eyebrows relax.

"Can I go home now?" Chad asked.

"I'm not sure what is happening next. I'll talk to the prosecutor from the AG's office. I'm going to step out and see if I can find her. Are you okay here for a little bit?"

Just then, a heavyset woman with grey hair popped her head inside the door. "Hey Stu, can I see you for a minute?"

"Excuse me," Stuart said to Chad. "That's the prosecuting attorney right now." He stepped out of the room and closed the door. Chad could see them through the glass pane in the door, but he could not hear what they were saying. The woman appeared to be doing all of the talking, with her hands moving as she became more animated in her conversation. Chad saw Stuart hold his hand up to stop her, and then he appeared to be trying to convince her of something. The woman had the last word, and then she left, abruptly. Chad watched Stuart turn and slowly come back into the room.

"I have some bad news for you, Chad. The AG's office has an eyewitness account possibly placing you with the victim yesterday. But I am also troubled by something you haven't told me. You bought a one-way ticket to fly to Phoenix, Arizona today? That's a bit suspicious, isn't it?" Stuart looked annoyed at Chad.

"It didn't seem relevant." Chad explained. "I wanted to get away from my father and find my mother. No one needed to know that part." Chad got choked up and summoned all of his energy to not cry in front of his lawyer.

"Well, it doesn't look good, for starters." Stuart said. "It looks like you planned the whole thing. It makes you look guilty and it makes you look like a flight-risk. Do you know what that means?" Stuart asked Chad, exasperated by this latest discovery.

Chad sat down at the table, put his head in his hands, and started sobbing.

"Look," Stuart said quickly, "I believe you, but you have to see what the prosecution is thinking right now. There are things we can be hopeful about: they still have to do an investigation, including physical evidence on the victim, and that may exonerate you. They need to interview the victim and the eyewitness. You have your account of your rescue attempt and the couple that rescued her, and no one would know that without being there. So, there are lots of things that can get you off the hook, but it is going to take some time. So hang in there and don't open your mouth to anyone unless I am here with you, okay?"

"Yes," Chad mumbled, wiping away tears from his cheeks with the back of his hands.

Before I go, though, tell me about this plane ticket. What was the deal there?"

Chad bit his lip nervously and then spoke, softly. "I was

going to find my mother."

"What do you mean?" Stuart tried to ask in a way that would not further upset the young man in front of him who suddenly looked very fragile.

Chad raised his head from his hands and wiped the tears from his eyes with the sleeve of his shirt. "My mother was the only person who was ever kind to me, who ever made me feel good about myself." Chad took a breath, regained his composure, and looked up at Stuart. "She took off in May, right around the time I was graduating from high school, and she never told me she was going. I knew she had to get away from my Dad; he made her so unhappy. He was always putting her down, yelling at her, mocking her. But I could go to her. She'd want me." Chad's voice cracked with emotion as he said the last part.

"She's in Phoenix now?" Stuart asked.

"Yeah," Chad said. "Well, I'm pretty sure that she's in Scottsdale. I found a postcard and some other things from her sister. It makes sense. I don't think my Mom was strong enough to go somewhere and start a new life all by herself, and she didn't have anyone except me and my Dad, and her one sister."

"So you were just going to fly out there, one-way, with no other plan, based on a hunch that your mother was there?" Stuart asked in a voice filled with disbelief.

"It's not like that. You wouldn't understand. I needed to be with her, and I knew I would find her." Chad choked a little on his words. "There is nothing for me here. I can't stay here."

Stuart took the cue to stop pressuring Chad. "Okay, Chad. You sit tight for now and rest assured I am working on this. I'll talk to your father about your mother's relocation and your plan to go see her."

"No!" Chad jumped up to his feet.

Stuart stepped back, startled. "Jesus, Chad, what the hell?"

"He doesn't know anything about it. He can't. Don't you see? He's the reason she disappeared in the first place. She had to get away from him. He's a miserable, mean drunk and I hate him for what he did to her. I'd rather rot here in a prison cell than let him find my mom and make her miserable again."

"Okay, I won't say anything to him now, but I'm quite sure he is going to find out as the investigation continues. Do you know where the postcard is and anything else that supports your story about the ticket to Phoenix?"

"It's not a story," Chad said, still riled up about his father. "It's in a knapsack in the station wagon that the police towed away and probably searched already."

"I see," Stuart said. "I'll look into it." Stuart paused for a moment and contemplated whether or not he should tell Chad something. He crossed his arms over his chest and said softly, "Chad, I have to tell you something. A guy from the *News Journal* is here snooping around. I told him 'no comment,' but he knows your identity and that the police brought you here as a suspect."

Chad put his head in his hands and thought of all those kids in school that had mocked him or ignored him, and all of the teachers who had pitied him or quietly despised him. Soon they would all be seeing his photo next to a caption describing him as a rapist.

CHAPTER 12

KELLY: SEPTEMBER 25, 2011

"MOMMY! YOU'RE BACK!" The girls shrieked and jumped up and down, clapping their hands as Kelly and Dan stepped into the foyer of their home. Despite her dark mood, Kelly felt her face lift into a smile. It was clear that in her absence the girls had picked out their outfits. Anna wore black tights under her father's giant Philadelphia Eagles football jersey and Grace paired her pink ballet tutu with a smiley-face sweatshirt. Kelly took a deep breath as her daughters squeezed her around the waist. She had longed to come home to them as she had lain in the hospital, and she had desperately yearned to hold them once again while she was tied up in the darkness, not knowing her fate. But now that she was actually here she was unable to take comfort in their embrace. Her skin felt like it was crawling. Her head and back ached, her thighs throbbed, and she felt an overwhelming urge to push past everyone and drag herself to bed.

Kelly's mother stood nearby, a strained smile on her face. Her short silver hair framed an expression that was obviously masking pain. Her hazel eyes were bloodshot from crying. She opened her mouth to say something, but nothing came out. Finally, she walked over to Kelly and wrapped her in a hug. Kelly felt her mother's body shake, and she heard a sob.

"It's okay, Mom. I'm fine. I just need to rest." Kelly lied.

She forced a smile as she said with what she hoped sounded like cheerful enthusiasm, "I am so glad to be home with my girls! But now I really need to rest. I'm sorry, girls, but I bet Dad and Gran want to play Uno or bake brownies."

Dan stepped forward, his hands in the front pockets of his jeans. "Yeah, how about both? Let's bake brownies and then eat them while we play Uno!"

Kelly's legs were heavy as she climbed the stairs to her bedroom. The soreness in her pelvis made her feel queasy. She shrugged out of her jacket, kicked her running shoes off, and slid under her down comforter. She had forgotten to draw the blinds, so the sun streamed into the room. Too exhausted to care, she put a pillow over her eyes and lay there, wishing for sleep. Despite her overwhelming fatigue, she felt as if low-grade electricity was running through her body, making her restless and jumpy. Horrible images and sensations kept flashing through the darkness in her head; the cold, hard floor under her back, the tight, rough ropes on her wrists, and the heaviness of that man over her, coming at her, entering her. She sat up in bed. The early afternoon sun shone brightly outside, and her whole family was one floor below her, safe. Her heart was racing. She picked up the jacket that she had dropped on the floor and found a vial in its pocket. Little blue pills rattled inside. The doctor had prescribed them in case she had trouble sleeping. Without reading the label, Kelly put two pills in her mouth, tipped her head up to look at her bedroom ceiling, and swallowed.

She went into her bathroom and ran her faucet. A battered and aged version of her face appeared in the bathroom mirror. Dark bags hung under her eyes and a red mark remained around her lips where the duct tape had been removed. Her hair was plastered around her neck and shoulders and the elastic ponytail holder still clung to the bottom of the matted mess. Her world had experienced a colossal shift since she put that elastic band in her hair the morning before; it had tipped on its axis and Kelly was just trying to hang on.

She swallowed some water from her cupped hands to help the pills settle. Then she sorely and gingerly sat down on the toilet to relieve herself. As she saw the purple and brown bruises spreading across her inner thighs she started sobbing, softly at first, and then causing her whole body to shake. With tears still streaming down her face, she dragged her body to the bedroom windows to shut the sunlight out, climbed back into bed and finally found sleep.

CHAPTER 13

MARIA: SEPTEMBER 25, 2011

MARIA FELT AS if she was crawling up the last flight of stairs to her apartment. It had been a hard workday and she was exhausted. Excruciating back pain had been stabbing at her all day. She paused at the door of her apartment and rubbed her back. As she was about to open the door with her key, it swung open, surprising her.

"Oh my goodness, you scared me!" Maria said to Juan as he opened the door with great force.

"I was just showing these people out." Juan spoke with anger in a manner that Maria had never heard before.

It was only then that Maria noticed a tall man in a grey suit and tie, and a tall blonde woman in a blue pants suit standing behind Juan.

"Maria?" The woman asked. "Maria Hernandez?"

"Yes?" Maria responded.

"Don't tell them anything." Juan hissed to Maria.

"Juan. Please!" Maria pleaded with him, "What is this about? You are scaring me."

"I'm Detective Helen Becker, with the Delaware State Police, and this is Detective Tim Hahn, Wilmington Police."

Maria's pulse raced and she started to sweat.

"It is nice to meet you, Maria. We have reason to believe that you witnessed a crime that we are investigating. You are not in any trouble and no one suspects you of any wrongdoing. We just need to talk to you."

Maria looked at Juan, whose eyes silently pleaded with her to be quiet and play dumb. "I'm, uh... I am not sure what you are speaking about."

"Please," the woman spoke gently, "I know this is a bit frightening, but just hear us out. We traced a phone call to the Wilmington Police Tip Line to your cell number, and then your cell account to this address. We also have talked to people at the Breck's Mill Art Gallery and to the person you work for at the Cleaning Angels. They all tell us you were scheduled to be at Breck's Mill at the time of the events being investigated. Please, we are just asking for your cooperation."

"Maria, don't talk to them until I can get someone at the LACC on the phone." Juan snapped as he pulled his cell phone out of his pocket.

"The LACC?" Detective Hahn asked to no one in particular.

"The Latin American Community Center," Detective Becker answered him. "It provides services to the Latin American population, including finding them lawyers."

Maria leaned against the frame of the front door to her apartment. She clutched at her side and back with both hands as she felt a painful stab seize her back and side again. She saw Juan talking quietly on his cell phone and the two detectives having a conversation as if they were in a grey fog. Her pain enveloped her and sealed her off from their world. She felt a warm wet rushing sensation between her legs and watched the clear viscous liquid pool on the floor and splash onto her shoes.

"Oh, my God!" Detective Becker pointed to Maria's feet. "Her water just broke. We have to get her to a hospital."

Juan ran to Maria and grabbed her just as she started to swoon. "Baby, are you okay?" His eyes looked right into hers with alarm and urgency.

"Yes. It hurts Juan, but it is time. My due date was October third, so I guess he or she wants to be a September baby." Maria managed a little smile through her gritted teeth.

"We have no car." Juan said to the detectives. "Can you take us to the hospital? Wilmington Hospital is just up the street."

"Let's go!" Detective Becker said.

CHAPTER 14

CHAD: SEPTEMBER 26, 2011

CHAD STARTLED AND opened his eyes to the white cinder block wall of his cell. His body was sore from the thin mattress that he had tossed and turned on all night. Stuart was shaking him with one hand, and holding up clothing with the other. A navy blue blazer and grey pants hung on a wire hanger.

"These may not be a perfect fit, but your father couldn't find anything in your closet that remotely met my description of clothing appropriate for your arraignment. So I got these from the public defender's closet. They are clean, at least." He thrust the hanger toward Chad. "We waived your preliminary examination because I saw no benefit. They will be able to show probable cause exists to hold you over, and they can even rely on hearsay evidence in this stage. I went through what they have so far and I don't see how we can change that at present. So, I want to speed up the process because you'll be held in the meantime, and my goal is to get your plea in and get you out pending trial."

"Trial?" Chad asked, still in a fog from his fitful sleep.

"I'm hoping we never get to that, but that's a conversation for later. One step at a time," Stuart answered.

Twenty-five minutes later, after a quick shower and shave, Chad was led into a courtroom by a prison guard who brought him to a table and motioned for him to sit in a chair next to Stuart.

"Clothing looks pretty good." Stuart tried to sound relaxed. Chad sat quietly. His stomach churned.

"This is just an arraignment today. The judge will enter the room. We will stand just before he enters and until he sits. He will probably take a moment to look at some papers in front of him, to get up to speed, and then he'll call you up. He will read the charges against you and ask how you plead to those charges. We went over the charges yesterday, but here is a copy of what the judge will be reading." Stuart pushed a piece of paper with the title *"Indictment"* in front of Chad. "I need you to look very calm and polite, and speak very clearly and loudly when you say, 'Not guilty, Your Honor.' Got that?" Stuart looked at Chad, who slowly nodded to show his understanding.

Chad turned to see the faces of the others in the room. His father sat in the last wooden row, with his arms crossed in front of him over a rumpled blue flannel shirt. He scowled at Chad and then turned his eyes to the floor. He did not recognize the other people sitting behind him. He assumed they were reporters or people who knew the victim. Then it hit him. He turned and whispered to Stuart, "Will she be here? The victim?"

"No, I don't think she's coming." Stuart paused for a moment and then added, before he regretted it, "Her husband is here, though. He's the tall guy with the striped shirt, no suit."

Chad's heart started beating fast as he slowly turned his head to see the husband. A tall man in a blue striped dress shirt sat alone in the second row. His head was tilted, as if he were examining something in his lap. Suddenly the man looked at Chad, with his eyes meeting Chad's eyes for a brief second before Chad looked away. His face immediately flushed with red-hot shame. This man thought he had raped his wife. Chad nervously fingered the piece of paper he had been giving a few moments earlier, which set out the substance of the crimes he stood accused of. He knew that he was supposed to enter a plea to those charges today, with all of those eyes burning in his back.

"Stand up," Stuart whispered to Chad, startling him. Chad quickly rose to his feet, staring straight ahead, as Stuart and everyone else in the courtroom stood.

A woman in a dark suit standing in front of the judge's bench announced, "Please rise for the Honorable Judge Silver." A short man with a receding hairline, wearing a black robe, entered the room. He walked over to his bench and sat, and immediately began flipping through a short stack of papers. After a moment, he looked up and spoke softly. "Mr. Chadbourne McCloskey, please approach."

Chad stood still for a moment, not certain what to do. He felt his legs shaking violently, and he hoped no one noticed. He felt Stuart's hand on his forearm, gently guiding him around the small table and toward the judge. Judge Silver looked a little worn, as if he shouldered a great amount of responsibility. To Chad's surprise, the judge's eyes reflected kindness. For some inexplicable reason, Chad thought of the disdain in his father's eyes, and for a fleeting moment, he wished this man sitting before him was his father.

"Mr. McCloskey, you have received a copy of the indictment and you are going to hear it read out loud to you right now. At various stages, we will pause and ask you how you plead to those charges. Do you understand this?"

Chad swallowed and said, "Yes, Your Honor."

"Okay then, Mr. McCloskey. You are going to have to speak a little louder, though. Can you do that?

"Uhm, yes sir," Chad responded louder this time.

The next few moments went by in a blur. Chad felt a buzzing in his head and his legs started shaking as he tried to stand straight and listen to words like *rape, kidnapping,* and *assault.*

When there was a pause, and he knew everyone was waiting for him to answer, Chad said "Not guilty, Your Honor," as Stuart had coached him. Judge Silver shook his head in a manner recognizing Chad's plea. Chad heard a collective murmur rise from the people seated behind him. The murmur ceased immediately when Judge Silver began to speak again. "Does the prosecution or the defense have any motions or requests at this time?"

"Yes, Your Honor," Chad heard the prosecuting attorney speak.

Judge Silver raised his eyebrows and looked at Stuart.

Stuart quickly added, "Defense has no motions at this time Your Honor."

"Okay, then, let's hear from the State." Judge Silver nodded to the prosecuting attorney as he spoke.

Chad glanced to his left to see the woman with the grey hair get up from the prosecution's table. She walked toward the judge purposefully and handed a stapled set of white papers to a clerk, who in turn handed them up to Judge Silver. She turned and handed an identical copy of the motion papers to Stuart. Chad could see Stuart's lips move quietly as he read them.

"Your Honor," the woman in the grey suit began. "The State believes that the Defendant is a flight risk. Accordingly, the State respectfully requests that the Defendant be held without bail, or in the alternative, that bail be set at one million dollars."

A murmur rose up from behind Chad's back again. Stuart leapt to his feet. "Your Honor, you seriously cannot be considering holding this young man until trial. My God, he has never so much as jaywalked, and he clearly poses no threat of flight or any danger to anyone."

"Mr. Harlan," Judge Silver looked at Stuart as he spoke. "I must assure you that it is my job to consider this matter and this particular request *seriously,* and that there is no evidence as of yet bearing on whether this man poses a flight risk or a danger." Judge Silver continued, "Certainly, your client has been accused of rather heinous and violent acts, and this request must be considered."

Judge Silver looked at the woman with the grey hair. "Would the State proceed with the basis for its request?"

The woman rose again from her seat, pushed back her chair, and began speaking from the spot between her chair and the table. "Your Honor, in addition to the evidence that the State has tying Mr. McCloskey to the horrific crimes described in the complaint and the indictment, we have evidence that Mr. McCloskey was planning to flee immediately on a plane to Arizona. Attached to the motion papers, at Exhibit A, you will find a copy of a ticket for a flight from Philadelphia to Phoenix, on September 25⁻one day after Ms. Malloy's assault and the same day that the police took Mr. McCloskey into custody. Your Honor, you will also see, at Exhibit B, an affidavit by Mr. Kenneth Sumner, the owner of Adventure Travel Agency, and the person who sold Mr. McCloskey the ticket. The affiant states that Mr. McCloskey appeared nervous and paid in cash when he purchased the one-way ticket on September 24-only hours after the crime...." As Chad listened to the prosecutor's words, and the evidence she described, he felt his stomach lurch. He realized how this must all appear to the average person, not to mention the victim's husband. He knew that at that moment even his father thought he was guilty of the horrific acts that he was accused of.

Judge Silver cleared his throat, loudly. "Mr. Harlan. Do you have anything helpful for the Court in considering this motion?"

Stuart stood up and pushed his chair back. "Your Honor. I have not been given any time to prepare to defend this motion. I have had no opportunity to depose the travel agent and, while we have evidence to explain my client's travel plans and their timing, I was not prepared to put his testimony on now. I can assure you that Mr. McCloskey is a law-abiding citizen and a decent young man who poses no threat of harm to the public and no risk of flight." Stuart paused for a moment. "Accordingly, the Defense contends that the State's motion is unwarranted, will cause undue hardship for my client, and that it should be denied."

Stuart sat in his chair, putting his right hand reassuringly on Chad's back as he did so. Chad was certain he saw a look of defeat in Stuart's face.

Judge Silver spoke immediately. "Mr. Harlan. I appreciate your concern with the amount of time you have had to prepare for this motion. However, your assurances are not sufficient to sway me in the face of a plane ticket and an affidavit of the person who sold the ticket to the defendant within hours of the crime." Judge Silver rubbed his chin for a moment as he thought. "The Court will set this motion for re-argument in two weeks, allowing defense counsel discovery related to Defendant's travel plans and other issues pertinent to this motion. In two weeks we will reconsider whether the circumstances warrant holding Mr. McCloskey without bail, or with a possibly prohibitively high bail amount, pending trial. Understood?"

"Your Honor," Stuart shot up from his chair. "What does that mean for my client now?"

Judge Silver looked at Stuart, and then at Chad as he spoke. "Mr. McCloskey will be held until the disposition of this motion, and then according to the disposition of the motion."

The murmur returned to the courtroom as the spectators and reporters reacted. *Prison. Locked cells. Violent inmates. Sadistic guards.* Chad had seen enough on television to know to be very frightened.

"The Court is adjourned," the clerk said loudly and unexpectedly. Everyone rose as Judge Silver got out of his chair and disappeared through a back door of the courtroom. Two men in DOC uniforms came over to Chad. One of them produced handcuffs.

"Come on!" Stuart complained loudly. "That is not necessary."

"It's procedure; nothing personal," one of the men said as he put Chad's hands behind his back and handcuffed him. Chad twisted his neck to see that his father's seat was empty and there was no sign of him among the other people rising from their seats, gathering their belongings and leaving the room. The tall man in the blue striped shirt, the victim's husband, stood and looked at Chad, and shook his head gently as if the weight of the moment was rocking him. Chad immediately felt the red burn of shame again creep up his neck and his face. He turned away from the man's eyes and bit his lip.

CHAPTER 15

KELLY: SEPTEMBER 26, 2011

AS SOON AS he returned home from the courthouse, Dan went upstairs to check on Kelly. A few hours earlier she had showered and dressed in her blue suit, preparing to go to the arraignment. But then Dan saw her crying softly and muttering, "I can't do this," as she undressed, popped a blue pill, and climbed back into bed.

Now it was two in the afternoon and Dan was growing concerned. Kelly slumbered under the covers. The curtains were drawn and the air in the room smelled of dirty laundry. Dan looked at the lump that was his wife and felt a mix of pity and resentment. She had always been so strong, resourceful and optimistic. She was the center and the light of their home and his constant source of certainty about their path together. Now she was sealed off in the dark, away from her family and the world, as if she was dead or wished to be.

He stepped over to the blinds and drew them abruptly, letting the sun stream in. Then he yanked up the old heavy window, and felt the air come in through the screen.

"What are you doing, Dan?" Kelly sounded annoyed. "I was sleeping."

"It is a gorgeous and warm day, Kel," Dan said, cheerfully. "I want you to feel it."

"Please close it up, I want to sleep." Kelly mumbled through the comforter.

"Enough, Kel. That is all you have been doing." Dan spoke to the open window. "Look, it sucks that you have been hurt so badly and that you have been frightened and I know I can't ever really know how it feels. But all you have done since you got home from the hospital is sleep in this dark room. This can't be the best way to deal with this. The girls miss you, I miss you, and you don't wash or eat or do anything that suggests that you are even trying."

"Damn you!" Kelly yelled, sitting up abruptly and pointing her index finger accusingly at Dan. "You have no idea how I feel. I thought I was going to die. I was so scared I almost couldn't breathe. I thought I'd never see you or the girls again." Kelly wiped her face with her hand and continued. "And some scumbag fucked me brutally and just for laughs. And then, after I was rescued, strangers took photos of my private areas and went inside of me once again to collect the DNA of the scumbag who had attacked me in the first place!" She took a deep breath and continued her rant. "And this morning I was supposed to go sit in a courtroom and see the monster that did this to me? Oh, and it turns out he's a teenager who has never committed a criminal act before in his life. Why now?" Kelly started sobbing. "Why me?"

Dan walked over and gingerly sat on the edge of their bed. Kelly looked up at his face. "I am still really tired. I keep taking these pills and then I sort of lapse in and out of terrified sleep."

"I'm sorry, Kel," Dan said. "I don't know what else to say."

"Every time I fall asleep I dream of it. I am running away through the woods, terrified. A man grabs me; he chokes me and tears at my clothes. The weird thing is, I can't scream. I open my mouth and nothing comes out. I can see people strolling on the river trails, walking dogs, jogging by, oblivious, and this guy is attacking me in plain sight." Kelly realized she had tears leaking out of her eyes again.

Dan softly raised his hand to her face and brushed the tears away with his fingers. He said nothing and just sat with her.

"I know it's not what you want to hear, Dan, but I need to lie down again. I'm sorry."

"Okay, babe, whatever you need."

Kelly rolled over and pulled the bed covers over her head. Dan walked back to the windows and closed the heavy blinds again, making the room very dark.

"Wait, Dan! What are you telling the girls?"

"I have been telling them that you are not feeling well, and that you will get better with rest."

"I wish it was that simple," Kelly mumbled to herself as Dan left the room.

CHAPTER 16

MARIA: SEPTEMBER 26, 2011

"IT'S A BOY!" The doctor shouted through his surgical mask as he held up a kicking baby with black hair that was slick with fluid from Maria's womb.

"Oh, my God, Maria," Juan whispered as he stroked his wife's head, "look at our beautiful baby boy."

"Is he okay, doctor?" Maria sat up to get a better view of her baby as the doctor carried him to a little table in the delivery room.

"He looks very good." The doctor responded as he proceeded to suction out the baby's nostrils and mouth. A high-pitched wail filled the room as their baby made his presence known. "He has a good set of lungs, too. Probably be a famous singer someday," the nurse beside the doctor joked. The doctor quickly cut and tied the baby's umbilical cord and, after a quick swabbing of his head and face, the nurse placed the infant on Maria's chest. Juan bent down to look right into his baby's face, with his cheek pressed against Maria's.

"He is beautiful," Maria sighed, exhausted and completely overwhelmed with love for her family.

"Does this little guy have a name?" the nurse asked.

Maria and Juan looked at each other and nodded. Maria spoke softly, her breath on her baby's face, "Miguel Juan Reyes. We are naming him after Juan's Uncle Miguel, who has done so much for us and who we love dearly."

Juan added quickly, "That is his name on the birth certificate. We will call him Michael mostly, and that will be his name at school." He leaned over and whispered into Maria's ear. "And I want you to be Maria Reyes, my lawful wife. Just hold on, that is coming soon."

Juan's overwhelming joy quickly washed away and was replaced by anxiety. He rubbed his left temple as he looked around the room at the nurses and doctors and all of their fancy medical equipment. He knew that an overnight stay in a hospital room with meals and continuous care would add up to a whopping bill. He had a job, but no medical insurance.

"I'll be back soon with some decent food for you." Juan walked toward the door purposefully. He was going to arrange to pay whatever it took to bring his son safely into this world, and he was going to return with food to nourish the mother of his son. Although he was tired after being up all night, he oddly felt stronger and more complete. As soon as Juan entered the hospital corridor, however, the sight of Detectives Becker and Hahn brought back the fear of forces larger than himself. He shuddered at the horror of Maria's deportation.

"Hello, Juan," Detective Becker waved slightly. "Is everything okay?"

"Oh, yes," Juan answered while purposefully striding by them. "We have a baby son, Mig, uhm, Michael."

As he walked away, he heard Detective Becker say to his back, "Juan, we'll leave you and Maria in peace right now, but we do have some unfinished business we'll have to attend to soon." Juan focused on the sound of his own footsteps on the linoleum floor and tried to calm himself with deep breaths, as he followed the signs to the hospital's Administrative Offices.

CHAPTER 17
CHAD: SEPTEMBER 26, 2011

CHAD LOOKED OUT the window of the van as it idled. The prison's grey concrete walls, metal bars, and tall iron fence topped with rolls of prickly barbed wire evoked a sense of impending doom. His hands shook uncontrollably, even as they rested, handcuffed together, on his lap. The two DOC employees in front of the van chatted easily with each other about the Philadelphia Eagles. As they went about their normal workday, Chad's own world was collapsing. Just at the time that he thought he would be happily reunited with his mother somewhere warm and safe and filled with promise, he was instead shackled in a van with metal bars on its windows, and about to be locked into a prison with ruthless and dangerous men.

Chad was led down a hallway to a small room with a sign above its door that said *Intake*. Once inside the room, he saw a tall muscular guard with a shaved head. As he stepped closer, Chad saw tiny beads of perspiration on the man's shiny head. "Get undressed," the man ordered.

Fear seized Chad as he began to loosen the tie and unbutton the shirt that he had worn to court a lifetime ago. He looked around the stark room and noticed a mirror. He wondered if anyone was watching from behind the mirror, and then he realized that he hoped someone was watching. What did this scary man want with him? His heart pounded in his chest as the large sweaty man approached him.

"These will be returned to your attorney," the man said as he bent down to pick up the clothing on the floor and shoved them into a plastic bag. He put the bag down and then produced a pair of blue pants and a matching shirt that resembled surgical scrubs, along with a pair of shoes that looked like cheap sneakers with Velcro fasteners.

"Here's your new wardrobe."

Chad quickly stepped into the baggy pants and shoes, and he decided against telling the man that the shoes were a little too big for him. As he pulled the shirt on he saw the letters *DDOC* printed in black.

"You're lucky, kid. Since you were coming from supervised custody, I didn't have to conduct a cavity search on you."

Chad did not know if the man was joking or serious. He shuddered again with fear as he wondered if a body cavity search might be a routine ordeal here.

Another guard yelled out, "McCloskey, he's in D-3-5-1."

"Got it," the sweaty man said. Together they escorted Chad through a series of doors in a long hallway. Each door opened in the middle and then shut tightly with a bang after they had passed through. Finally, they entered a loud, open area, with cells on every side. Chad glanced up and saw about five tiers of cells, one after the other, stacked sideways and vertically, like an enormous beehive constructed with grey bars, and layers of concrete flooring. Almost every cell in the hive had men in the same blue uniforms, leaning against the bars, sitting on their cots, or pacing in their cells. Their voices and sounds mixed together and reverberated throughout the entire space, filling Chad's ears. Men of all ages, sizes and colors talked, laughed, fought and yelled all at once.

They walked up two flights of stairs with Chad between the two guards. At the third level, they turned and walked along a narrow hallway in the middle of the beehive. Chad walked within inches of the bars to the cell on one side, and on the other side he could look straight down or up past iron fencing into the heart of the beehive. A sudden shrill whistle from a nearby cell startled Chad. A tall wiry man with black hair and the same blue uniform reached through the bars of his cell as if he wanted to touch

Chad. He wolf-whistled loudly and then yelled, "Fresh Meat! I got dibs on this one. He is sweet! My, oh my, Fresh Meat!" The man grinned evilly and opened his eyes wide at Chad. The dark blue ink of tattoos covered his forearms and the backs of his hands, and ran up out of his collar and around his neck to his chin.

They walked past the tattooed man's cell, but not far enough for Chad. "This is it. D-3-5-1. This is your new home; all six feet by eight feet of it." The bald guard motioned for Chad to step inside. He slammed the cell door.

Chad stood still on a small square of dark grey concrete enclosed by cinderblock walls. Two narrow bunks came out of the wall, one over the other. Each bunk held a thin, striped mattress and a beige canvas bag. A small metal sink and toilet were bolted to the floor against the wall opposite the bars, and Chad would have no choice but to use them in full view of guards and prisoners. He scrambled on to the top bunk and flopped down on his back, with his right arm over his eyes to hide the tears.

"Hey, Fresh Meat!" The tattooed man's voice boomed down the hall to Chad's cell. "What's the matter, Fresh Meat? You don't like it here? You feel lonely? You just wait until I get close to you. You won't feel lonely anymore. You will be my new best friend. And it will be all my pleasure. Ha, ha, ha!"

Chad sobbed quietly into his arm.

CHAPTER 18

KELLY: SEPTEMBER 27, 2011

KELLY DREAMED THAT a large man with a beard and terrible breath had pinned her down and was tearing her clothes off. Despite his brute force, he was gently tapping on her arm. When Kelly opened her eyes, Anna was standing at her bedside and tapping her on her left forearm.

"Mama, I have been trying to wake you up. You were yelling in your sleep." Anna bit her lip and tried not to cry. "Mama, what is really wrong with you? I miss you so much and I'm scared." Anna started sobbing.

"Shhh, it's okay," Kelly said, reaching out to stroke her daughter's hair. "I am so sorry Anna-Banana. I have just been sick and I needed sleep."

"But it smells in here like something serious, like someone's dying."

"Mommy needs a shower and some fresh sheets, that's all. I am not dying, I promise."

"Then what is happening? We have been with Gran and Dad for four days straight now and you're never around. Dad's always shushing us and telling us to leave you alone and Gran is even worse. She changes the subject every time we ask about you."

Kelly smiled a little, picturing her mother trying to be sunny and helpful while she deflected questions of an uncomfortable nature. "I'm getting better, Anna. I'll be back to normal before you know it." Kelly felt like a hypocrite, knowing she would never feel normal again.

"Mom, there is something else. I want to talk to you about something but I don't know if I can." Kelly watched her daughter squirm and look down at her feet.

"What is it, baby?" Kelly sat up in her bed, alarmed.

"A boy in my class, Joey Slater, brought in an article today from the paper. He told everyone it was about you. He held it up high over my head when I wanted to see it. Mrs. Stenson took it away from him and sent him to the principal's office. She told our class that your name wasn't even in the article, but everyone believed Joey."

"What do you think the article said?" Kelly asked, still stroking her daughter's head.

"Everyone said that you were attacked near Rockford Park. Joey Slater used the word 'raped.'"

Kelly shuddered at the sound of that word coming out of her eight-year-old daughter's mouth. "Well, Anna," Kelly started slowly, gathering her thoughts. "You know I always want to be honest with you, right?"

"Uh-huh," Anna uttered as she nodded her head up and down.

"But I also want to protect you. So, Dad and I decided that the best thing was to be honest with you about my not feeling well and needing time and rest, without telling you anything that is too scary."

"But Mama," Anna said, "if the kids at school know about it, then I should know, too. You *are* my mother, for gosh sakes!" The anger in her voice startled Kelly.

Kelly thought for a moment. "First of all, I do not think that your classmates—including Joey Slater—truly understand what the word *raped* means, or he would not have been joking about it like that. But it is true that a man attacked me. I was running along the river, and he caught me and put me to sleep with some kind of drug and he hurt me. When I woke up he was gone and I went to the hospital to be treated."

Anna quickly climbed into the bed and rested her head on her mother's chest. "I'm scared, Mom. Is this man coming for us?"

"No, baby, we are completely safe. The man was arrested and he is in a prison cell somewhere. He cannot hurt us." As Kelly said this confidently to her daughter, she felt herself shudder. *What if they had the wrong man? What if he was not alone? Was there someone still out there that wanted to hurt her, or worse?*

"Are you okay now, Mom?"

"Yes, baby, I am going to be fine. Smelly and tired maybe, but that's all." Kelly faked a laugh and gently stroked Anna's head.

"I'm glad Mom. But I want you to get up now. Please. It feels like summer today and it smells really good outside." Anna pinched her nose again.

Just then, Dan walked into the room. "Anna, I told you not to bother Mom."

"It's okay Dan. I needed it.... Is it really like summer outside?"

"It is amazing, Kel. It's seventy-five degrees and the sky is blue and clear. Why don't you come out in the backyard with us and we'll have a late lunch there. It will be good for all of us." Preempting her refusal, Dan quickly gathered clothing for her to change into. He chose a powder-blue Adidas warm-up suit and a worn white T-shirt commemorating a Bruce Springsteen concert they had been to five years earlier. "Look," he said, as he laid the clothing on the bed gently, "you can even wear your flip-flops today." He placed a pair of pink flip-flops next to the clothing.

"I'll see you out back in a few minutes." Dan waited until Anna left the room before speaking again. "Kel, the doctor's office called to say all of your tests were negative. They wouldn't share any details, but you can call them for more. They said some of them need to be taken again in six months, but that is good news." Dan waved his hand in front of his nose, to pretend he was waving away the malodorous air of the room, hoping to make Kelly laugh. "Since we are having a little lunch date, maybe you could at least, you know, shower."

Kelly said nothing and did not laugh. But, to Dan's relief, she got out of bed slowly, collected the clothing and started toward the bathroom. She felt bruised and tired and every step toward the shower was a strenuous feat.

A moment later, Kelly felt the warm stream of water and started to wash her hair with both hands. Something in the soapy white water rushing down off of her body and toward the drain lifted her mood. She found herself scrubbing vigorously, every inch of her body, and even enlisted the help of a scratchy loofah pad that had previously hung in the shower unnoticed. She scrubbed and rinsed and scrubbed again, until her hands were puckered and her skin felt tender. Kelly looked at her face as the condensation slowly cleared from the bathroom mirror. She recognized the eyes, but her skin was drawn, her cheekbones were more pronounced, and she looked sharper and older at the same time.

When she returned to her bedroom, Kelly noticed that Dan had stripped their bed and opened up their bedroom windows. She was surprised to find that the warm breeze coming through the windows lifted her spirits. Suddenly she could not wait to get outside. Five minutes later, she sat with Dan and the girls at their backyard dining table. Kelly's fingers played with a napkin next to a plate with a turkey sandwich and fresh strawberries. She tilted her face up to feel the warmth of the sun.

"Aren't you going to eat your lunch, Mom?" Anna asked.

"No, sweetie. You can have it." Kelly answered.

"We ate our lunch already, Momma, at school." Gracie chimed in.

"Okay, if it's not turkey you want, I know what you can't refuse." Dan quickly disappeared into the back door of the house. He reappeared a moment later with a tray of brownies. "Kel, your mom and the girls made these brownies for you." Then, after Kelly refused to register any response, Dan said, "Girls, don't you want to see Mom eat some of your hard work?"

Grace and Anna giggled and nodded.

Kelly took a brownie off the plate and popped half of it into her mouth. She was surprised to enjoy the chocolate taste in her mouth and the squishy texture of the brownie. She hadn't eaten much in days, but she suddenly felt hungry. She popped the other half in her mouth and said, "Maybe one more."

"Excellent. These are good for you I'm sure. I think they call it comfort food." Dan said, smiling at his wife and daughters for the first time in days. He reached over gingerly and put his fingers through Kelly's thick hair, which was still damp from her shower. The girls each ate a brownie and then ran off to climb a small apple tree that grew in the corner of their yard.

"Dan," Kelly's voice grew somber again, ending their rare moment of levity. "What have you learned about this case?"

"I have been talking to the police every day, and a lot has happened. As you know, the young guy who was arraigned, Chad McCloskey, is in prison pending trial. I haven't met him or anything, but I did see him at the arraignment." Dan hesitated a moment before continuing. "He actually looks like a normal guy, Kel. I mean, he looks like a kid you'd see playing baseball at Rockford Park or having pizza with friends at Trolley Square. He does not look like a monster."

"Is that your professional opinion, Dan?"

"No, of course not. I don't mean to upset you, Kel. I am just trying to explain that he wasn't what I expected. He looked like he was lost or scared or something."

"I bet he's scared. If he's the scumbag who did this to me he should be scared." Kelly snarled.

Dan held up his hand to her to signal that he needed a few minutes to speak uninterrupted. "Please let me explain where I am going with this, Kel. I'm on your side, remember?"

Kelly breathed a loud sigh.

"He claims he did not do it." Dan continued. "He told the police that he found you in a little gardener's shed on the Breck's Mill property, bound, blindfolded and gagged. He said that you were completely knocked out."

Kelly looked up at Dan's face as she saw flashbacks of waking on the cold bumpy stone floor with her hands tied and her eyes blindfolded. She recalled the acrid smell of something familiar, and at that moment she realized it was the smell of fertilizer that filled her nostrils while she lay on the cold hard floor. A gardener's shed was her prison.

"That's a little convenient, don't you think? Why wouldn't he just call the police or an ambulance or something if he found an injured person?" Kelly asked, feeling her face redden with anger.

"He says he was too scared, so he brought you to a place in the trail where he knew you would be rescued. This is where his story gets interesting. He can describe in detail the couple and the dog that showed up when you were rescued. And his story as far as location and timing is corroborated by a phone call that the police got from a woman. An eyewitness called the police and told them that she saw a man carry a body in a blanket into the woods by Brecks Mill."

"So?" Kelly asked, exasperated. "Just because he left me somewhere to be found or 'rescued' as you put it, does not mean that he is not the one I needed rescuing from in the first place!"

"Kel, please. Geez, I know you are hurt and angry and all that, but I am not your enemy." Dan said. "The police are still running DNA tests on this guy, a background check, interviewing folks and even searching his house, okay? So, if he is the guy, they'll nail him." He looked at her, trying to figure out if he could continue. "But," he hesitated, "there is more that I learned. Do you want to know, or is this too much for you?"

"No, Dan, I want to hear everything."

Dan placed his hand on top of Kelly's hand on the table. He was heartened by the fact that she did not pull away. He hesitated before telling her the next part. "Kelly, there is possibly someone else involved."

"What? Why didn't you tell me?"

"Well, first of all, it did not seem like a good idea to share this with you while you were curled up in the fetal position in our dark bedroom. I didn't want to make things worse. Also, I wanted to wait a little bit in case the police could give us more specifics." Dan paused. "It turns out the woman I just told you about, the eyewitness, said she saw one man shoot and carry away a woman fitting your description along the trail by Breck's Mill, and then, about an hour later, she saw a different man carrying a woman wrapped in a blanket into the woods."

Dan looked at Kelly for her reaction. He thought that she had the same look that Gracie had when she was trying to build the perfect sand castle or memorize words for a spelling test. Her eyebrows were knitted together and her lips were drawn tight in a line. "The evidence, especially if they have DNA, will say for sure," Kelly mumbled, without any apparent emotion.

Dan squeezed her hand. "I love you, babe. I know you have been through hell, and I know it is going to be a rough road for you, but we are all here to help. Take your time, tell us what we can do to help you get through this, lean on us."

Kelly sat gazing straight ahead, quiet for at least two minutes. Then Dan saw her lift her left hand to her cheek. He knew she was wiping away a tear. Then, after Kelly caught her breath with a shudder she said softly, "I am going back to work tomorrow."

"What?" Dan asked. "Kel, Margaret came over when you were sleeping yesterday. She told me not to disturb you, but she asked me to assure you that all of your cases and obligations were covered and everyone at the firm is fine with you taking off whatever time you need. Christ, you just got cleared as far as the concussion. Don't you want to take some time off to heal completely?"

"Dan, I don't need time. I don't need rest. I am lying up there trying to sleep or drug myself into some altered state with sleeping pills just to block out those horrid thoughts and memories that keep replaying in my brain, poisoning me. I don't know what I need, but lying around is making me feel like I am losing my mind."

CHAPTER 19

CHAD: SEPTEMBER 27, 2011

DETECTIVES BECKER AND Hahn walked carefully up the decaying steps and onto the porch. After pushing the doorbell button a few times and hearing no sound, Detective Becker pounded on the front door. "Hello? Is anyone home?" She walked over to a window and peered inside at Charlie McCloskey who was slumped over the morning newspaper at his kitchen table. He startled when she rapped on the glass with her knuckles.

A moment later, Charlie opened the door. "What the hell is this?" Charlie scowled as he pulled an old bathrobe tightly across his chest. He smelled of whiskey, and he had several days' stubble on his chin.

"Excuse the interruption, sir, but we figured we were most likely to catch you at home in the morning before work." Detective Becker held up a paper and continued speaking. "Sir, we have a warrant to search your house and its contents. Will you be peaceful in complying with this request or will I need the help of the officers I have waiting here?"

Charlie curled his lip in scorn, spit right next to Detective Becker's feet, and stepped aside. "Come in, I have nothing to hide. You'll find a mess, I'm sure, but as far as I know, that's not a crime." He shuffled back to the kitchen and resumed his position at the table. The detectives and officers went to work.

Detective Becker went straight to Chad's bedroom. An old pizza box peeked out from under the unmade bed. Some clothing sat on a beanbag chair in the corner. It looked like an average eighteen-year-old male's bedroom, with one notable exception: the pizza box was actually a treasure trove. It had been carefully lined with aluminum foil, and held an array of pine cones, acorns, dried flowers, fragments of bird eggs, small rocks and numerous feathers. There were also small plastic vials containing tiny items and with labels marked *tooth of red fox, falcon's beak,* and *skull of chipmunk.* Detective Becker closed the pizza box carefully, taped it shut and put it in a clear plastic evidence bag.

In Chad's closet the only thing that Becker found remarkable was a small wooden cigar box. She opened it slowly and found an assortment of tiny tools and containers of various sizes and shapes. She put on a brand new pair of plastic gloves and gently examined the tools and other contents of the box, which included a tiny tweezer, a small set of scissors, cotton swabs, empty vials and a pack of blank labels. A moment later, she had wrapped the cigar box with its contents in another evidence bag. She put it with the pizza box and carried them together against her chest. As she walked through the kitchen, Charlie McCloskey looked up.

"What's that you got there?" Charlie grumbled as she walked by.

"It's just part of our investigation, sir." Detective Becker continued walking toward the door.

"That's the stuff he used when he collected his little treasures from the woods and river," the old man yelled at her back as she passed by. "An innocent hobby of a boy, for Christ sakes!"

Detective Becker resisted the urge to yell back to him as she walked purposefully to her car. She slid the bags and their contents carefully into the back seat and locked the car.

When she re-entered the house, Charlie stood by the door, agitated. "Why the hell do you have to take his special boxes?"

"I can't say, sir, except that it may be evidence of a crime." Detective Becker answered in her most professional and detached voice. Then, as she started to walk back to the bedroom, she paused for a moment and said quietly, "I'm sorry."

"That boy does not have a violent bone in his body. Those were just things for collecting stuff from the woods." Charlie stopped for a moment to wipe spittle off of his mouth with the back of his hand.

"I'm sorry, sir, I am not following you," Detective Becker said.

"Ever since Chad was a little boy, he liked to bring home things he found in the woods; feathers, rocks, that sort of thing. I never really got it, but it was a hobby. His mother helped him. They got library books and special kits and everything. It was their thing; they shared a love of the woods and its creatures."

"Again, I am sorry, sir," Detective Becker continued, "but I'll leave that to the experts to tell me exactly what the contents of that box are and if they have any relevance to this matter." She bit her lip, turned her back, and walked away to resume her search of Chad's room. She noticed that Chad had a bookshelf filled with books related to the topic of plants and animals. She picked one off the shelf titled, *Trails of the Brandywine River Valley*. Inside its cover, flowery cursive handwriting read:

My dearest Chad: Happy 14th birthday! Remember always to follow your passions and preserve what is beautiful. But please do not forget that sometimes you have to let go of things that don't deserve your love and care.

Love Always,

Mom

Detective Becker was surprised to feel a lump form in her throat. She knew that Chad's mother had left him unexpectedly and that he was a troubled young man living here in this old house with the broken man slumped over in the kitchen.

"Helen." Tim Hahn's voice in the doorway to Chad's bedroom startled Detective Becker. She turned to face him. "I searched the father's room and didn't find anything of interest. Just a few empty Jack Daniels bottles, a pile of dirty laundry, some half-eaten bags of greasy snack food... oh, and signs of large rodent activity." He shrugged his shoulders as he reported. "Pretty depressing, actually."

"Okay, thanks." Detective Becker said.

"Do you need any help in here?"

"Yes, please." Detective Becker pointed to the books on the

shelf. "Would you please bag up the books regarding plants, animals and the Brandywine River trails?"

Hahn looked at her with his eyebrows raised in confusion. "Okay, if you say so." He went to work gathering evidence bags and labels and perusing the books.

"I just have to go through the drawers in this dresser and then I think we are almost done. There's no basement, and other than the two bedrooms, there's the kitchen, a small family room, attic space and a few closets."

As she spoke, Detective Becker methodically searched the drawers of Chad's sole dresser. She opened the drawers, gently sifting through the clothing in each drawer, and then closed the drawer. "Man, this kid was clean," she said to Hahn. "Not even a pack of cigarettes, a bottle of something or even a dirty magazine." Finally, as she moved boxer shorts in the top right drawer of Chad's dresser, she found a manila envelope containing a handful of photographs; color Polaroids and crinkled black-and-whites of different shapes and sizes. Detective Becker immediately realized that the common figure in all of them was a petite dark-haired woman with large, sad eyes. She had seen those eyes before, in the young man awaiting trial on kidnapping and rape charges.

A half hour later, as she followed Hahn out of the house, Becker saw Charlie still sitting at the kitchen table. He had moved only to pour Jack Daniels into his coffee mug and then to stare at the newspaper's sports section on the table in front of him.

"We are all done here, sir. I apologize for any disruption, and I am sorry for your circumstances." Detective Becker spoke to Charlie's back, as he did not turn around or make eye contact in response to her voice. The kitchen door closed behind her with a thud and she gratefully breathed in the fresh morning air and the smell of the Brandywine River.

CHAPTER 20

MARIA: SEPTEMBER 27, 2011

MARIA STRUGGLED TO keep her heavy eyelids open as she held baby Miguel to her breast and tried to get him to latch on to her swollen nipple. His wailing drowned out the sound of Detective Becker's gentle knock on the open door.

"Excuse me."

Maria looked up to see the woman who had been to her apartment standing in the doorway to her hospital room. The visitor averted her eyes and looked uncomfortable. Alarm flashed through Maria's body.

"I'm so sorry to disturb you right now. It looks like you have your hands full. I am Detective Helen Becker. We met two days ago at your apartment—just as this little guy decided to enter the world." She paused for a moment and finally looked directly at Maria. "I honestly just need to ask you a few questions."

Maria immediately sat up straighter and responded, "Hello." Surprisingly, once Maria changed her position the baby settled down and began to nurse.

Detective Becker lingered by the door, again with her eyes averted.

"Does Juan know you are here?" Maria asked.

"No." Detective Becker responded. "Where is he now?"

"At work... he couldn't afford to miss again." Maria looked around the hospital room, as if Juan were hiding behind a curtain. "I know he does not want me to talk to you."

"I'll be as brief as possible. I'm sorry about the timing, but as I informed you two days ago, we are sure you are the person who called the police about events relating to the abduction and rape of a woman named Kelly Malloy."

"I, uhm, I am not sure if I should be talking to you," Maria said, hesitantly.

Detective Becker ignored Maria's concerns and kept speaking. "You have no need to worry. I'm only here to investigate this case, I am not investigating you, okay?" She looked at Maria with understanding in her eyes, hoping to avoid the reason for Maria's reticence. But then she decided to be blunt. "Ms. Hernandez, I am not at all concerned with your status here. That is not what I need to talk to you about. You have my word on that."

For the next ten minutes, Detective Becker took notes as Maria recounted what she saw only three days earlier from her perch in the Breck's Mill window. She answered the detective's questions, explaining that she did not know or recognize the two different men or the woman that she saw that day. She spoke freely until Detective Becker asked her a question that made her uncomfortable.

"Why did you refuse to give your name and phone number to the police when you called to report what you had witnessed?"

"Please," Maria pleaded with Detective Becker, "don't ask me that question when you know the answer. We have done nothing wrong." Maria started to cry. "And I have so much to lose."

Detective Becker knew that any person hearing Maria's account would have asked the same question. "Okay." She said as she closed her writing pad. "You're right. That is not important. Let's not worry about that. Thank you again for your time. And, congratulations on your beautiful son."

As Detective Becker climbed into her car in the hospital parking lot, Juan was straining to push open the revolving glass door to enter the hospital. Two nights of sleep deprivation since his son's birth, combined with exhausting work framing a house coupled with his anxiety over the detectives' unfinished business, had left him completely drained. He was relieved that he could take Maria and Baby Miguel home to their own apartment that evening, away from expensive doctors and probing police. He stopped for a moment on his path to the elevators and pulled his cell phone out of his pocket. He stood in a quiet corner while he dialed the number.

"Hello, you have reached the office of Sara Nuñez. I am away from my desk right now, but I will return your call as soon as I am able to."

Juan waited for the beep. He took a deep breath before he spoke quietly into Ms. Nuñez' voicemail box. "Hello, this is Juan Reyes and I am calling again about the status of my citizenship. I have pressing circumstances and I cannot wait any longer for my citizenship status to be final. Please, please, please call me back at 302-555-6321." Juan snapped the phone closed, angry about the desperation in his voice. He liked to be cool, confident and in control. But his world was spiraling out of control.

Only a few minutes later, as he stepped out of the elevator into the maternity wing, Juan's heart leapt as he heard his cell phone ring. He stepped into a restroom and answered.

"Hello? Juan Reyes speaking," Juan said softly.

"This is Sara Nuñez, returning your call. I just got your voicemail. Is everything okay?"

"No, not really. My wife, Maria, is being questioned by the police because she reported a crime that she witnessed. I am afraid they might find out that she is not here legally and they might deport her. On top of that, we just had a baby and I don't know what will happen to him if that happens."

"Oh, my gosh," the voice on the other end of the line said. "You had a baby! Congratulations. A boy or a girl?"

"A boy. His name is Miguel Juan Reyes," Juan said quickly. "But you don't understand. My wife entered the country illegally, and now our baby is here. The LACC sent me to you years ago, and I completed my citizenship application a long time ago. I have been waiting patiently, but please tell me, when is that going to happen? What can I do to make it happen right now?"

"Well, I am away from my office right now, Juan, so I don't have your whole file. I got your voicemail and called you right away. I do recall submitting your citizenship application. Based on my recollection and the documents that I have on my home computer, it seems that your approval and final steps should actually happen any day now. I'll make some phone calls to INS when I get in tomorrow morning and I'll let you know."

"Thank you." Juan said. "I am sorry that I sound impatient but we have police snooping around right now and it is making me nervous."

"We'll sort that through in the morning, Juan. For now, rest assured, no one is deporting a mother of a newborn baby. Oh, and by the way, your baby is an American citizen because he was born here. So that one is easy. And you are here legally as well. Maria is our immediate concern. We'll sort it out tomorrow."

"Thank you." Juan tucked the phone in his pocket and looked around, making sure no one had heard his conversation. Then he hurried back toward the hospital room that contained his whole world, his family.

CHAPTER 21

KELLY: SEPTEMBER 28, 2011

KELLY STEPPED OFF the escalator and walked quickly across the lobby of the New Castle County Courthouse. Her heels clicked on the floor and her right hand firmly clasped the handle of her briefcase as she headed toward the exit. She kept her eyes down in an effort to avoid making eye contact with someone who would feel compelled to start an awkward conversation. She had already endured her co-workers' feeble attempts to make everything seem normal. Margaret was the only one who had been natural and helpful. She had even made Kelly laugh, commenting that Kelly's newly cropped hair "might work on Posh Spice, but not on a thirty-something attorney."

Despite the awkwardness, Kelly was a blur of efficiency. She had successfully argued a motion to compel production of evidence in an employment discrimination case, and in fifteen minutes she had a conference call regarding a settlement of another matter. Her mind was focused on clients' problems and the numerous steps to their solutions, mercifully leaving no room for the terrifying flashbacks and bottomless pit of despair that had been paralyzing her.

As she rounded the corner toward the exit, Kelly spotted Jack Barnard. He had just finished coming through the security check at the courthouse entrance, and he stood only twenty feet away from her. She ducked behind a column, frozen. She was in no mood to discuss the Johnson appeal.

She sheepishly peeked around the column to see if Jack Barnard had moved on. He was still there. As Kelly watched, he finished putting his keys back in his pocket, recovered his briefcase as it came through the x-ray scan, and then he bent down to tie his left shoe. *Just hurry up and get the hell out of here*, Kelly thought. Her conference call was now twelve minutes away.

Suddenly, a light reflected off something metallic on Barnard's finger, catching Kelly's attention. Her mouth dropped in horror as she recognized the large crescent-shaped scar on his wrist just below the palm of his hand, and his chunky gold ring with a red stone. It was as if an electrical jolt had coursed through her body. Shaking, Kelly walked quickly out of the courthouse, no longer caring who saw her, and not hearing them if they spoke to her anyway. Fear, fury and disgust all competed within her as she dialed her cell phone and tried with all her might to keep her composure. She saw goose bumps rise in the flesh of her wrist and she felt her knees shake, all as her body remembered the futile struggle to fight off her attacker.

"Margaret, it's Kel. Please call John Staley at Energy Enterprises and tell him I can't do the settlement conference call today. Try to re-schedule it for later in the week. I need to go somewhere right now, and I'll check in with you later, okay?" Kelly heard her voice grow shaky as she tried not to cry.

"Are you all right, Kelly? You sound weird. Are you sure you're ready to be back at work?" Margaret asked, with genuine concern.

"I'm fine. I just realized I have to meet with someone and it is urgent. I'll check in later." Kelly shut her phone closed as she turned and walked toward the Carvel State Office Building. She walked through the lobby, checked the directory on the wall to find the floor for the *Delaware Department of Justice*, and strode quickly to the elevator.

"Hello," Kelly spoke to a middle-aged woman sitting behind a reception desk. "I need to speak with Deputy AG Sam Schultz."

The woman looked up at her. "Do you have an appointment with Mr. Schultz?"

"Yes," Kelly lied. She had known Sam since their first day of law school. They sat next to each other in most of their first-year courses, alternately panicking and laughing about the trials and tribulations of a first-year law student. They navigated life in the District of Columbia together, and spent endless hours in study groups. The summer after graduation, they both wound up in Delaware, preparing for the Delaware Bar exam. She knew Sam and she trusted him. But also, as an insider at the Attorney General's office who also knew Jack Barnard, he was the only person Kelly felt she could talk to about her appalling realization.

Kelly watched Sam walk toward the reception area. With his thin frame, freckled and bespectacled face and shock of red hair he bore a resemblance to Howdy Doody—a resemblance that he used to disarm defendants and their lawyers and to charm jurors. In reality, he was an extremely effective and methodical prosecutor with an impressive conviction record.

"Hey, Kel. How are you doing?" His face showed anguish as he walked up to Kelly and gave her a hug. "I know you have been through hell, Kelly. I didn't even know you were back at work already."

"Sam, you are not going to believe what I came here for, but I don't know where else to go." Kelly's voice cracked as she tried not to break down.

"Geez, Kel, come on, let's go to my office. We'll talk there." Sam put his arm around her shoulder and steered her around to walk down a hall. After passing a few closed doors, Sam guided her into a messy office.

"I'm sorry to interrupt you like this. Were you busy?" Kelly asked as Sam gestured for her to take the seat opposite his desk chair.

"Yes, very. Never too busy for you though, Kel, so let's get down to business. What is going on?" He looked straight across his desk and directly into Kelly's deep blue eyes. He felt that familiar flutter he experienced when they had been students together. For three years he had gazed at her eyes, studied her skin, and even surreptitiously smelled the scent of the shampoo in her hair. His desire for her was unrelenting, and yet she acted as if he were a big brother.

Kelly got up from her chair abruptly to close the door to his office. She started to pace in front of Sam's desk. "You know about my attack at the river, right?"

"Well, yeah, I heard about it here and read something about it in the newspaper. I wanted to call you right away, but I guess I didn't really know how to handle that sort of thing between old friends. I am so sorry, really." Sam leaned forward in his chair and spoke quietly, as if he was afraid to disturb Kelly in any way. "I know that they have a guy in custody, a young turk named Chad McCloskey, and that it has been assigned to an AG."

"Well, he is not the guy who did it." Kelly said, her voice breaking.

"What? You're certain?"

"Yes, I know who did, though."

"Hold on. Let me get the person assigned to your case to listen to this." Sam looked uneasy as he spoke.

"No, Sam. You have to hear me and tell me what to do. I know that Jack Barnard attacked me." She looked him right in the eyes and said, "Jack Barnard, esteemed member of the Delaware Bar, is the asshole that drugged me, raped me and left me bound and gagged in the woods."

"Kel, do you know what you are saying? Do you have proof of this?" Sam asked.

"Yes, it all makes sense now that I think of it. But I didn't realize it until a few minutes ago when I spotted him in the courthouse. He has the exact ring and scar that my attacker had, not to mention that his giant white hand matches what I saw, too." Kelly took a deep breath and looked down at where her fingers nervously played with a suit button. "I don't think I told the detective about the scar. I only remembered that just now when I saw it. It's him."

"So you want to accuse a member of the Delaware Bar that we have known for years of attacking you and brutally raping you—based on a glimpse of his hand?" Sam raised his eyebrows in disbelief.

"It was not just a glimpse. His hand was the only thing I could see when the scumbag was raping me, because I had a blindfold on. So I focused on remembering that detail since it was the only thing I could see. Also, he specifically threatened me the night before I was attacked—only... I did not even think of that until today." Kelly swallowed hard and banged her fist on

Dan's desk as she spoke.

"What are you talking about? You say he *threatened* you?" Kelly noticed that Sam was clenching his fists, and his face turned bright red and then an ashen gray.

"My God, Sam! Can't you handle this conversation?" Kelly asked, sounding annoyed with him rather than concerned. "You are my friend and you are a brilliant prosecutor. Please, I need you to tell me that you know what to do here!" Kelly pleaded with Sam.

Sam was silent. The image of Jack Barnard on top of *his* Kel— violating her. *Bastard. Fucking bastard!* For the first time in his entire career of prosecuting violent criminals, he completely understood the desire to kill another man.

Oblivious to Sam's inner turmoil, Kelly continued with the facts that supported her case against Barnard. "He screwed up and filed an appeal a day after the appeal period had expired. Of course, I had no choice but to move to dismiss it. And the Court had no choice either—it's a jurisdictional matter. It was a sloppy procedural mistake that is practically *per se* malpractice. He completely lost his composure and started screaming at me and threatening me personally."

Sam took a deep breath and unclenched his hands. "Did anyone else hear these threats?"

"Yes," Kelly said. "My secretary Margaret heard them, at least. Maybe some other people in my office. He was on speakerphone and very loud."

Sam scribbled a few notes on a legal pad.

"Oh, my gosh!" Kelly exclaimed, "I just thought of this: I was attacked as I ran along the river near Breck's Mill. I can't tell you how many times I have seen Jack Barnard down there fly-fishing in the morning when I run by. He has definitely seen me there and I am certain that he knew that was my routine."

Sam focused on his notes to keep calm. "Kel, this is definitely adding up. But, it is going to be delicate. We'll need to start real strong, given his position with the Delaware Bar. Is there anything else you can think of that helps?"

"Only that the guy has a reputation for being a womanizer and a brute with women when he does not get his way. I've heard rumors of course, but I also experienced a little of that personally. Do you remember that night we were out celebrating our bar exam results? We were at O'Malley's Tavern and Barnard kept pulling at me and refusing to take no for an answer."

Sam's eyes grew wide with the memory. He remembered the jealousy, but also the feeling of inadequacy as he left Kelly to fend for herself. He tried to sound casual with the recollection. "Yeah, I do sort of remember that. The guy was a total asshole."

"I have also heard that he was arrested for assault in high school—although that may have been expunged. And I think he has been through a messy divorce or two. You can probably get some stuff from women he has bullied or similarly mistreated." Kelly finally sat in the chair. She had a look of determination on her face as the case against her attacker solidified.

Sam looked at his watch. "Kel, you are really, really sure about this ring and scar thing?"

"Yes, I'm sure of it. It took the wind out of me just now when I saw him. I saw his ring and his wrist scar, and that big hand as he tied his shoe. I was sickened by it—it was such a moment of clarity, of certainty."

"Okay. I promise you, I'll get in touch with the right people here and we will figure out how best to get Barnard. DNA would be a beautiful thing, but also, interviews of women he had relationships with, and a check to see if there has ever been any record of arrest or even a complaint against him that is relevant to this type of behavior. Of course, I'll look over the evidence they have so far against Chad McCloskey, in case anything points to Barnard. I'll call you once we get rolling on this."

Kelly stood. As Sam walked her to his office door and opened it, she leaned in and kissed him on the cheek. "I can't thank you enough, Sam. I will feel a hundred percent better when this guy is nailed. I know you are the man for the job."

Sam blushed. "Well, if I'm not, at least I'll know the person who is."

"You were always too modest, Sam. You deserve to be the attorney general of Delaware by now." Kelly turned and walked away.

Sam lingered to watch her walk until she turned the corner toward the elevator and was out of sight. He knew that the uneasiness in his stomach was not from his suppressed feelings of love and desire. This time it was terror. By being indecisive and insecure in the past, he had fallen short when he had a chance to protect her. He could not let that happen now.

CHAPTER 22

CHAD: SEPTEMBER 28, 2011

CHAD RESTED ON his side on the narrow bunk in his cell facing the cinderblock wall. Other than meals, showers and the one-hour supervised time in the rec room each night, Chad passed his time in this position: lying quietly and feigning lifelessness seemed to be his best option.

"Hey, you! Fresh Meat!" Chad heard the disturbing calls from a cell far too proximate to his own. He kept looking at the wall. "You can't ignore me, Fresh Meat. Fresh Meat! Fresh Meat! Fresh Meat! Fresh Meat! I am gonna keep chanting until you talk to me."

Chad shouted at the wall, "Shut the fuck up!"

"Oh. A tough guy," the scary man continued. "I just want to know what you did to get in here, Fresh Meat."

Chad continued to ignore him.

"Hey, Fresh Meat!" His tormentor would not relent. "I got a job for you. Tomorrow you can pick up my soap for me in the shower." The man started whooping loudly and Chad heard other inmates' voices join the laughter. He felt the hair rise in the back of his neck in alarm, but there was nowhere he could go and nothing he could do. So he continued to face his wall and pretended not to hear them.

Against the din of his tormentor, Chad heard the clink of keys on his prison door cell. Alarmed, he turned around to see the guard opening the door and another inmate entering. The man was thin with a newly shaved head, and tattoos covering his arms. Chad noticed he even had tattoos on his neck, peeking out from under his prison garb. A long thin scar ran down the side of the man's face. The guard closed and locked the door quickly and walked away without saying another word.

Chad swung his legs over his bunk and jumped down. "Um, hi."

"Hey," his new cellmate grunted, barely looking up.

"I'm Chad." Chad said, extending his hand for a handshake.

"That's fucking great," the man said. "I'm locked in a tiny cell with a prep school asshole."

Chad quickly withdrew his hand. He was surprised and hurt by the man's words, and humiliated for not knowing proper prison etiquette. He started to climb back up into his bunk when he felt a hand grasp his left ankle.

"Where the hell do you think you are going?" The man growled.

"To my bunk." Chad said, forcing himself to look the man in the eye.

"I don't think so, asshole. I get the top bunk. I always get the top bunk." The man glared at Chad. Then he looked away, in the direction of Chad's tormentor two cells down. "Isn't that right, Paco? Don't I always get the top bunk? Tell this prep school asshole who I am."

"Hey, Fresh Meat," the man responded. "You have the privilege of bunking with a leader of the Latin Kings. If you want to stay alive in here, you better do as he says. Maybe he'll make you his number one Bitch." The man laughed loudly.

Chad felt his knees get weak, and a wave of nausea gripped him. He swallowed hard, clenched his fists and, fighting the urge to cry, he tried to look brave and uncaring. "Whatever. I don't give a shit where I sleep, okay?" He sat on the lower bunk with humiliation, fear and rage all churning inside of him. Then suddenly, he heard his own voice yelling, "Oh, and by the way, my name is not Fresh Meat or Prep or asshole. It's Chad!" Chad was shocked by his outburst. He sat silently, waiting for his new cellmate to pounce. After a moment though, he looked up and saw that he was quietly chuckling and shaking his head.

"Man, oh man. Okay. That's more like it, amigo." The thin man with the tattooed neck looked at Chad with what Chad hoped was a tiny flicker of respect. "Don't worry about what that loco dude Paco said. I am only into chicks."

Chad resumed his position facing the wall—this time on the lower bunk. He heard the thin man climb up on to the bunk above him. Then he heard him mumble through the mattress, "They call me Rico."

Chad relaxed a little, now that he felt his cellmate was less likely to kill him in his sleep. He closed his eyes and tried to forget his cinderblock confinement. He brought into focus in his mind a picture of his mother smiling, sitting next to the gurgling Brandywine River and holding a straw picnic basket. Sunlight streamed down through the trees of the riverbank, creating a patchwork of sunlight and shadows on her happy face. He finally found his escape in slumber.

CHAPTER 23

KELLY: SEPTEMBER 28, 2011

KELLY TOOK A deep breath and tried to gather herself before stepping through her garage door and onto the slate floor of the mudroom. The sight of her daughters' colorful rain boots and muddy sneakers in cubbies comforted her. She stood quietly in the mudroom, straining to hear Dan's voice coming from the kitchen as he helped Anna with a homework assignment. While nervously fingering Grace's yellow hoodie, she concentrated on his steady calm voice. She wanted to go to Dan, tuck her head under his chin and cry into his chest. She wanted him to know that she had come face-to-face with the man who had turned her world upside down, and that he was still out there. But for now she had to be calm, comfortable and strong in front of her daughters. She walked tentatively toward the kitchen.

"Mommy!" Grace shrieked, looking up from a Disney coloring book and clutching a purple crayon. She jumped to her feet and ran over to embrace Kelly with her slender arms.

"Well, that's what I call a welcome," Kelly laughed. "Boy! It feels good to hug you!" She looked across the room where Dan and Anna still sat side-by-side, with a math workbook on the table in front of them. "How about you two? No hugs for Mom?"

"Hi Mom," Anna said, with one finger twirling a long lock of hair. "Dad's helping me with long division, and it really sucks."

"Hey!" Dan said loudly, causing Kelly to jump. "Anna!

What have we told you about saying that word? You just lost half your allowance this week for that, and we do not want to hear that word again. Understood?" Dan and Kelly were silent as they both glared at Anna. "Yeah, well that sucks, too!" Anna yelled as she got up, turned from the table and ran upstairs to her bedroom.

Dan quickly rose and started to follow her, flush with anger.

"Dan!" Kelly said, as she reached out and grabbed his forearm, stopping him. "Please stop. We'll talk to her later. I think you and I need to talk right now."

"She's been impossible lately," Dan said, waving at the homework books left open on the kitchen table as he spoke. "I even got a call from her teacher today saying that she left her science class on a supposed bathroom break and just disappeared. A teaching assistant had to go search the entire school property before she found her sitting on the little kids' swing set. She would not explain herself to her teachers or to me at all."

"Why didn't you call me?" Kelly asked.

Dan was silent for a moment, looking at his feet and then into his wife's eyes. "You have enough to deal with at present. Besides, I think her behavior is related to your behavior lately, so maybe it's not a good idea to involve you."

Kelly bit her lip to remain calm and said to Grace, "Baby, please go up to your room for a bit. Mom and Dad need a little alone time."

Gracie looked at her father for a moment, and Kelly saw him nodding his affirmation. She quietly gathered her coloring book and a fistful of the scattered crayons on the table and left the room.

"Gee, Dan, I'm sorry. Have I not been a model of good behavior lately?" The anger and bitterness in Kelly's tone made Dan flinch. "Maybe because I was tied up and raped by someone who's still out there, I am still feeling just a little off! Maybe you could suck it up for a little while and try to help with the kids and help them get through this without heaping more guilt and blame on me."

"What the hell are you talking about?" Dan rarely displayed anger. "I've not gone to work since you were attacked. I have tiptoed around you and the subject, and answered your every need. Jesus Christ, Kel! Something horrible happened to you. I get that. But, you know what? We are all still here!" Dan stopped for a moment. He couldn't find the words.

"I came home to tell you something really important, and instead of finding my husband ready to listen, to comfort me, I get criticism and blame about my shitty parenting!" Kelly continued her rant.

"I was only telling you what's going on with our daughter. Kel, I don't know what to do. I am trying my best."

Kelly paused for a moment and looked at her husband. She knew she had been unreasonable, but she was not in an empathetic mood. She quickly changed the subject. "Dan, it's Jack Barnard. He is the guy who raped me."

"What?" Dan looked up at her. "Who the hell is Jack Barnard? What are you talking about?"

As Kelly explained her case against Jack Barnard, Dan took her hand in his and led her to the family room sofa. He listened quietly, soaking in every detail. He knew that his wife was a successful attorney because she had an incredibly sharp memory and was meticulous in her attention to detail. He knew without a doubt that Kelly had figured out the identity of the monster that had deliberately and irreparably injured his wife and their family.

As Kelly described her morning encounter with Jack Barnard at the courthouse, and the moment when she knew for certain that she was looking at her attacker, she began to cry with loud sobbing sounds that were unlike anything Dan had heard before. Her mournful wailing frightened him. He instinctively reached his arms out and wrapped them around his broken wife. He noticed Anna and Grace peeking around the corner of the staircase. Dan motioned them away quietly by nodding his head toward the stairs and mouthing, "*Go back upstairs, now!*" The girls were clearly frightened, too, and they quickly ducked back up the stairs.

After a few minutes, Dan felt Kelly's body relax a little, and her sobbing eased. She lifted her head and looked at Dan. Her mascara was streaked and pooled under her eyes and a line of snot ran out of one of her nostrils. "Well?" Kelly shuddered and caught her breath. "What do you think of all this?"

Dan put his left hand on her chin while he gently dabbed at her eyes and then her nose with a tissue.

"Dan." Kelly said again. "Please, say something."

"I want to kill this fucking bastard!" Dan's eyes were ablaze.

"Daddy? What is happening?"

Kelly froze in horror as she saw their daughters again peering around the corner of the bottom of the stairway. She also felt a twinge of hurt and jealousy as Anna addressed her question to their father, as if she was not even there.

"I thought I told you girls that Mom and I needed some time alone." Dan said in a tone that sounded less like anger and more like tired resignation.

"Please! What's going on?" Anna said. "Why is Mom crying and who are you going to kill?" Anna twirled her hair nervously and Gracie started crying.

Dan sat mute for a moment. He exhaled deeply and tried to regain his composure while trying to think of what to say.

"Girls," Kelly spoke before Dan could. "It's time for a real family meeting."

The girls came into the room almost shyly. Gracie sat on the couch next to Dan, while Anna sat in the armchair across from the couch, with her arms protectively crossed in front of her chest.

"You both know that I have not been feeling well lately, and that I was resting after I was in the hospital." Kelly looked at her girls' faces as she spoke, trying to watch their reaction to her news. "Well, I was hurt by a man, and he is about to be in a lot of trouble and put away somewhere so he can't get out. He was mean only to me, he does not want to hurt you or Daddy and he can't do that, anyway. I am getting better every day and I need you both to try to be brave and patient. Can you do that?"

Both girls nodded their head. Dan continued to sit quietly as Kelly continued. "And I want you to know that you can ask me about this, and that you might hear people talking about it at school, and that it might be a little scary or embarrassing for you, but we are all going to be fine." Kelly looked at her daughters as she spoke. Gracie looked down at her hands in her lap, while Anna continued to nervously twist a long lock of hair around her finger. Kelly looked up at Dan when she said the last sentence, as if she was reassuring him specifically.

"And Anna," Kelly continued talking. "I know you were embarrassed when you heard kids at school talking about my attack, and I know you are angry that I have not been around for you while I was recovering. But you are old enough now to know how to deal with those emotions. You can talk to Dad or me, or you can go see a counselor at school if you want. But you do not have a license to be rude to your teachers or your parents or to skip class and ignore rules. Understood?"

Anna rose from her chair crying and ran to her mother. She hugged her as she sobbed, "I'm so sorry, Mom. I'm scared."

Grace got up and tried to put her little arms around them both, an awkward three-way hug. Dan moved over and wrapped his arms around all of them saying, "We're going to be okay. We are the Mighty Malloy Family!"

*****

Kelly and Dan climbed into bed. They were exhausted and emotionally drained by the day's events. Streetlights in front of their home cast a warm glow through the bedroom windows. Dan glanced at Kelly sideways. In the soft light he noticed that her cheekbones were more pronounced than ever, sharper against her pouty lips and her big dark eyes. He thought that her new short hairstyle made her look vulnerable, although he was sure that she had chosen it to look stronger. He was surprised to feel arousal stir in him, and then an aching as he stiffened. He turned on his back completely, looked at the ceiling and emitted a loud sigh.

Kelly knew that he was frustrated and feeling disconnected from her. She could not fathom ever wanting to have sex again, but she was surprised to feel a sense of loss, as if she was mourning the death of that part of their relationship. She closed her eyes and saw a continuous reel of images of their bodies coming together over the years. First there was the night in Key West, their bodies twisting and grinding on the wet sand and the stars in the sky behind Dan's face and shoulders over her. Then their slow lovemaking in front of the living room fireplace while babies slept upstairs. Kelly remembered Dan guiding her into a new position, trying to emulate a picture from the Kama Sutra open on their bed. She recalled their tearful and tender lovemaking on the squeaky little bed in her childhood home on the night of her father's burial.

"Kel?" Dan whispered into the space above them.

"Yeah?" Kelly whispered back.

"I, uhm, I... miss you." Dan whispered, hesitating a little as he murmured the words.

Kelly felt a flutter of something in her stomach at Dan's words. It was not desire she felt though; it was fear. She missed him, too. She ached to hold him and to connect with him and to press against his strong arms and chest. But she winced at the thought of sex. She felt her thighs tighten as if precluding the possibility. She turned in bed toward her husband, bent her left elbow and rested her head on her hand. "Babe, I miss you too." She let out a sigh. "I miss you too, but.." she couldn't finish the sentence. She had no words for it.

Dan moved toward Kelly slowly. She felt the pull of his warmth and of his quiet strength. He wrapped his arms around her and squeezed her gently. "It's okay, Kel. I love you and I am happy just to hold you." Dan said in his quiet husky bedroom voice that Kelly loved.

Kelly inhaled the smell of his skin and felt the back of his shaggy hair with her fingers. "I am going to go talk to someone, I think." Kelly loosened her arms around Dan a little.

"What do you mean? Talk to whom and about what?"

"I think I'm going to talk to a counselor. I got a business card for someone from the doctors or the police, I don't remember. My body is healing, but inside my head is still a mess." Kelly thought of the business card that she had deliberately hidden in the recesses of her recipe box on their kitchen counter.

"I think that is great, Kel.... I love you."

A moment later, Dan snored softly. Kelly gently extricated herself from his arms and rolled over. It seemed as if she had just fallen asleep when a loud ringing sound pierced the silence of Kelly's dreams. She was covered in sweat and out of breath as she desperately tried to run away from a ferocious brown wolf. She braced for the tearing of sharp fangs, while the shrill ringing woke her. She leaned over to grab the phone on her night table.

The red letters on her alarm clock read 11:45. Dan woke and struggled to put a pillow over his head in response to the ringing phone.

"Hello?" Kelly half-greeted and half-asked the telephone's mouthpiece in a groggy voice.

"Kel! It's Sam. I'm sorry it's so late but I was down in the Kent County courthouse all evening and just got back to plow through my inbox. I have the DNA lab results."

"Sam?" Kelly asked as she scratched her head, still trying to shrug off the deep sleep. She watched Dan turn over and remove the pillow he had put over his head a moment ago.

"Kel, we finally found some DNA that is going to be useful, from the clothing you wore on the day of the attack. We just got the test results and it does not match the guy they have been holding, Chad McCloskey. Tomorrow morning I expect to get an arrest warrant and a request for DNA from Jack Barnard."

Kelly sat up straight at the edge of the bed, fully awake. "What if he does not agree to DNA testing?" Kelly asked.

"I can file papers to compel that, but I doubt he'll refuse. If we already have him arrested, he will look guilty by refusing, and he'll know his refusal will be in vain too, because the court eventually will order it. Plus, Barnard is a lawyer and he has a gigantic ego, so I bet he thinks that he was too smart and too careful to leave DNA."

Kelly felt a wave of fear as Sam confirmed that her attacker was still out there, and not random at all. He *knew* her. He *chose* her specifically to violate and hurt and humiliate. With the phone in one hand, she hastily got out of bed and walked to the security alarm panel on the wall by the doorway to their bedroom. Its red light and the word *armed* gave her some comfort. She stepped into the hallway and whispered, "Sam, am I in any danger?"

Sam exhaled deeply. "No way, Kel. There has been no way that he knows we are even on to him, and tomorrow will be like a blitzkrieg with an arrest, a quick DNA test and, hopefully, grounds to hold him until trial." Sam paused for a moment, trying to think of something else to help calm his longtime friend. "Oh, and don't forget, we have a witness who saw a man who looked like Barnard shooting you and carrying you away into the woods."

Kelly vaguely remembered a reference to a witness. "What's the deal there? Who is she?"

"Some woman called the Wilmington police tip line to report your attack. She has been difficult to speak with. I am afraid she is an illegal immigrant, so she is a reluctant witness. I'll fill you in on that later in the week as we get further."

Kelly recalled her run through the woods on that fateful day; the dazzling new sunlight on the river, the sweet smell of a September morning and her running shoes moving over the soft earth. Somewhere in the midst of that beautiful and tranquil moment, Jack Barnard was lying in wait to attack her and to destroy her. And, beyond that, a nameless woman silently watched in horror.

"Sam?" Kelly asked, with hesitation. "This is a little embarrassing, but where did they get a DNA sample? I thought they told me that he used a condom."

"Yeah, I guess it is a bit awkward, between old friends. But you and I are both professionals, and so we'll have to get beyond that." Sam cleared his throat. "They found a small semen stain on your running shorts, Kel. Some must have spilled out of the condom as he got off of you or as he took it off." He tried to sound solid, matter-of-fact, as if he was discussing evidence with a colleague regarding an unknown victim. "Hey, Kel?" Sam waited a minute for a response. Getting nothing but silence, he continued. "This is going to have rough spots. It is going to be filled with a world of hurt, and painfully intimate physical details and even moments of humiliation for you."

"I got a taste of that already, Sam, when they were poking around inside of me for evidence and taking photographs of bruises on my private parts." Kelly tried hard to remember where her running shorts were when the monster completed his act. She remembered only that they had been yanked off of her legs and over her shoes.

"It is really hard for me to talk like this with you, uhm, about you, and I have prosecuted rape cases before. I can't even imagine how it makes you feel."

"Or Dan," Kelly murmured.

"Yeah, of course. Dan too. It's going to be really hard on Dan, too."

As Kelly sat in the dimly lit hallway listening to her dear friend, she realized that her hand holding the receiver was shaking uncontrollably. "Sam?"

"Yeah, Kel?"

Kelly winced a little at the sound of his voice. His love for her came through in every word. She loved him and trusted him like a best friend, but she never could love him romantically. "Thanks. I can't thank you enough for being here for me." Kelly started crying quietly.

"Shhh, Kel. Come on, it's going to be all right. We have got this guy as good as nailed now. Kel, I was going to fax you over a copy of the arrest warrant and the complaint and supporting affidavits, but I kind of think you shouldn't have to read all of those details right now. Okay?"

Kelly continued to sob softly. Sam was silent and helpless on the other end of the line.

Finally, he heard her speak. "I guess you're right Sam. I know you've got this. And I am not ready to see the details."

"I'll call you tomorrow after he is arrested and let you know where we are." Sam said hastily. "Good night, Kel. Hang in there."

CHAPTER 24

JACK BARNARD: SEPTEMBER 28-29, 2011

JACK BARNARD PULLED back his sleeve to expose his thick gold Rolex watch. It was eight thirty-five and the waiter had not even brought their first course. His gesture had the desired effect.

"Wow, that is a gorgeous watch," the twenty-eight-year-old woman with wavy blond hair and tremendous breasts exclaimed as she extended her arms across the table to examine it up close. Her name was Sandy, or maybe Shelly, he wasn't sure.

Barnard had been fixed up on this date by a sales rep from a legal copy service company. She had been described as a "sure thing" to Barnard, and he knew what that meant. If he had to buy dinner and drive to Philadelphia to meet her, he *better* get laid. Bringing her to the swanky Fountain Restaurant at the Four Seasons Hotel and then driving her back to his penthouse in his Jaguar would do the trick. Her inane conversation became white noise as Barnard pictured what he would do to her when he got her there. Once she was intoxicated with too much wine and the ride in his new Jag, she would be putty in his hands. He tried to picture her with her dress off.

"Jack? Jack, what do you think?"

"Oh, I'm sorry. I guess I was thinking about one of my cases there for a moment. I'm sorry, I am just under a lot of pressure."

"I've told you enough about myself. Why don't you tell me

about you?" She twirled her hair in her fingers and bent over a little so Barnard could see more of her cleavage.

"Uhm. I grew up in Wilmington. Went to Concord High School, then Texas Tech for college, and I played linebacker there," he pointed to his Texas Tech ring in case she had missed it. "Then Widener Law School, and then became a trial attorney, opened my own shop four years out and never looked back."

The woman, named Sandy—or Shelly—giggled. "Jack, I'm not interested in your résumé. Who are you? What have you done other than go to those schools, play football and practice law?"

Barnard paused while their waiter placed their first courses on the table. *Thank God,* he thought. He finished it in three quick bites. "Okay, well, my dad was a lawyer in Delaware and he was a ball-breaker. He was always the big man in the community, in the newspaper for all his good charitable works, paying for inner-city kids' basketball uniforms, getting ball fields named after him, you know—the big saint and hero. Everywhere he went people knew him and thought he was such a great guy."

"You sound like you didn't think so. I think that..."

As his date kept talking, Barnard dug into his entrée. He saw flashbacks of his father flaunting his infidelity, or his mother crying at night after she suffered another indignity, or worse—a hand to the back of her face for complaining about it. He hated his father for doing these things, but he hated his mother even more for letting him. He couldn't respect her and he stopped feeling sorry for her.

"Well which is it, hero and saint or ball-buster?" Sandy or Shelly was starting to annoy him.

"A little of both, I guess." Barnard remembered how his father came to all of his football and basketball games, always looking like the supportive father, only to smack him across the head and call him a *loser* when they were alone in his car because of a dropped pass or a missed foul shot.

When the waiter brought the dessert menu, Barnard waived him off. "Just a check, please." Then he leaned in toward the table and said quietly, "I have a much better idea for dessert."

*****

As Barnard brought the blonde up the elevator, she was just starting to slump over. He had put his arm around her and held her up as she shuffled toward his door. He opened the door to his penthouse and moved her quickly to the bedroom. He did not want her to lose consciousness; that was no fun. She giggled as he threw her on the bed and started tearing at her dress. He wanted her naked and under him and at his disposal.

"Oh, you like it rough, huh?" She giggled.

He wished he had gone easier on the wine. She was too easy already, and maybe close to passing out. He had to hurry. "I do like it rough. And you do, too, because I know you are a bad girl." He grabbed a pair of handcuffs from his bureau.

She laughed a little, as if she wasn't sure if he was joking or not. Her face registered concern.

Now Barnard was aroused and had to hurry. He had mastered the balance of fear and physical dominance, consensual and coerced. The trick was to not go over to the side where the woman would know with certainty that she had actually been victimized, that she hadn't played along willingly with a game she regretted. Barnard was always careful to not leave a mark.

*****

The phone rang next to Jack's disordered bed, waking him up. "Hello," Barnard growled into the phone. The sky was turning from black to orange outside the floor-to-ceiling bedroom windows.

"Jack, it's Micky. I just got back to the station after my shift and I saw arrest warrant papers with your name on them."

"What? Who is this?" Barnard's head throbbed from the Scotch, the wine and the crazy bitch who wouldn't stop pawing him when he was trying to sleep, as if they had some intimate connection. A tumble of blond hair stirred next to him in bed and then rolled away.

"Jack, focus. It's me, Micky. You know, your friend from the old neighborhood...."

"Oh, yeah. What the hell are you calling me at this hour for?"

"I have night patrol duty all this week. I got back to the station at six this morning and was pouring a cup of coffee and chatting with some of the guys when I found out they are getting ready to execute an arrest warrant. They are coming for you, buddy, and it has something to do with that attack by the river last week."

Barnard hung up the phone. Panic surged as he went into flight mode. He dressed quickly and then emptied his dresser drawers and closet in huge armfuls, pressing jeans, shirts, suits, shoes and socks into a large suitcase with wheels.

"What are you doing? What's going on?" The blonde stirred.

"I have a case blowing up and I have to get on a plane as soon as possible."

The woman sat up in bed. Her mascara had smeared under her eyes and her hair was matted from hairspray and Barnard's rough foreplay. "How am I supposed to get back to Philly?"

"I don't give a—" Barnard caught himself mid-sentence. He couldn't leave this woman here, in this condition, if the police where coming to his home to arrest him for rape. "I mean, I hadn't thought about that. I am in a tremendous hurry, so I'll get you to the airport and then put you in a cab from there."

As the blonde freshened up in the bathroom, Barnard grabbed a billfold thick with cash that he kept for emergencies, plus his wallet and his passport and shoved them all in his briefcase. Moments later they were driving 80 miles per hour on I-95 North.

Mercifully, the woman kept her mouth shut and leaned against the car window sleepily. Barnard went over it in his mind. *How could they finger me? I was too careful. I hadn't left a trace.* He went over the details in his mind, in order. *No one could have seen me that morning by the shed. I checked and checked that morning and I've been there at that same time countless other mornings. Malloy could not have seen me... I hit her from behind and did not approach her until she was knocked out. Then she was blindfolded. I didn't leave any DNA, nothing under her fingernails because her hands were tied behind her back, she was unconscious most of the time, and I used a condom.* He remembered peeling off the condom and sealing it carefully in a ziplock bag. Afterward he'd dipped the condom in a bottle of chlorine bleach and then flushed it down his toilet. *I left no fingerprints because I wore gloves—except when I had to take them off to use that tiny little syringe or take off that skin-tight slippery condom. But I left with both those items....*

Red and blue flashing lights and screaming sirens came up behind him at that moment. Three police cruisers surrounded him.

CHAPTER 25

CHAD: SEPTEMBER 29, 2011

"HEY, FRESH MEAT." The man named Paco began his taunts as they entered the recreation room. The biggest prisoners went off to the area with free-weights and a few other guys lingered around a ping-pong table. Chad spotted a television set and some chairs. "What did you do to get in here? You look like one of those rich white boys who cut up his parents one night when they are sleeping." The man laughed loudly.

Chad kept his head down and walked toward a chair in front of the television set in the corner.

"Hey, Fresh Meat. Maybe you got drunk at the prom and raped the prom queen. Is that what you did?" He pointed at Chad. "Answer me! I am talking to you, bitch!"

Chad sat in a chair and pretended to be immersed in the morning news. His stomach churned and his cheeks grew hot as he felt the other inmates staring at him, waiting for his response. Suddenly he heard his name called and he saw a burly guard motioning for him to follow. He rose quickly from his chair and followed the guard out of the room while his tormentor continued.

"You're getting lucky this time, Fresh Meat, but I'll see you real soon."

Chad was led to a small room furnished only with a table and two chairs, and a clock on the wall. A moment later Stuart entered the room in a rumpled blue suit and his briefcase in hand. He was out of breath as he exclaimed, "I have really good news Chad. Your DNA doesn't match the semen found on the victim's clothing. I'm going to file a Motion to Dismiss in a few days, once I get everything together and a final lab report. But I'll also pursue a quicker option by asking the AG to enter a *nolle prosequi*, which is a fancy term for dismissal of the charges against you. They have to do this if the evidence shows they no longer have probable cause to believe you are guilty."

Chad looked at his young attorney. He wanted to share in Stuart's optimism, but he still feared the sadistic inmate, the burly guards and the cinderblock walls. When Chad looked at Stuart, he saw a man-child with a skinny neck and pimples on his chin. Even his ill-fitting suit made him resemble a child playing dress-up in his father's clothing. "What does that mean? I mean, what does that mean as far as me getting out of here? Is it definite, probable or just a possibility?"

"Well, we still have things a little muddied up by the witness seeing you moving the victim around, and maybe your purchase of that one-way ticket out of here on the day of the attack, so we have to work though those parts. But still, the DNA result is really good news."

He continued before waiting for an answer. "And if I am getting out, when?" Chad swallowed hard and with difficulty, thinking of the man in his cellblock who kept harassing him.

Before Stuart could answer Chad's question, the door to the small room opened slowly and the guard who looked like a linebacker poked his head back inside the room. "Excuse me. Sorry to interrupt," he spoke to Stuart as if Chad wasn't even there. "Counselor, I need to talk to you for a moment."

Stuart stepped outside, leaving the door open. Chad heard them speaking to each other but he could not decipher their words. He realized a third person was speaking now, so he looked up and saw a Wilmington police officer's uniform. Chad tried to interpret the expression on Stuart's face. *Disbelief? Shock? Sadness?* Suddenly, the police officer stopped talking and all three men looked at Chad. Chad saw his young lawyer briefly put his hand on the police officer's arm and Chad heard him say something about "bearing bad news."

Chad stood abruptly and remained standing next to the table, frozen with terror. *What now?* He was convinced that some other incriminating evidence was revealed and now he was going to rot in this prison, with its impenetrable cinderblock walls and stagnant air filled with fear, frustration and loneliness.

"What! Please, just tell me. Get it over with!" Chad pleaded with Stuart as he returned to the room.

"Chad," Stuart started slowly, "I just got some bad news about your father."

"My father?" Chad asked in disbelief.

"Yes." Stuart sat down again across from Chad and motioned for him to sit down again, too. Stuart began rubbing the nonexistent stubble on his chin and began speaking. "A group of women walking along the Brandywine River early this morning saw a pickup truck half submerged in the water. They called 9-1-1 and the rescue folks pulled your father out of the cab of that truck. There's no official cause of death yet, but the officer just told me that, based on their initial investigation, they think he was in the river since late last night." Stuart stopped speaking and looked across the table at Chad. He was surprised to see the color return to Chad's face. "Chad?" Stuart asked, "Are you all right?"

"Um, yeah," Chad said, expressionless. It was not at all the reaction that Stuart had expected. "Are they sure it was my father?"

"The police told me they pulled his license out of a wallet in his pocket." Stuart saw nothing that resembled grief or sadness on Chad's face. "Should I get someone, like a grief counselor or a doctor or something?"

"No, really, I'm fine. Actually, I am quite relieved."

"What?"

"Well," Chad started, "for one thing, I thought you were coming in here to tell me the police had more damning but bogus evidence against me."

"Chad, we're talking about your father. He's dead." Stuart spoke as if Chad hadn't heard him accurately the first time. "Do you want me to get someone trained that you can talk to about this—to uh, help you process this?"

"You don't get it," Chad said a little too quickly. "My father was a no-good, drunken, bitter, son-of-a-bitch who made my mother miserable and then ultimately drove her away. He made me feel small, weak, like a loser. And the worst part is…" Chad started to choke up as he spoke. Stuart averted his eyes as tears welled up in Chad's eyes. "The worst part is, he deliberately and constantly tried to make us feel like shit so he could keep us with him, keep us too small and weak and lost to go anywhere and break free from him. I wish this had happened years ago. My mother and I would have been a lot better off."

After a long silence, Chad wiped his eyes with the shirt of his prison uniform.

"Well, I am sorry for everything you have been through and sorry about your mother. But the good news is, I think I can get this thing dismissed based on the DNA. But it may take a little while." Stuart closed his briefcase on the table and stood. "Oh, and I will find out from the Warden's Office or Social Services about making funeral arrangements for your father. I'm certain they will take you to the funeral, too, of course, once it is arranged."

Chad sat silently, his head staring down at the table in front of him. "Thank you. I don't know how I can ever repay you."

Stuart, feeling a little embarrassed at this remark, shrugged his shoulders and replied, "I'm just doing my job." He laughed a little and made an attempt at lightening the mood. "Why do you think the State pays me the big bucks?"

As Chad waked back to his cell with the guard right behind him, his thoughts were whirling. Pictures of his father over the years flashed through his head. In one image he was chopping wood and screaming for his "no good, lazy son" to come collect it. In the next he was seated at the kitchen table, staring at his mother's pot roast in disgust and telling her that "there was only one thing she did worse than cooking," and that was "everything."

Chad felt a sudden lightness, despite the prison guard and the metal bars and locks everywhere. He was free of his father forever. There would be no more of his derision, contempt, orders, opinions, bitterness or bullying. He was free of Charlie McCloskey's misery, at least.

CHAPTER 26
KELLY: SEPTEMBER 29, 2011

THE RHYTHMIC TICKING of the antique clock on her desk lulled Kelly into a trance. The girls were at school and Dan was at work. Exhausted, Kelly struggled to concentrate on her laptop screen. Outside the window she saw a bright red cardinal perched in a branch of a young oak tree. Then the phone next to her elbow rang shrilly and unexpectedly, jostling her.

"Kel, it's Sam. We have Barnard in custody. The bastard was tipped off by someone; probably a friend in the police force. He was driving on I-95 early this morning when we stopped him. He said he was going to visit a friend, but then he got a little foggy on the details when we asked him who, so we could verify. He also had his passport in a suitcase filled with his clothes, so that didn't look so good for him, either. In any event, we had the arrest warrant signed first thing this morning, so the police were able to nab him. He's had his initial appearance already and now we start preparing for a preliminary hearing, which is scheduled for October seventh."

"And the preliminary hearing is what, again?" Kelly asked, growing frustrated by her lack of knowledge on criminal law and procedure.

"That's where we show the judge that there is probable cause to believe that the crimes have been committed and that Barnard committed them, and why he should be held over to answer in Superior Court. We can use hearsay evidence at this juncture and, of course, probable cause is a pretty low standard of proof, you know, in contrast to the beyond a reasonable doubt we'll have to establish at trial."

"What about the preliminary hearing with the guy they're holding, Chad McCloskey?" Kelly asked. "I didn't even attend that."

"Well," Sam replied, "I was not on the case then, but I saw from the record that they waived the preliminary hearing. Like I said, it's not a high burden for the prosecution. We have a witness report of a man with McCloskey's description and his car transporting you, unconscious and wrapped in a blanket, into the woods where you were rescued. Then we have evidence that he was about to leave town, with a one-way ticket to Arizona that he purchased immediately after you were attacked. That was certainly probably cause to hold him over for this crime before the DNA results, and for now, it's still sufficient probable cause. He could still have been involved in your attack, along with someone else who did leave the DNA sample on your shorts, or he could at least have been an accomplice."

"Will I have to testify at Barnard's preliminary hearing?" Kelly tried to swallow the dread that was climbing up her throat.

"Kel, I know that testifying in front of Jack Barnard is going to be really difficult for you. But Barnard has retained a hotshot defense attorney who is brutal. So, yes, you are going to have to try to mentally prepare for this. You'll just tell your story to the judge, giving him specific reasons why Barnard poses a danger to the public, and to you. You will have to describe the horror, pain and trauma he inflicted on you with the attack, and how you saw his hand, with the unique ring and scar. I'll probably ask you to also describe his recent verbal threats against you, how he knows your running routine, and maybe even about his aggression toward you years ago when you refused to dance with him."

"Can I tell the Court that I would be terrified for my safety if he was out free pending trial?"

"Yeah, Kel," Sam said softly, "you should mention that too." He sat helpless, phone in hand, as he heard Kelly start sobbing. He felt a familiar pull, an old tug in his chest and stomach, as he yearned to be next to her, to hold her in his arms and to make her feel safe. "Kelly, it is going to be okay. I am going to nail this guy, with a boatload of evidence to show he poses a real danger to the public and he's a flight risk. He's in custody now, he will not touch you before trial no matter what happens at the preliminary hearing, and he will be put away for a long time." Sam then surprised Kelly with a little laugh that sounded like a snort. "Barnard is unwittingly helping us, too, with his arrogance. But his arrogance will be his Achilles heel, Kel, you wait and see." "Unfortunately, Sam, being arrogant is not a crime."

"Kel, DNA is everything and we will nail him."

"But we don't have a DNA match, do we?" Kelly said in a defeated tone.

"Not yet, but we got his sample already and it is in the lab's hands. That's what I mean about his arrogance. There was press there already when they led him in for his initial appearance, so he took the opportunity to grandstand, making some declaration about volunteering his DNA to avoid any further miscarriage of justice. I thought his lawyer was going to bust a gut. It's like Christmas for a prosecutor when the defendant thinks he is smarter than his own counsel." Sam laughed through the phone. "He said the same thing at his initial appearance, in front of the judge. So, we immediately obtained a cheek sample and a blood sample and they were both delivered to the lab."

"Why would he give that up so easily?" Kelly asked, worried that maybe she was wrong about Barnard's guilt.

"Kel, think about it. The guy knows evidence and he knows grandstanding. First, he made this big gesture to convince the public and the Court that he's innocent." Sam lowered his voice for the next part. "But, I think that he is arrogant enough to believe that he committed the perfect crime, and that there is no DNA trace to worry about. He used a condom, which he probably disposed of carefully, and he never had to struggle with you, remember? He thinks there is no semen, no blood, no skin under your fingernails, no fingerprints; he is convinced he is clean here."

"But I thought you said you have a sample from my shorts?" Kelly surprised herself when this question came out without any semblance of embarrassment.

"We do, Kel. It has been confirmed and it is protected in the lab. I guess your shorts were in the right place when he removed his condom and he has no idea. I have the report: there was definitely semen on your shorts. But we are keeping that under wraps until we have to disclose it through discovery. We did not need that to get the arrest warrant. For now, it is our smoking gun."

Kelly pictured a disheveled and red-faced Jack Barnard peeling a condom off of himself over her discarded running shorts and inadvertently sealing his fate. She clasped her hands together and made her knuckles turn white. She felt bile come up into her throat and though she swallowed hard, she started to gag.

"Kel?" Sam asked. "Kel? Are you OK?"

"Sam?" Kelly recovered herself and replied, hesitantly, "I'm scared. I can't explain it. I know he is in custody, but you know how well-connected this guy is. You mentioned that he even got tipped off by someone inside about his impending arrest this morning. Are we safe on all the physical evidence, you know, the custody of it? It's not going to disappear or be swapped out or altered, is it?"

"No, Kel. I am being very, very careful on this. I have a dependable and trustworthy guy on it. He is maintaining custody of the specimens and the reports, and on top of that he split the specimens and is preserving the split samples somewhere else. Even I don't know where they are."

"Okay, Sam. Thank you again for everything. You are the only thing keeping me sane at this point." Kelly felt a twinge of guilt toward her sweet, steady husband as those words left her lips. She put the phone back on its receiver, and quickly walked over to the alarm panel by the mudroom door. She felt a little paranoid turning the alarm on mid-morning while she worked at home, but she needed to feel safe. She went and sat back down in front of her laptop, went back to working on a brief, and mercifully lost herself in someone else's problems for almost two hours.

*****

"Hey, Kel!" Sam's voice boomed through the receiver into Kelly's ear. She pulled it away from her head and looked at the clock on her desk.

"Do you have the DNA results?" Kelly asked, breathlessly.

"Geez, Kel, I'm good but I am not a miracle worker. I just submitted them this morning, remember? I am using an independent lab that has the quickest turnaround time I know of, but they are never same-day results." Sam spoke quickly, brimming with excitement. "I had a chance to talk by phone with the eyewitness who called the Wilmington police tip line, Maria Hernandez. Her boyfriend has an immigration lawyer through the Latin American Community Center, Sara Nuñez. She doesn't practice criminal defense, but she explained to Maria that she had no choice but to cooperate as a witness. So Maria talked to me. She gave me a lot of information and it is all consistent with her call to the tip line. She saw someone matching Jack Barnard's description shoot you with something as you ran by Breck's Mill and then she saw him carry you away. But later she saw someone matching that other guy's description. Sounds just like the kid they locked up already, Chad McCloskey. He carried you into the woods from a different spot near the mill."

"That's great, Sam. With DNA and my testimony, she is like the nail in his coffin!" Kelly's heart pounded.

"I agree, except we have a few issues with her."

"What do you mean?"

"She is a sweet woman, Kel, not much more than a kid. Her lawyer told me that she came from Mexico and is living with her Mexican boyfriend. The good news is, she speaks great English. The bad news is, she is not legal yet. He has a green card, and they are working on it, but right now they are not comfortable having anything to do with this. And, to make matters worse, they had a baby just a few days ago."

"So what does this all mean, Sam?" Kelly asked. She had taken a course in immigration law a zillion years ago in law school and only remembered the basics.

"Worse-case scenario? I guess she could be deported. Their kid's a citizen because he was born here, but she obviously can't leave him here. She is terrified, and reluctant doesn't even begin to describe the kind of witness she'll make."

"Why did she come forward then?"

"She told me that she knew you had been hurt badly and that maybe she was the only one who saw these men and what they did. She was scared, but she felt like she had to call the police because it weighed too heavily on her conscience."

"Sam, I want to meet her. I want to tell her we'll do what we can to protect her and her family. I want to thank her and get an immigration lawyer from my firm to help them. Is that possible?"

"Kel, you know that can't happen. You are a victim and therefore a witness in this case, and she is a witness. You can thank her and help her when this whole proceeding is over. But you'll have no contact at all with her before then. Got that?

"It's just that this guy... this selfish monster... has wrecked so many people's lives. First, some kid, who already had a miserable life, may have been falsely accused and then locked up for this. Now, this scared woman, with a new baby and a tremendous amount at stake, is fearful that she is going to be deported." Kelly stopped to catch her breath and wipe away a tear with the back of her hand. "I should also mention that I have become toxic to my husband and daughters, who, I am afraid, will be affected for the rest of their lives."

Sam heard her sobbing again and bit his lip. "Kel, I'm sorry about all of that, but these are the circumstances of every victim that I work with. It is time now to suck it up, look forward and do what you can to fix whatever parts of this can be fixed. We have a job to do. You just listed more reasons why you have to help me put this guy behind bars forever, so he can't wreck any more lives, and so you and this woman Maria and the boy Chad can all get some closure." He softened a bit. "I am just saying that we all want the same thing, and crying is not going to help, okay?"

Kelly took a deep breath and wiped her face with her sleeve. "Sorry, I am not a robot, Sam. I'll try to toughen up. But, I do think it will help our case and me if I can meet with the woman, Maria. I want to help her if I can, or at least try to make her feel safer. And I need to thank her."

"Okay, Kel. I'll see what I can do to reach out to her or her lawyer with some assurances, at least in the short term. But you will have no contact with her until this is over. Are you hearing me?"

He continued, "And while we are on this subject, if we get to a point where we're convinced that there's no basis to pursue prosecution against Chad McCloskey, I was thinking I'd have to try to smooth things over with him, and thank him for helping you, because he'll still have to be a witness for us, too."

"I am not too warm and fuzzy about him though, Sam," Kelly replied. "He should have called 9-1-1 when he first found me. Why in hell would someone leave me bound and lying in the woods?"

"Come on, Kel, I have explained this already. The kid had a rough life and he may have been just a scared, messed-up teenager reacting with bad judgment to a very frightening set of circumstances. If his story pans out, it seems to me he had good intentions and he did go out of his way to get you somewhere where you'd be rescued. He claims that he watched over you until that happened, too—don't forget that."

"Are you getting soft on me, Sam? Where are you going with this?" Kelly asked, with irritation sounding in her voice.

"There's good press in it for the kid. Remember, his arrest for the crime was on the front page. And, hopefully, an apology and a thank you improves his feelings about the police and prosecutors—after what he was put through—because we need his testimony." Sam paused. "I guess you should see for yourself who these people are, what they have been through also, and how they fit here. Maybe it will help you become less angry and possibly even a little grateful."

Kelly winced when she heard Sam's growing frustration. She thought he was being unfair, judging her to be angry instead of grateful.

"It's all coming together, you'll see." Sam said. "I gotta run, call you soon."

"Thank you, Sam. Later."

"Later."

As Kelly hung up the phone, she caught her reflection in a gilt-framed mirror that hung on the wall across from her desk chair. Her new chin-length hair was a mess. Her eyes were sunken into her head, and there were dark circles under her eyes.

She was shocked to see this shrunken and frail-looking person where her reflection had once beamed health and confidence. Sam's words echoed in her head, "*become less angry.*"

She recalled the odd way that her daughters had looked at her when they got out of the car to walk into school that morning. Their faces were a mix of fear, worry and—something else. "Oh, my God," Kelly exclaimed out loud as she realized it was disgust and embarrassment that she saw in her girls' faces that morning.

I have got to move forward. I need to get better, Kelly said to herself as she grabbed a pencil and her legal pad. She scribbled the words *Resolutions to Get Back on Track* on top of the page and underlined them for emphasis. She began scribbling furiously, realizing that with each promise to herself, she was gaining back what the monster had stolen from her. A toxic stew of anger, fear, bitterness and self-loathing had filled every facet of her life since the attack. Sam's frank words, coupled with the memory of her daughters' facial expressions that morning, were the wake-up call that she needed.

Kelly felt stronger with the mere act of writing the words. Her resolutions unfolded:

1. Eat at least three meals a day.

2. Shower, wash hair and blow-dry it.

3. Make beds and keep house reasonably tidy.

4. Plan a vacation for Christmas (unless there is a trial, and then plan it for Spring Break).

5. Call or talk face-to-face with at least one friend every day.

6. Schedule time alone with Dan weekly.

Kelly sat and chewed on her right thumbnail while she contemplated her list. She went back to resolution number 4 and edited it.

4. Plan a vacation to ski or snorkel for Christmas (and if there is a trial, get it rescheduled or get it reassigned—you are going on this vacation!!!).

She added another edit to resolution number 6.

6. Schedule a weekly date with Dan and try to get back to sexual intimacy.

Writing the words *sexual intimacy* still gave her a knot in her stomach. But Kelly yearned for a connection with Dan, and bit her lip with resolve to not let that bastard Barnard ruin the closeness she had shared with her husband. She underlined that one twice.

After tapping the paper a few times, and reading her revised list over, Kelly realized that she was not finished.

7. *Make sleeping eight hours a priority—take pills if necessary.*

8. *Be more patient and fun with the girls.*

9. *Exercise????*

The last resolution drifted alone and in a very noncommittal fashion, with no words to compel Kelly to action and no requirements regarding type or frequency. Before her attack, Kelly's daily run was essential to her good health of mind and body. It revved her up and stoked her energy and confidence for whatever adversity she faced in her day, while it also cleared her head and fatigued her body, helping her to rest and relax.

After reading her list, Kelly realized that resolutions 6 and 9 had a lot in common. She yearned for them both, felt terribly unhealthy and unsettled without them, and yet terror seized her as she visualized embarking on either activity. After sitting and mulling over her list one more time, Kelly put an asterisk next to resolutions 6 and 9 to remind her to concentrate particularly on those. Then she realized her final resolution related to those important tasks.

10. *See the counselor/therapist who specializes in my issues.*

A moment later, she walked to her kitchen and opened the recipe box. She found the business card of the woman who had been described to her as a *Rape Crisis Counselor* and an *Interventionist*. But when Kelly gingerly flipped the business card over in her fingers it just read, "*Sally M. Jeter, MD, Ph.D.*"

CHAPTER 27

CHAD: SEPTEMBER 29, 2011

CHAD WAS STARING at the bottom of the cot above him, his hands clasped behind his head as he lay flat on his back. A guard had informed him that his attorney was coming to see him, even though Stuart had already been there that morning. He had been waiting almost two hours since the guard told him this, and he began to get anxious. He desperately needed news about his release. He closed his eyes and allowed himself to imagine his reunion with his mother. He pictured a white stucco home with a red tile roof and a wraparound porch filled with comfortable rocking chairs. Behind the house a fiery sunset burnished tall jagged mountains. A screen door opened and shut as his mother ran toward him. Her arms would be extended as she ran toward him, because she needed to embrace him as soon as possible. She ran easily, as if on air, with her head up and a wide smile on her face. Just as she was about to wrap him in her arms, Chad heard the loud clanging of his cell door. His eyes opened to the familiar off-white concrete and brick illuminated by his prison's fluorescent lighting.

"Hey, kid," the guard called to Chad. "Up and at' em, your lawyer is here."

Chad sprang to his feet and followed the guard out of his cell and down the hall. To his relief, the scary guy Paco was not in his cell, and Chad's procession to the room where his lawyer waited was uneventful.

"Chad," Stuart said as he sprang up from the chair he had been sitting in to shake Chad's hand. "It's good to see you. I have really good news."

"My case has been dismissed?" Chad blurted out.

"We never even got that far, Chad. It was the darnedest thing. This morning, the police arrested another suspect for this crime. They have all sorts of evidence that points to him. They are just waiting for test results on this guy's DNA."

"What do you mean?" Chad was shocked and relieved but afraid to believe it was real. "Are you sure? Who is this guy?"

"He's a big shot trial attorney, ironically. His name is Jack Barnard. I got some information out of the AG's office—some in the course of regular discovery in my defense of your charges, but some of it I guess would be considered off-the-record. But it sounds pretty airtight."

"Well, what does that mean for me?" Chad asked. "How long does it take to get DNA results?"

"The AG's office said the DNA results should be ready in a day or two. They have expedited the testing. Of course, this guy Barnard is denying everything, but the DNA results should be the clincher. If you're a religious man, Chad, you better pray that Barnard's DNA matches the DNA found on the victim." Stuart continued speaking, putting his hand on Chad's left shoulder as he spoke. "It's a good thing this guy left some semen behind."

Chad blushed at the word. He had never had sex. He had seen the pictures in his father's magazines, and he had brought himself to climax while looking at those pictures, but he had never gotten close enough to a girl to even kiss her.

"So, what now?" Chad asked.

"Well, we wait a day or two for the DNA results, and then, if everything goes as we hope, you are out of here and back to your life." Stuart said.

Chad felt a knot in his stomach as he thought about his life. His father was dead, he did not know where his mother was, and he had no one.

"But the other thing I came about was to tell you that a lady from the Delaware Division of Family Services is here. She said technically, because you turned eighteen, you have aged out of their services, but this is a bit unusual, so they're going to help you anyway."

"What are they going to do for me?" Chad asked, exasperated.

"Well, first of all, they've made funeral arrangements. They tracked down the priest of the church where your parents— mostly your mom, it sounds like—attended services. They got a plot at that church's cemetery and arranged everything. All costs are being tallied and we'll sort that out later. It seems your father did not have a will or any life insurance."

"There's a surprise," Chad said sarcastically. "Why should he think of me or my mother?"

"Well," Stuart continued, "the good news is, your father owned that house and property free and clear. The house is a tear-down, but the property next to the Brandywine down there is now considered prime real estate and it will fetch a really good sum."

Chad smiled at the phrase *tear-down*. He happily pictured the forlorn farmhouse with the chipping paint and the sagging porch being knocked into pieces by bulldozers and cleared away in truck beds, leaving a clean slate of possibilities.

"What do you mean by 'good sum'? Who gets that money?"

"Hopefully you can track your mother down and get her involved in this process. Under the law, the money will go to her, and then of course to you. The lady from DFS said that a realtor thought you could get up to $800,000 for that property. Then, any debt your parents owed would have to be satisfied by those proceeds, but so far it seems your father was big on paying cash for everything. So, it is probably just funeral-related expenses you're looking at, which will run around ten grand, and any taxes and fees related to the sale of the home."

"Wow," Chad said. "I never would have guessed that place was worth much. It turns out the old man left us something after all. I'm sure he would have managed to piss it away if he had the chance."

"Well," Stuart continued, "this will all take a while to sort out. We need to get you out of here. Then we need to sort through the financial stuff."

"And," Chad interrupted him mid-sentence, "I need to find my mom."

"Yes," Stuart said. "I'll let you know if I find anything useful on that subject."

"I am going to find her even if no one else can," Chad said.

"That may be, Chad. I believe you are capable of many things. But for now, I just need you to hang in there and keep safe. You are going to be walking out of here real soon, I am confident of that."

Chad swallowed the lump in his throat, thinking of the scary man lurking in the recreation room, the cafeteria, and the shower room.

CHAPTER 28
KELLY: OCTOBER 1, 2011

KELLY TRIED TO picture Maria Hernandez as she drove west from the city. Sam told Kelly not to meet with the witness, but Kelly saw no impropriety in talking to Maria's boyfriend's immigration lawyer. Besides, she reasoned, she was not going to discuss the case at all. She hadn't informed Sam, because she did not want him to tell her not to. She had to do something.

The apartment buildings, supermarkets and gas stations of the city were replaced by rolling green hills and thick woodlands punctuated by an occasional farmhouse, barn or small country store. In recent years, parts of Hockessin had been developed with new roads and cul-de-sacs lined with tidy lawns and tremendous brick houses that Dan sarcastically referred to as McMansions. Chain stores and restaurants followed, and eventually even a strip mall.

But Kelly noticed with sadness the impossibly small and dilapidated dwellings on the outskirts of Hockessin that were home to Latin American immigrants. Many came to the area for seasonal farm work, and then they remained after getting jobs in landscaping, housecleaning, construction and food services. These were the circumstances of people who worked very hard and yet, due to their precarious status in this country, could not buy their own home and invest in it with certainty. With a sigh, Kelly thought again of Maria Hernandez.

The *Offices of Sara M. Nuñez, Esquire* occupied the bottom floor of a small two-story grey building in a parking lot framed by fields. A man and a woman sat in a waiting area, and a toddler with curly black hair played with a toy truck on the floor. Kelly walked over to the reception desk only to find it empty. "Hello?" she asked tentatively, to no one in particular.

"Hello?" A stocky woman with long shiny black hair and bright red lipstick stuck her head out of a door. "I don't have a receptionist on Saturday mornings." She walked over to the reception area to speak with Kelly. "I am Sara Nuñez."

"Yes. Hi, I'm Kelly Malloy. You probably recognize that name. I am not here to talk about that matter at all, I am just here about Juan's citizenship."

Nuñez looked uncomfortable and spoke quickly. "I am terribly sorry, but this family here has very pressing matters, so I can only give you two minutes of my time. I do represent Juan in his application for citizenship. That's why he called me about, uhm, these recent developments."

Kelly cut her off brusquely, "I'm not here to talk about that."

"Well, I can tell you that Maria Hernandez is terrified that her discovery here will lead to her immediate deportation. She has to worry even more now, with the baby. And, her husband is very close to getting his citizenship. She is distrustful of police and anyone having to do with law enforcement, so this has been very hard on her."

"Oh, I am so sorry," Kelly said. "I really just wanted to help her."

"Help her? How?" Nuñez' cynicism at Kelly's remark came through loud and clear.

"Well, my firm, Sherling and Vine, has an excellent immigration law specialist in Philadelphia. He is really good, and also I think he is connected."

"Connected?" Nuñez asked with her cynical tone again.

"Oh, I didn't mean anything improper," Kelly felt a blush creep up her neck. "I mean, immigration is his specialty, it's all he does. He always knows who to talk to at INS--or CIS— whatever it is called, and he presents his clients in the light most favorable to a speedy and desirable outcome. He'll take Juan's case on a *pro bono* basis," Kelly felt herself becoming self-conscious. Nuñez had not greeted her with a handshake, and she did not invite her into her office. Kelly realized what she must look like to Nuñez: a well-off, well-connected white woman driving in here with her expensive car and designer briefcase, and acting as if there was a quick fix for the complex and terrifying circumstances of a complete stranger.

After a long silence, Nuñez said, "Well, I am certainly not a specialist. I help clients referred by the LACC in a wide range of matters, not just immigration. And as you can see, I do not have the resources of a big firm. Why don't you email me the name of that partner of yours and I'll talk to Maria."

"Uhm, ok," Kelly said awkwardly. "Should I call you, then, or just wait to hear from you?"

"I'll call this immigration lawyer and talk to Maria. Then your partner can communicate directly with you." Nuñez looked at Kelly. "No offense, but everything would be easier if you would stay out of it during the pendency of this other matter." Then she beckoned with a wave of her hand and the man and woman got up and walked toward her office door. Kelly smiled uncomfortably as the woman passed her, tugging on the hand of her toddler who still clutched the toy truck.

A moment later, Kelly exited the building and kicked some dusty gravel from the parking lot. Her Volvo looked out of place. She wished she had borrowed Dan's pickup truck. She felt humiliated by Nuñez's reaction to what must have appeared to be naiveté on her part, but she also admired the way Sara Nuñez had cared so deeply about her clients. Although she was a fellow attorney, Nuñez had sounded as if she were protecting her own family member.

"Hey, Kel!" Sam's excitement filled up Kelly's car as she drove back to Wilmington. "I have something important to talk about. Are you driving?"

"Yeah, but it's ok. I have you on speaker."

"At Jack Barnard's preliminary hearing and arraignment, we will have more than enough evidence to detain him until trial."

"Oh, my God, Sam! What are you saying?" Kelly pulled her car over to the shoulder of the road to concentrate.

"It's good, Kel." Sam let out a little laugh that Kelly recognized as a sign of relief. "The DNA evidence is in, and it is positively your man, Jack Barnard. Kel, you nailed it!"

Kelly felt her body shudder as she sat parked on the side of the road. Fear? Repulsion? Relief? It moved like electricity through her, and rose up in goose bumps on her arms. He *was* the monster! She knew when she saw his hand in the courthouse, but that moment was one of terror. Now she knew for certain, and now he was in custody. For the first time since her attack, Kelly felt vindicated, and hopeful.

"So, what now, Sam? What do we do?" Kelly exhaled, trying to calm herself.

"I'm going to kick ass at this preliminary hearing. First your testimony, and then eyewitnesses, police reports and then, *BAM*! We'll show them a DNA match that cannot be questioned." Kelly could tell from Sam's tone that he was enjoying himself.

"My testimony? Do you still need that with the DNA evidence?" Kelly felt the dread return as she pictured herself describing in detail the humiliating and intimate details of her attack in front of a jury, counsel, onlookers and members of the press, as well as the monster himself, Jack Barnard.

"It will be okay, Kel. I will come by to prep you at eight o'clock on Monday morning, so we can all take this weekend off from this case. After I see you on Monday I have meetings with our other witnesses."

"Oh God, Sam. Try to leave Maria Hernandez out of it if possible... I can't be responsible for her deportation. She just had a baby!" Kelly noticed that her knuckles were white from clutching the steering wheel.

"Kel, where are you? The connection is breaking up."

"Oh, I'm just out running errands in Hockessin."

"Oh, yeah, that's a bad spot for cell phones. Listen, Kel, I'll do what I can do. Our number one priority is to make sure this prosecution is sound, and that Jack Barnard is held pending trial and then convicted. It is a high burden at trial, Kel: we have to prove his guilt beyond a reasonable doubt, so I don't want to make any promises about Maria Hernandez."

"Okay, Sam. I'll see you Monday at eight. I'll get Dan to take the girls to school."

"Goodbye, Kel. See you Monday."

As Kelly heard Sam end the call, she wiped a stray tear with the back of her left hand while she turned the key in her car's ignition with the other. Her thoughts turned to Dan. *"I'll get Dan to take the girls to school,"* she thought, as if Dan was merely some instrument at her beck and call. Just that morning, before the sun came up, Kelly had rolled over to find that Dan was not in bed next to her. After checking the bathroom, Kelly had crept downstairs and found him sleeping on the sofa in the family room, with the television light flickering and the sound of ESPN turned down to a soft murmur. He slept on his side, with his legs bent in order to fit his long frame on the couch. A recent copy of *Architectural Digest* lay on the rug beneath him and a wide chasm of loneliness stretched between them.

CHAPTER 29
CHAD: OCTOBER 1, 2011

CHAD CLIMBED OUT of a police car and into the bright sunshine. He walked slowly toward the fresh mounds of dirt and the dark coffin perched next to a newly dug rectangular hole. He became self-conscious as he walked, aware that a Philadelphia TV news crew was there, filming from just outside the perimeter of the cemetery. He thought of the headline, *Rape Suspect Attends Drunk Father's Funeral, Mother is Still Missing.* He was also embarrassed by the fact that only three people—probably the guys Charlie drank with—came to the funeral.

Stuart strode next to Chad with his hands buried in the front pockets of his wrinkled black suit. He positioned himself between Chad and the news cameras and he thoughtfully produced a pair of dark sunglasses for Chad. Stuart had told him that he was there to ensure that Chad did not talk to the press, but Chad liked to think that Stuart was there as his friend. With the sunglasses covering his eyes, Chad scanned the few people standing around, desperately hoping to see his mother. She was nowhere in sight.

"Hello, Chad, I'm Father John," a man said as he extended his hand to Chad. Chad looked at his worn but kind face and realized that he had no recollection of ever meeting this man before. "I thought I'd say a few words about your father and then maybe you could say a few words."

Chad briefly pictured himself delivering a eulogy that revealed to all in attendance that his father was a miserable, mean drunk. "Thank you, Father John, but, um, I think I don't feel right speaking today. I'd appreciate it if you'd handle it for me."

"Well, is there anything you'd like me to know about your father that I can recount in my comments?"

Chad looked up into the man's kind blue eyes and said, calmly and with certainty, "No, Father." He swallowed hard. He wanted the priest to understand what type of man Charlie McCloskey had been and how he had made his wife and son suffer. But he stood mute, waiting for the service to begin.

"Okay. Well, then," Father John said, "let's get started."

Chad was directed to sit in one of four white wooden chairs placed next to the freshly dug grave. They had been reserved for the family. Chad self-consciously sat with two empty chairs to his left and one to his right. Stuart stood right behind him. Chad knew that the news footage would reveal to its viewers that the alleged rapist sat alone, because his no-good drunk of a father didn't even have four family members who could be bothered to come to his funeral. Chad purposefully kept his head up and his face expressionless. He tried to conjure up a vision of a man who was decent, not capable of a brutal attack on a woman, and nothing like the man about to be deposited into the ground inside a wooden box. He wondered if his mother would see a tape of this moment on an evening news program somewhere. He briefly thought about Kelly Malloy watching the news, too, intensely scrutinizing his expression and trying to determine if he could be her attacker.

He blocked out the words of Father John, not wanting to hear the hackneyed remarks about the "good," "devoted" and "loving" father and husband, and all of the other bullshit Father John would be required to say. Instead, Chad focused on his plan to reunite with his mother in Arizona. He replayed the picture of his mother coming out of her home and running toward him joyously against the backdrop of a warm sunset.

Chad awoke from his trance when he heard the *thwump* of a shovel-full of dirt hit the top of his father's coffin. He hadn't even noticed when they lowered it into the ground. Father John was declaring out loud that his father had originated out of dust, and "to dust he shall return." Chad felt the same feeling of relief, of a complete unburdening, that he had experienced when he first learned of his father's death.

As the service ended, Chad stood slowly, uncertain as to what to do next. He felt Stuart's hand at his elbow. "You okay, Chad?"

"Yeah, I guess so." Chad looked at his young lawyer again, grateful for his presence. "What now?"

"Well, now we go thank the good padre and shake hands with the three old cronies who managed to show up." And with that, Stuart gently led him over to the old priest and the three mourners at the funeral. Chad shook their hands and accepted their condolences, and then walked away without remembering their names or caring who they were.

Moments after Chad was returned to his seat in the police cruiser, Stuart ducked his head into the open door behind him and said, "Hang in there, Chad. I'm coming to see you tonight, and I'm hoping to bring you some good news."

*****

Chad sat alone at a small table, staring at the clock on the white wall; eight thirty-five. At that moment Stuart burst into the room, out of breath. "I've got good news, my man!" He clapped Chad on the back and then he walked around the table and pulled out a chair. He changed his mind and started pacing back and forth. "The DNA results are in and Jack Barnard has been conclusively proven to be the bastard who abducted and raped Kelly Malloy."

"Are you sure?" Chad asked, hesitant to really believe that his nightmare might be ending.

"Absolutely sure. This is science, guaranteed and respected by all."

"Wow!" Chad grabbed Stuart and wrapped him in a bear hug. "Oh, my God! Thank you! Thank you!"

"Okay, Chad," Stuart said, a little awkwardly. "You don't want to suffocate your attorney, do you?"

"You mean the best defense attorney in the state?" Chad joked.

"Well," Stuart said, his eyes shining behind the thick round lenses, "certainly the best one you have ever had." Stuart chuckled. "Although this won't hurt my ability to get business and charge hefty fees for my services—should I ever decide to leave the poor downtrodden folks I get to represent now."

"Well, I guess I can take some solace in the fact that I advanced your career." Chad joked again. "So... when do I get out of here?"

"Soon. I called the AG and asked them to file a *nolle prosequi* like we discussed. The lead prosecutor, Sam Schultz, didn't get back to me until about an hour ago. He has been pretty busy, as you can imagine. He said he will consider dismissal now that the DNA results match Barnard, but only after he checks out a few things. He claims they are not ready now to dismiss and let you walk, because they still have probable cause that you were somehow involved in this crime."

Chad pumped his fist into his palm. "This is bullshit!"

"I know it's hard, Chad, but you have to hang on." Stu took out a legal pad and scanned his notes of the conversation he'd had with Schultz. "This Schultz guy says he has a duty to protect the victim and the public, and until he is very comfortable that he does not have probable cause to believe that you were either participating in this attack or were at least an accomplice to it, he is not dismissing. He also said he has a duty to not continuing your prosecution if that changes, and he will look into that now." Stu's eyes scanned the pad. "He mentioned that he needs to check out your rescue story with the couple that found the victim. Also, he wants to check out your plane ticket excuse with the people who interviewed you when your mother disappeared, the ones who searched your belongings and car. He said he needs to probe a bit regarding notes in the file about an old postcard to your mother—notes that support your story about the plane ticket and the bus company, confirming your mother went to Arizona. He has some follow-up questions for lab guys as well. He sounded earnest and everything, but he said he'd been consumed with getting Barnard these past few days... so, now he can turn his attention to this. You are not going to like this either, but he mentioned it's now Saturday evening, he has some hearing prep scheduled for Monday morning, and then he can get to this. He thinks realistically he can be ready for this decision by Wednesday. I'm sure it's not soon enough for you, but I'll call him Monday morning and start bugging him again, I promise."

Chad gulped. *Four more days and nights to endure.*

Stu tried to encourage Chad, saying, "And of course, when you walk out of here, there will be the obligatory press conference. That will be your chance to show the world that you're a nice, decent guy who was guilty only of being a Good Samaritan. Your chance at some good press... and of course, I'll get a chance to speak as well."

"Okay, Stuart. I'll let you do most of the talking anyway, like usual," Chad tried to joke.

"Oh, and I have one more piece of important news to tell you." Stuart said. He hesitated for a moment, as if he did not know how to bring up the subject. Then he opened his briefcase and quickly located a few pages stapled together. "A detective has located your mother."

Chad stood, stunned. "She's okay, right?" He felt his throat tighten. "Please tell me what you know. Please." Chad begged.

"She's fine Chad. And she is not in Arizona, so it's a good thing that you didn't go through with that harebrained idea of flying off to the Sun Devil State with a one-way ticket and spare change in your pocket."

"Where is she?"

"She's living in Oregon with her sister." Stuart replied. "The detectives figured it out after they did some computer-based searches of the fifty states. You know, court records, motor vehicle, that kind of thing." Stuart's eyes scanned the pages briefly to refresh his memory. "She did live in Scottsdale for a short time. There were some payroll tax records showing she worked there for a little bit, but that's about it. Next she moved to Eugene, Oregon. She filed a petition to change her name from Louisa McCloskey to Louisa Chadbourne. And recently, she got a new driver's license in Oregon. Her address, her driver's license information, all of the details are right here, Chad. This copy is for you." Stuart held out the three-page report, stapled in the upper left corner.

Chad took the report from Stuart. His eyes scanned the information, catching important snippets. First he made sure he saw his mother's name, as well as her birth date. They were right there, assuring him that this information actually revealed his mother's whereabouts, and that she was alive and, presumably, happy. He read out loud what was listed as her current address, "23 Morning Mist Lane, Eugene, Oregon, 97405." He immediately replaced his vision of the red-tiled roof and white adobe ranch against stark mountains of Arizona with a smart blue shingled house with white trim, a white picket fence surrounded by lush evergreens, and colorful flowers in its window boxes. The picture of his mother coming out of her front door to greet him remained identical, however—and that was really the only part that mattered.

CHAPTER 30

KELLY: OCTOBER 3, 2011

KELLY WANTED TO ask Dan why he was sleeping downstairs on the couch, but she could not. She knew the answer was bigger than anything she could solve right now, and she was sure she could not handle whatever reaction he would have to the question. She had made a plan to deal with her anger, her bitterness and her aching loneliness, and she was going to embark on it as soon as Dan and the girls had left the house.

After Dan and the girls slammed the mudroom door and loaded into Dan's pickup, Kelly picked up the telephone and dialed.

"Hello, Jeter and Associates," a woman's nasal voice answered the phone after a couple of rings.

Kelly looked around her kitchen as she spoke self-consciously. "Yes, uhm, hi." She paced back and forth as she spoke. "I'm calling because my family doctor, Dr. Johnson, told me that he spoke with Dr. Jeter about my circumstances and she agreed to see me relatively promptly."

"Well," the woman said, "Dr. Jeter isn't in yet. I'm the office manager, the early bird. Dr. Jeter's practice is full at present. I wasn't aware that she was accepting new patients."

Frustration, fatigue and anger welled up and tears spilled out of Kelly's eyes. "Can you please just ask the doctor? I am sure she'll know what this is about." Surprising herself, she added, "It's sort of an emergency."

"Oh, wait!" the woman blurted out. "Here it is! Dr. Jeter left a post-it note on my computer last night. It says I should fit Kelly Malloy in today. The doctor's booked until five, when she usually leaves, but she can see you then."

Kelly thought for a moment about the girls' schedules, dinner and the unfinished brief on her desk. "Okay, I'll be there at five. Thank you very much," she said, remembering her *Resolutions to Get Back on Track* list and the vision of Dan sleeping on the couch.

"Oops. No, wait a minute. She has to be somewhere this evening, so let's make it lunchtime," the woman said. I'll have to schedule you between noon and one, when she usually catches up on her paperwork. So, we'll see you at noon."

"Okay, yes, whatever you have." Kelly was relieved. "I'll be there at noon."

A knock on the door brought her back to the present. "Hello?" It was Sam at the mudroom door as Kelly hung up the phone. Sam declared, "I just saw Dan and the girls driving down the street."

"Yup, good old Dan. He's my rock," Kelly said as she turned and walked back toward her kitchen. Sam wasn't sure how to respond to Kelly's comment or her sarcastic tone, so he quietly closed and locked the door behind him and followed her into the kitchen. He unloaded papers and folders from his briefcase onto Kelly's kitchen table, and she put a tray of donuts and a mug of coffee in front of him.

"Too much sugar and cream, just like you took it in law school."

"You're just jealous because I can eat like this and keep my girlish figure," Sam joked as he helped himself to a jelly donut.

"What is all of this?" Kelly asked.

"I brought copies of a lot of stuff that I'll leave with you, but we don't need to go through all of that now. I do want you to be familiar with all of this for the preliminary hearing, though, and ultimately, for trial. There's the complaint, police reports, papers relating to the arrest warrant and—oh, you'll want to see this—a copy of the DNA report."

Kelly snatched the DNA report out of Sam's hand.

"Jeez, Kel. You're going to give me a paper cut."

Kelly read the document carefully, trying to absorb every detail. Sam watched her eyes darting back and forth as her lips moved silently. "I had a couple of criminal law classes in law school and I can barely understand this thing. How is your average Joe on the jury going to get this?" Kelly asked, waving the report toward Sam's face.

"No problem, Kel, I've done this a million times." Sam assured her. "First, we establish chain of custody—you know, making sure everyone knows this was in fact Jack Barnard's sample, and it was unadulterated. And then my guy at the lab testifies, after establishing he is an expert in this area, that he performed the testing and that he prepared this report. I ask him questions about the report and he breaks it down into plain English for our jury members."

"Okay, Sam,"I'm sorry. I know you are the best and I know I need to stop worrying."

"Kelly, I'm telling you. This is airtight. We have witnesses that put Jack Barnard at the scene, and better yet, we have this DNA match. This DNA test has a margin of error that is so infinitesimal, it's as good as telling the jury that it is flawless, certain, perfect." Sam smiled a broad grin.

Kelly walked to Sam and wrapped her arms around him. "Oh, Sam! I can't thank you enough. You have no idea!"

Kelly and Sam did not hear the truck in the driveway or the door open. Dan stood, dumbfounded, as he watched from the kitchen hallway. Kelly dropped her arms quickly and stepped away from Sam.

"Oh, hi, babe," Kelly said, hurriedly. "I was just thanking Sam for putting this guy away. He was just showing me the DNA report that is foolproof."

"Great," Dan said, flatly. He walked stiffly toward the kitchen. "I just came back to get my cell. I forgot it." He spoke without looking at them. He walked to the kitchen counter, found his cell phone, and tucked it into his pocket. He turned and headed out the door without a word.

"Dan!" Dan stopped but did not look back. "Please wait a second." Kelly hurried over to the door, stepped outside and onto a stone path that led to their driveway. "Dan, we have to talk. Please. That was just a friendly hug, a grateful hug. Sam has done so much for me, for us. He's going to put this guy away, he is going to give us all peace of mind, finally." Kelly looked at Dan with growing desperation. He stood silently, looking down at Kelly's feet. "Come on, Dan, what are you thinking?"

"What am I thinking? What am I thinking? I'm thinking that I don't know my wife anymore. I am thinking that she is so wrapped up in herself and her needs that she can't see that the rest of her family is suffering, too. I'm thinking that I don't like to come home, especially—when my wife has been incredibly distant toward me—to find her arms around another guy! I'm sorry I didn't go to law school and I can't prosecute rapists and I can't be your big hero right now. But you know something, I am your husband, and the father of your children and I am not sure you give a crap about that right now. That is what I am thinking!"

Dan turned and walked swiftly to his truck. He climbed in, pulled the visor down so that Kelly would not see that he was fighting tears, and backed quickly out of the driveway.

Kelly stood next to the door to her home for a few minutes, until her sobbing subsided. Dan's words had stung, but Kelly was also strangely grateful for them. She wiped the tears off her cheeks with her shirtsleeve as she thought about his tirade. He'd get over the fact that she was hugging Sam: Kelly knew that Dan trusted her and he understood her relationship with Sam. But the rest of what he said rang true. Kelly had been consumed by her anger, her grief and by her desire to get revenge. She couldn't remember the last time she literally cared for her daughters or husband or had connected with them or shared in any meaningful way.

"Sam," Kelly said as she re-entered the house, "please, just get me through the basics for the preliminary hearing. We have to make this quick. I need to spend some time mending fences today."

"No problem," Sam said as he stood up from the kitchen counter stool. "Let's get started."

*****

Four hours later, Kelly sat in an empty waiting room with a dry potted fern in the corner clinging to life, and an array of magazines offering low-fat recipes and Caribbean vacations. She read the framed diplomas on the wall; *University of Pennsylvania's Perelman School of Medicine* and *Villanova University, Summa Cum Laude.* Kelly noticed that Dr. Jeter had graduated from college only two years before she had. She was calculating Dr. Jeter's age and surmising about her marital status when the door to an office opened and a tall woman with long, fiery red hair strode toward her with her hand extended.

"Hello, Kelly. I'm Sally Jeter," she said as she approached.

Kelly stood and shook her hand. "Hello, Dr. Jeter. Thank you for seeing me so soon."

"Oh, no bother. I learned a long time ago to build this hour into my schedule just in case. And if no one needs me that day, I can catch up on paperwork or run an errand." Dr. Jeter smiled warmly. "And please, call me Sally." She gestured toward her office door. "Let's go into my office. Would you like anything? Coffee? Water?"

"No, thank you, I am fine," Kelly responded as she watched Sally turn on her heeled boots and walk into a handsomely furnished office. Kelly followed her and sat down on a brown leather sofa.

"So, Kelly," she began, crossing one long leg over the other, "why don't you start by telling me why you are here?"

"I thought my doctor, Dr. Johnson, covered that already."

"Yes, I spoke to Dr. Johnson. And I read newspaper articles about your attack and about your case. But just try, if you could, to tell me why you are here, now."

As Kelly sat gathering her thoughts, Dr. Jeter opened a brown bag that peeked from her large handbag. "And, if you don't mind, I'll eat while you fill me in." She pulled out a sandwich and a banana. She held the banana up to Kelly. "Are you hungry?"

"Oh, no, thank you," Kelly said, hurriedly. "I'm fine."

"Well, we know that you are not 'fine,' Kelly, or I wouldn't have the pleasure of meeting you today." Dr. Jeter smiled warmly again. "You seem like a strong, capable woman, but I know you must need to talk to someone about the attack."

Kelly bristled when she heard the word "attack." As she prepared to speak, facts, emotions, images all flashed in her head in a jumbled mess. "I'm not a big believer in psychiatry and therapy and all of that. I just feel like I should tell you that right off. I've never been to a therapist and I don't think I know anyone who has."

"You would be surprised to discover who comes to me and my colleagues, Kelly. Many of my clients are people who are very successful, accomplished, popular, and strong—whatever you think of when you think of people who would never need the likes of me. It is okay to need a little professional guidance to get you through rough patches in life, and there should be no shame in it."

Kelly liked that Sally used the word *clients* and not *patients*. "I'm sorry, I didn't mean to offend you. I guess I'm just a little uncomfortable with the territory."

"No offense taken. Your discomfort is normal. Also, you will get more comfortable sharing with me—I have that effect on people," Sally said, drawing a smile from Kelly.

"I respect you tremendously, Kelly. I know you are a strong woman, a lawyer, a wife and mother, and an athlete. I also know that some terribly wicked man did horribly painful things to you. And, although I wouldn't suggest for a moment that I know how it feels, I have a pretty good idea of what you have been through and what feelings you may experience as a result." Sally paused for a moment to take a bite of her sandwich. She held her right hand up as she did so, to signal that she was not finished with her thought. After she swallowed, she continued speaking. "You are going to have to dig deep and self-examine and explain to me fully and honestly in order for me to help you try to sort this out and move on."

"Hah!" Kelly feigned a laugh angrily. "Move on. Just like that?" She paused for a moment. "You sound like my husband. And I am sure it is on the mind of others who have not said it, like my co-workers, my clients, my kids."

"That's it, Kelly!" Sally blurted out. "Anger is something you are feeling. Tell me about it."

Kelly sat still for a moment, and then her words came in a rush, streaming out so quickly that she did not realize that she was spitting a little as she spoke. "Anger! Yes. White-hot, all-consuming anger that makes me want to kill this man!" Kelly hit her balled fist against her other palm. "Anger that fills me up and makes it impossible for me to eat, sleep, think. I am angry when I sit in traffic and when it rains and when the checkout person at the supermarket is slow and I am angry when my partners expect me to plow full-speed ahead into a trial schedule as if this never happened, and I am angry at my husband when he...when he...." Kelly sat mute for a moment searching the wall behind Sally for clues to finish her sentence.

"When he what?" Sally asked. "When or why are you angry at your husband?" Sally realized she did not even know Kelly's husband's name yet, or very much else about Kelly, for that matter, but this seemed like a productive path to pursue.

Kelly put her face in her hands and spoke softly, with her words falling onto her lap. "I am angry at Dan because he keeps going on about his day as if this is all going to be okay. He is there for me; he cooks, he takes care of the girls...our daughters. He is patient, gentle....he is concerned...."

"Sounds like a real bastard," Sally said, shocking Kelly with her sarcasm.

Kelly looked up from her hands at this comment. "What?"

"Come on Kelly. It sounds to me like you just described the husband you can't possibly get mad at. I mean, he's loving, gentle, helpful, patient and supportive. He's a good father who is hands-on with the kids. Why are you angry at him?"

Kelly sat quietly for what seemed like an eternity. She thought of Dan. She recalled him at her side in the hospital, his hand stroking her head right before the woman came in to put her legs up in stirrups to take photos and specimens for evidence. She saw him balling up her sweaty sheets and opening her blinds to sunlight as he persuaded her to go outside and get some fresh air. She bit her lip as she pictured him lying next to her every night in bed, his beautiful chest moving up and down quietly as he breathed, his boxer shorts covering the swell of unanswered desire, his eyes staring up at the ceiling, wondering when she would ever touch him again. Then she recalled him sleeping on the couch, alone, unreachable. She started to cry. Huge, sloppy tears poured down her cheeks, and loud sobs escaped from her mouth. Sally deftly pulled tissues out of a box and handed them to Kelly.

"That's good, Kelly. It's okay. Go ahead and feel it. No one is here to hear you and no one is judging you. Let it go." She put her hand on her shoulder.

Kelly kept her head in her hands the whole time, except to dab the wetness and the black smears of mascara off of her eyes. She looked up and said quietly, "I have no reason to be angry at Dan. I just am."

Sally spoke gently. "It sounds like you might be using a coping technique called *displacement*. You direct your anger or emotion at the wrong person, or the wrong outlet. Dan didn't cause your anger, but he's an easy target for it. We need to figure out better coping mechanisms right now, Kelly," Sally said softly. "Do you want to take a breather?"

"No." Kelly looked up, wiping her eyes. "You've hit the nail on the head already. I'm starting to think that I've been deliberately hurting Dan, and I don't even know why. He doesn't deserve it."

Sally waited a moment for Kelly to wipe her eyes and blow her nose. "You said he doesn't deserve it. Just like you did not deserve the hurt that was inflicted on you by your attacker. Maybe you want your husband to feel some of that too, to 'get it.' Or, at the very least, possibly you just are venting your hurt and anger onto the closest target."

Kelly looked at Sally in earnest, very interested in what she was saying, desperately looking for some sense in her feelings, searching for some form of a solution. "One thing I want you to think about today is whether you can use a different means to deal with the anger and hurt. Try to recognize Dan again as your ally, because he can be a great source of comfort or strength for you now."

Kelly thought about Sally's words for a moment. She had never experienced this type of anger. This anger seeped out of her skin and permeated every minute of her day. "I don't know, Sally," Kelly said. "I've been angry before. You know, at a nasty opposing counsel or an uncooperative client, or even the jerk that drives right behind your car or cuts you off on I-95, but this is a whole different animal."

"Well," Sally said, "with those other examples, how do you respond to your anger? What do you do to make you feel better?"

"I guess I swear sometimes, if my girls aren't with me." Kelly chuckled a little, uncomfortable with that admission. "And I usually vent to my co-workers or to Dan." Kelly thought for a moment. She nodded her head as if remembering something important. "And, often, I put on my running shoes and I run."

"You *what*?" Sally said.

"I run almost every morning, for forty-five minutes, or an hour, whatever I have time for and feel like." Kelly sat as in deep thought, remembering how her morning run made her feel. "It's cathartic." She continued. "I'm moving along, arms and legs pumping, breathing, moving, through the new day. Somehow it defuses or eliminates frustration, anxiety, anger." Kelly looked at Sally's eyes, "Don't get me wrong, the underlying problems are not necessarily solved, but my physical reaction to them usually is. And often I have worked up some sort of plan to deal with the problem, or at least I've put it in perspective when I'm finished with my run."

Hmmm," Sally said crossing her legs. "Are you running these days?"

"No," Kelly said. "Not since the attack." She looked down at her folded hands on her lap. "I was running when I was attacked."

"Yes, I saw that it in the newspaper," Sally said matter-of-factly.

Kelly sat quietly and thought for a moment. She decided at that moment that she liked Sally. She liked her directness. Despite her warmth, she did not try to soften the facts or talk around them.

"It sounds to me like you have a ready and healthy support system here to help you through this, Kelly. You have a loving and supportive husband, and a physical and healthy outlet in your running. You just have to get yourself to a place where you are not avoiding them or demonizing them." Sally twirled a long strand of her red hair in her fingers as she spoke, reminding Kelly of Anna. "Do you think maybe you blame yourself—you know, for running alone along that river that day? Or even Dan, for not protecting you?"

Kelly felt Sally's gaze on her, waiting for her reply. "I don't know," she said, her voice cracking a little. "I can't blame Dan for anything. He wasn't there when it happened and I know if there had been anything he could have done to protect me, he would have. I don't know why I have been angry at him."

"Why don't you tell him that tonight?" Sally said. "Just tell him that you realize you have been treating him differently and you are not sure why, but that you do not and cannot blame him for this." Sally stood up, signaling that she was starting to wrap up their session.

Kelly looked at her watch and was surprised to see that the hour had passed.

"That's enough for a homework assignment." Sally smiled at Kelly and put her hand on her shoulder. "Letting go of your anger in whatever positive way you can, and not directing it toward people who are there for you. Try to lean on that wonderful husband of yours. I am sure he is feeling guilt and anger also, and he will be relieved to be able to share this with you, rather than feel like it is a rift between you."

"Uhm, okay." Kelly rose from her chair. "I'm not real clear, and I am a little embarrassed. But I have to get to the point since it is time to go. Are you telling me to be physically intimate with my husband?"

"Kelly, sex can be complicated after you have been a victim of a sexual assault. So, you'll know when you are ready with Dan." She smiled. "You could try to have sexy thoughts about him. Admire the things you love about him and try to recall those feelings even if you are not ready to act on them. That will help you get there eventually."

"Uhm, okay. Thank you." Kelly extended her arm to shake Sally's hand.

"Can you come back in two days?" Sally said. "Is that good for you or do you want to come just once a week?"

"Two days is good," Kelly said, "unless you have some time tomorrow." Kelly was surprised at how much this session had meant to her. She felt like she could be open with Sally—and Sally had wise words and perspective, but mostly she was honest and nonjudgmental.

"I think two days is a good idea, Kelly. I'll see you at the same time, noon. "You have some homework to do with Dan and you need to digest what we discussed today. You can bring lunch if you want. I'll be eating." Sally pointed to the remnants of the turkey sandwich that had been her lunch. She retrieved a business card off of her desk. "I am writing my cell phone number on this card and my home phone, because I'll feel better if you have access to me right now."

"Thank you," Kelly said as she took the business card and tucked it into her wallet. "There is a lot going on with the investigation and prosecution of this case, and I will be busy— but I may also need some professional guidance in the next few weeks."

"Well, feel free, Kelly, I am glad to be of service." Sally laughed and added, "A little glad to hear that lawyers can't solve everything."

*****

After leaving Sally's office, Kelly sent a text message to Dan. She was not yet ready to talk to him. She needed a time where there would be no interruptions, where she might actually have a chance to bridge the endless chasm between them and to connect with him again somehow.

I'll get the girls from school this afternoon.

Dan's reply seemed terse. *OK.*

At day's end, Kelly watched as the children streamed out of Brandywine Elementary School. She saw Gracie first, with her big smile and her ponytail high on her head. Gracie waved and jumped up gleefully as she spotted her mother in the carpool line. Behind Gracie, Anna reluctantly approached her car. She looked down at her feet as she shuffled out of the school, with a heavy backpack slung over one shoulder. As her little sister tapped her on the shoulder and gestured toward Kelly, Anna merely nodded, glanced up to confirm her location, and then put her head back down to continue shuffling toward the car. Kelly's heart was heavy as she realized how Anna must have been feeling. She had not been there to help her daughter struggle with fear, sadness, and even embarrassment in the wake of her attack.

"Hey, Mommy!" Grace shrieked. "I am so glad you are here to get us."

"Yeah, to what do we owe this pleasure?" Anna remarked sarcastically.

"I have been missing my girls too much!" Kelly twisted

around from the driver's seat in an awkward attempt to face them as they entered her car. Grace climbed over and into a booster seat behind Kelly, while Anna sat and quietly pulled her seat belt across her chest and lap. With her body still twisted around to look at her daughters, Kelly declared, "I'm making your favorite dinner tonight. Can you guess?"

"Lasagna?" Gracie asked.

"You got it!" Kelly answered happily, turning to look straight ahead and to turn the key in the ignition. "And I'm making a chocolate layer cake."

"Yippee!" Grace exclaimed, clapping her hands.

Kelly glanced at her older daughter's face in the rearview mirror as she waited for the car in front of her to start moving out of the carpool line. "What do you think, Anna?"

"Store-bought lasagna and cake, right?"

"No, Miss Smarty Pants," Kelly said trying to sound lighthearted, "from scratch. Well, except the noodles are from a box and I will use a cake mix. But I'll add egg and oil and stuff to the cake mix and I'll make the icing with real butter and cocoa and stuff."

"So, what, you are like our mom now?" Anna shot back at her.

For the briefest of moments, Kelly felt anger well up in her and she wanted to punish her surly and disrespectful daughter. But she remembered what Sally had told her, and she also remembered the stinging truth of Dan's words. She took a deep breath and relaxed her white-knuckled grip on the steering wheel.

"I'm sorry you are angry with me, Anna, but it does not give you the right to be mean to me or rude, okay? I am here and I love you and I am ready to talk about anything."

Anna looked out the car window as she spoke. "Well, it's just that I don't get it. You haven't talked to us or done anything with us in a really long time. You're always in your bed sleeping, or talking with that Sam guy. Dad, Gracie and I are, like, invisible." A tear rolled down Anna's cheek. "Now you are sitting here in carpool trying to look like every other mom. And, you're baking from scratch? I mean, that's something you never did, even before the, uhm, before you changed."

"Mommy," Grace interrupted, "carpool is moving."

Kelly looked up and noticed that the cars in front of her had left, and she was blocking a long line of parents in their cars waiting to move forward and collect their children. She knew that they dared not honk at her, the one that they all watched and wondered about. She put her foot on the accelerator and started moving slowly down the road. She gathered her thoughts. "Girls, I want you to listen to me carefully and not interrupt for a moment. Can you do that?"

"Yes, Mommy," Grace responded right away. Kelly looked quickly in her rearview mirror at Anna's face and saw that she was slowly and silently nodding her assent as she continued to stare out the window.

"First of all, I love you and Daddy more than anything in the world. I know that I have not been around very much—or at least not really *with* you when I am around. I'm so sorry for that. I am not making excuses; I just want you to try to understand why. That bad man attacked me, and I was hurt very badly. And I was changed. After the attack I felt an incredible amount of sadness and anger, and a feeling of being unsettled all of the time.It is taking me a little while to feel normal again, but I am getting there. I never, ever stopped loving you guys, I just sort of got lost there for a while. And I am grateful for Daddy for being such a big help and I am so sorry if you felt like I was abandoning you or mad at you for something." Kelly had a hard time finishing her sentence, as she was getting all choked up. She heard a soft sobbing in the back seat and was surprised to see tears on Anna's face when she glanced in the dashboard mirror.

A short drive later, Kelly took a deep breath as she steered the car into their driveway and parked in the garage. She turned around quickly to continue talking to her daughters before they started to leave the car. "Girls, I want you to know I am taking some concrete steps to show you that I mean this. I'm taking a little break from work, for at least six months, which includes your Christmas and spring-break vacations from school. I'm not going to work at all. I just want to make your meals, drive you to school and sports and play dates, help you with your homework, and take a few fun trips here and there."

"Awesome," Grace said, unbuckling her booster seat.

As Kelly stepped out of the car, Anna came over to her slowly. With tears streaming down her cheeks and her arms outstretched, she met her mother and wrapped her in a tight hug. "Oh, Mom. I've missed you."

Kelly stood in the garage for a few minutes, feeling her older daughter's arms around her and stroking her hair with her hand. She realized how much she had missed their connection, their warmth.

*****

Kelly tidied up the family room in anticipation of Dan's arrival as the girls finished their homework in the kitchen. She built a fire with newspaper, kindling and logs. It did not crackle and jump like the fires Dan made, but it did give off a cozy glow. With the fresh flowers she had put on the coffee table and a few flickering lights, the room looked soft and inviting. The smell of lasagna baking in the oven and a chocolate cake cooling on a rack filled the air and Kelly felt as if she was right where she belonged, a boat moored safely in the midst of a storm. She heard the door open and saw Dan walk into the room slowly. He moved tentatively. His eyes took in the fire glowing and the flowers on the table.

"Dan, please, come sit with me here. I want to talk to you." Kelly said as she gestured to the couch and then sat down. Dan still had his coat in his hand as he sat a few feet away from Kelly. He looked at her almost quizzically, but he did not speak.

"So what is going on now?" Dan asked, dumfounded.

"What do you mean?" Kelly asked.

"I mean you seem different than you have been for a long time. I don't know, peaceful maybe?" Dan asked arching his eyebrows to signal that he was having trouble labeling the change in his wife. "You made a fire, you are cooking something that smells really good, and you look like you are actually happy to see me."

"Dan," she looked directly into his eyes and she took his hand in hers. "I have been suffering since the incident in ways I can't even explain."

"I know, babe." Dan whispered back, choked up with emotion.

"But what I am saying is, I want it to stop. The evil that man unleashed on me does not need to keep seeping into our lives. I want to feel a little bit like I'm back in control, that I'm still a healthy, functioning person who sleeps and eats and showers...." She squeezed Dan's hand, "and who loves."

Dan looked back up at Kelly as he heard these words, and she wasn't certain, but she thought she saw a pained expression in his eyes at the word *loves*.

"So what can we do to help you?" Dan asked, inching closer to Kelly on the sofa and meeting her eyes with his.

"Well, *you* have already been so helpful. You have been patient with me, and have really stepped up with taking care of the girls and everything. I am really grateful for that. And I love you."

"Oh, my God, Kel, I love you, too. You know I do. And I... I miss you."

Kelly continued, "I know it sounds funny, but I sat down a few days ago and wrote a list. Simple things to get it back together, to make me feel whole again." She took the list out of her pocket and handed it to Dan. She continued speaking as Dan studied the list. "I saw a woman today, a counselor. She's experienced in helping people cope with traumatic events, including sexual abuse. I was really nervous and cynical about it, but I was so desperate for something to change." Kelly looked directly into Dan's eyes to see if he saw her differently, because she felt different. "Her name is Dr. Jeter and she is already helping me. I feel comfortable talking to her and sort of hopeful for the first time since the attack. She made me realize that I can take deliberate steps right now to get back a lot of things I have lost."

Kelly stopped for a moment, and carefully chose her words. "I think I felt at first like I was ruined. I was hurt and humiliated and angry and scared and basically not functioning. But then it became deeper and darker than that. Those feelings were festering over time... they made me angry and withdrawn and unable to see beyond myself, and I couldn't see what I was doing to you and the girls." She checked Dan's expression again, which was one of concern but perhaps also longing. She squeezed his hand again. Dan placed his other hand over hers, eager for the touch.

Kelly continued. "Oh, babe, I am so sorry. But I am also feeling hopeful. I can climb out of this hole, and I can function... and I can love, and be a mother again....and a wife."

"Well," Dan sighed, "I'm not sure how we do this, but I am definitely happy to try."

The girls poked their heads in the room. "Is it dinnertime yet?" Anna asked.

"Yes, it is," Kelly replied. "Please wash your hands and set the table and I'll get the lasagna out and make a salad."

"Wow," Dan said, standing up. "Did you just say you baked lasagna?"

"Yes," Kelly said with a smile. "And—don't have a heart attack— I baked a cake, too."

"Oh, my God, what have you done with my wife?" Dan joked.

"I'd say she has returned." Kelly answered. "Well, at least she is on her way back." Dan and Kelly embraced, with the rapt attention of their daughters lingering at the edge of the room. "Oh, and one more thing Dan," Kelly blurted out, as an afterthought. "I want to tell you my other big news. I already told the girls. I'm taking a sabbatical from work."

"What?" Dan asked. "What does that mean?"

"It means my cases and clients can be taken care of by other lawyers. Everyone is okay with me staying home to take care of myself and my family for a while, and then I'll go back to work when we are all ready." Kelly stated this with complete conviction in the soundness of her plan.

"Are you sure, Kel?" Dan asked. "You love your work."

"I love my family, too, and right now, I need to focus on my list." Kelly gestured toward the paper still in Dan's hand. "Besides, lawyers at the firm have taken sabbaticals for everything from travel, to divorce, or even just burnout. It's okay. I know they'll hold my spot for me, and we have enough money saved. Plus, some of the time off will be accrued paid vacation, and the firm will continue our medical benefits the whole time."

Dan shrugged and handed Kelly back the list. "Hey, I'm totally behind you if this is what you want. I like the idea of homemade dinners and knowing the girls are going to be picked up and driven around and all of that. In fact, I will feel like I am on vacation." Dan laughed again. Kelly realized she had missed his laugh.

"Speaking of vacations," Kelly interrupted, "I want to start planning a vacation for Christmas. Maybe we should go back to St. John, or go someplace else warm and restful for us all to recover from a rough fall, and, unfortunately, a trial." Kelly noticed that her mention of the word "trial" caused Dan to back away slightly.

"I love St. John." Grace said. "Remember we drank out of pineapples there and we saw colorful fish and collected seashells?" She giggled. Kelly was grateful for the perpetual optimism of her youngest, and the cheerful diversion.

Anna walked over and squeezed herself between Dan and Kelly. "Mom, I know the trial is going to be really hard on you. I'm sorry I have been kind of bad lately. I've been really scared, but I know you are going to be fine because you are brave."

"Thank you, baby." Kelly said, hugging her. Kelly looked at Dan as she spoke, trying to explain in words that Anna would understand. "I know that they have evidence now that will make it a short trial and the bad guy will be found guilty. So that helps a lot." Kelly saw Dan arch his eyebrows, looking for more information. Kelly mouthed the letters "D-N-A" to him. Then she continued speaking, "With this evidence, they might even be able to convince the bad guy to admit his guilt and go to jail without a trial."

Dan spoke up. "Putting this guy away with or without a trial sounds very good to me. Now, we have a delicious-smelling lasagna to eat, and the details of our day to share over dinner, so let's enjoy that now, okay?"

*****

Later, after cleaning up dinner and getting the girls through their bathing and bedtime routines, Kelly sat on her bed watching Dan's reflection in their bathroom mirror as he brushed his teeth and hummed to himself. He was wearing a pair of worn blue boxers. Her eyes ran appreciatively over his flat stomach, his long muscular legs, and the way his right bicep flexed as he moved his arm back and forth to brush. She felt a longing and a pulling in her that quickly and surprisingly became a throbbing, hot arousal. *"Try to have sexy thoughts,"* Sally Jeter's words rang in Kelly's head. She quickly jumped out of bed and threw off her cotton boxers and worn T-shirt. She grabbed a short satin nightgown out of her underwear drawer and pulled it over her head. When she saw Dan grab the dental floss, she knew she had a moment to light the cinnamon-scented candle that stood on her night table. She climbed back into bed and put her hands behind her head to try to appear casual. She smiled as she felt the throbbing, moist sensation between her thighs, *a drought broken, a dam breached*, she thought. She was overwhelmed by the long-lost hunger for her husband's flesh.

Unaware of the inferno waiting in his bed, Dan casually flipped back the covers and slid between the sheets. "Oh, the candle smells really nice," he said, good-naturedly. He leaned over and gently kissed Kelly on the cheek, and then turned to lie on his back.

Kelly climbed on top of Dan so quickly that she caused him to flinch. She put her lips over his and kissed him hungrily. Dan kissed her back, tentatively. He kept his hands at his sides, resting on the bed. She ran her hands through his hair, along his neck, and traced his collarbone. Then she slid down under the covers, running her tongue straight down the middle of his chest, over his muscled stomach and to the top of his boxers. She sat up a little and started pulling at his boxers.

"Whoa! Whoa!" Dan said. "Are you sure?" Dan was breathing heavily and his face bore a grimace of pain. He felt such an urgent swelling between his legs and throughout his whole groin that he thought it might kill him.

Kelly sat up over Dan, and shook her head "yes" violently. She removed his boxers and flung them on the floor. She tucked her head under the comforter, eager to touch him and to taste him.

Dan groaned, "Oh, my God!" With all the restraint he could summon, he whispered, "I can't take much of this, babe. You know it has been a while. I want to be inside of you."

Kelly ducked her head out from under the comforter long enough to say, "Not this time. This is exactly what I need." She found herself pleasantly aroused as she did so.

Several minutes later, Dan lay on his side stroking Kelly's

bare shoulder. "My God, Kel. That was amazing. Thank you, baby." He wrapped his arms around her. "Maybe next time I can, you know, please you a little, too? I'd like to make it a joint enterprise," he said, smiling.

"I know it is hard to imagine, but that was exactly what I needed," Kelly said. "The whole thing kind of took me by surprise, and I just went with it. I needed to remember how beautiful and special your—uhm—parts are to me." Kelly giggled. "I think I also needed to be in control this time."

"Hey," Dan said, "feel free to control me like that any time. I'm at your disposal." He grinned at Kelly with his whole face— an expression Kelly had not seen in a long time. He wrapped his arms around her and pressed his body against her back. Kelly felt safe, hopeful, and almost whole.

CHAPTER 31

CHAD: OCTOBER 4, 2011

CHAD LAY IN his usual position, on the thin bottom bunk facing the cinderblock wall. The bunk above him shielded him from the bright lights of his cell and he closed his eyes trying to focus. *Just hang on. Almost out. Almost home.*

His cellmate, Rico, had been escorted to the visitation room to see a relative or a friend, and the cell was quiet for a change. Chad had no one to visit him, other than Stuart. He wished desperately for him to appear, and to tell him he was free of this place.

"Wake up sleeping beauty. It's shower time." A guard opened his cell door. Alarm cursed through Chad. "I'm not feeling well. I really just need to sleep."

"That's not going to work, inmate. You said that yesterday and you checked out at medical. No fever, no symptoms, nothing. You are starting to stink, and trust me, you do not want to upset your cellmate."

It's not my cellmate that I am worried about. Chad thought.

The guard tapped Chad on the back. "Come on, you have no choice."

Moments later, Chad stood in line with other inmates waiting for the showers. He held a scratchy white towel tightly around his waist with one hand and a bar of soap in the other. He nervously scanned the line and was relieved that he did not see his tormentor, Paco. A guard stood just outside the bathroom entrance, hopefully within shouting distance.

An inmate left the shower farthest from the guard when it was Chad's turn. "Go ahead," Chad said awkwardly to the man behind him, "I'm not ready yet."

The man shoved Chad hard, "That one has the worst water pressure, get your ass in there."

Reluctantly, he walked to the defective shower. With the noise of the showerheads and the inmates chattering as they showered or waited in line, Chad hoped desperately that the guard at the doorway would hear him if he yelled. He hung his towel on a hook and turned on the water. He quickly scrubbed his head and shoulders with soap and just as quickly began to rinse so he could finish and get out. His eyes were shut for the briefest of moments to protect them from the soapy rinse. A strong hand curled around his right wrist. He opened his eyes to see Paco, in only his underwear, standing just outside the stream of the shower. He held a metal shank in front of Chad's face.

"Shhhhhhhhh," Paco said. "If you make a sound, Fresh Meat, I will fucking cut your throat open before you can finish your first word." Paco released Chad's wrist to turn off the water. He motioned to a tall, muscular man behind him to go watch for the guard. "Now you come with me and don't do anything stupid or you know what happens." He waved the shank again, just below Chad's chin. He grabbed his victim and pulled him quickly out of the shower and behind a wall to the bathroom stalls.

Chad was pulled into a stall with Paco and the door was locked behind them. As Paco pushed him forward, he put his hand out to the wall over the toilet, with his body bent over the toilet. Chad tried to turn around and Paco growled, "Don't move. You know what I want." A sharp blade was pressed slightly into Chad's buttock. "There's a little taste of what I can bring if you do not cooperate. And," he laughed a squeaky, eerie laugh, "I just branded you as my bitch."

Hot tears rolled out of Chad's eyes as he felt two hands grab his hips and start to pull him backwards.

"Don't touch that kid now, or ever, or you and every sad

fucking excuse for a relative you have will die." The deep, confident and powerful voice of Chad's cellmate, Rico, caused Paco to immediately release Chad.

Chad turned around to see a panicked expression on his attacker's face. Paco whispered. "Say you wanted this or I will kill you later."

"I can hear you, Paco, you dumb shit. This kid's under my protection. Touch him and you're fucking dead."

Paco unlocked the door and it swung open. Rico stood calmly and clearly in control with his arms crossed as Paco scurried out of the stall and ran out of the shower area. Chad walked out with his hands down, trying to cover his genitals. "Go get a towel, kid, I got your back."

Chad walked quickly around the wall to his shower and grabbed his towel off the hook where he had hung it only minutes ago. The shower area had been emptied, and there was no guard in sight. He wrapped the towel around his waist and stood there, shaking violently.

"Look man, I still got to take a shower, so just stand there for a minute and you'll be fine. No one is going to mess with you now, okay?"

Chad shook his head slowly. He couldn't move his feet if he wanted to. He stood like that for what felt like an eternity, while Rico showered and sang loudly in Spanish. When Rico came out of the shower wrapped in a towel, he walked to where their clothing hung. Chad followed behind. They silently put on their DDOC garb, slipped on their shoes and walked out of the shower room.

Back in their cell, Chad curled up on his bunk. A tiny droplet of blood soaked through his pants where the shank had marked him. It was a superficial cut that would leave a lifelong scar.

"Listen to me, kid." Rico said quietly through the bunk. "Don't say a word to your lawyer or the guards or anyone about that and you will be a lot better off. Got it?"

Chad swallowed hard and tried to speak without crying. He took a deep breath. "Yeah," is all he could manage to say. It was enough for Rico.

The entire cellblock seemed eerily quiet, and Chad knew it had something to do with what had happened. *Rape.*

I was almost raped. He closed his eyes and tried desperately to soothe himself with the comforting image of his mother. But the bound and bruised body of Kelly Malloy now blocked it out.

CHAPTER 32

KELLY: OCTOBER 5, 2011

KELLY SAT IN a worn leather chair watching Dr. Sally Jeter take the lid of off a chicken Caesar salad. Recounting the events of the past two days was almost as pleasant as the events themselves. She thought that she sounded like a normal, functioning mother and wife.

"How about physical intimacy with Dan, has there been any change there?" Sally asked between forkfuls.

"Well, yes." Kelly paused for a moment to get her thoughts together. "I talked to Dan alone, in a quiet setting where we had each other's attention. I told him I was sorry for shutting him out and I told him that I loved him and missed him."

"How did that go?"

"It was welcomed. My gosh, it felt like a waterfall crashing over us after a drought. We were touching all night, hugging on the couch and touching feet at the dinner table. It was like a wall had disappeared and we were finding our way back." Kelly smiled.

"Anything else? How about in the bedroom?"

"Boy, you are a pushy broad," Kelly joked. "Yes, we finally had some physical intimacy. Not our normal lovemaking, I guess. I am really not ready for that yet." Kelly looked at Sally and searched for the right words. "Let's just say we had intimacy, emotional and sexual, and it felt really good to be close. I think that we are at least on the right path."

"Okay," Sally said smiling. "No need to say more. It sounds like you are on the right track."

Kelly looked out Sally's office window, which faced east toward the Christiana River and the poorer part of town. She saw a blue line of city buses waiting for passengers, and an expanse of deteriorating row homes and apartment buildings. Her thoughts immediately turned to Maria.

"Kelly. What are you thinking of? You sort of drifted away there."

Kelly paused for a moment, trying to identify what she was feeling. "I think I am carrying a lot of guilt."

"Guilt?" Sally probed. "You mean about the attack? Or about Dan and the girls?"

"Well, no. At least not right now," Kelly laughed lightly. "Believe it or not, there are other lives I have managed to screw up lately."

"What are you talking about?" Sally asked with a perplexed look.

"Well, since you read about the attack, you know there is a young man they have locked up right now who may be innocent. In fact, it may turn out that the only reason he is locked up is because he helped me out."

"Yes, I read about that guy. He's just out of high school, right?"

Kelly nervously played with her wedding band as she spoke. "Yeah. Anyway, for reasons I shouldn't really go into, I am starting to think he may be telling the truth."

"Well, if it is as you say it is, he'll be out of prison before long." Sally said, trying to reassure her client.

"It's more than that. According to my friend Sam, who is the prosecuting attorney, this kid has a really tragic story. He had an abusive father and his mother abandoned him." Kelly stopped playing with her wedding band and started bending a paper clip that she had lifted off of Sally's desk. "Now, on top of all of that, he has been labeled a rapist and thrown into prison with some scary people."

"Hmm. That is sad, Kelly, but you need to remember that it is not your fault. You are both victims here of the same tragic circumstances." Sally looked at Kelly to make sure she was really hearing her.

Kelly continued, "And then there is Maria."

"Who's Maria?" Sally asked, confused.

"She is a woman who witnessed parts of the attack. She has critical testimony and she'll be subpoenaed for trial." Kelly explained.

"Many people have been witnesses in trials, Kelly. You know that; you have seen it hundreds of times. It can be frightening, but she'll get through it." Sally said in a matter-of-fact manner.

"I wish that was the problem," Kelly quickly responded. "It turns out Maria is an illegal immigrant. She has been living here under the radar and working hard without bothering anyone. And now, because she helped me, she has been discovered by the authorities to be here illegally. The AG involved assures me she will not be deported during these proceedings, but still it is very difficult for her. The man she lives with, the father of her baby, is here legally, and he's close to getting his citizenship. They desperately want to get married and be free of all of this worry."

Kelly decided to omit the part about giving Sara Nuñez the name and phone number of her law partner in Philadelphia.

"Kelly, I want you to accept that you are only human, you are also a victim, and you can only achieve what is possible. But, it is clear to me that you are a person who sets a goal, takes action and achieves that goal. Go with that instinct. I know you'll figure it out. Although we have only had two sessions, I have seen your fighting spirit and I know that's why you are making such tremendous progress after your attack."

"Thank you," Kelly said, gathering her handbag. "That means a lot to me. I think you're seeing improvement only because I am very ready for things to improve. I was a complete mess after the attack, and I guess I kind of curled up into a ball there for a little while."

"Well, you are squarely on the right track. Many people would have been derailed for a long time after such a traumatic experience. What do you say we schedule a week from now? I think you are in a good place and know what you need to focus on. Come back next Thursday and we'll talk. And of course, you have my numbers if an emergency develops before then."

"Thanks, Sally. I doubt I'll need to bother you before Thursday. Goodbye." Kelly closed the door to Jeter & Associates and strode into the hall. She had planned a little detour before heading back home.

*****

Kelly pulled the scrap of paper out of her wallet one more time to check the address that she had copied off the police report, *1402 N. King Street, No. 2-B*. Five minutes later, she pulled into a parking spot on King Street. Two young men in oversized dark hoodies and droopy jeans loitered by the parking meter as Kelly quickly stuffed quarters into it. One of them emitted a long and low whistle, making Kelly's face grow hot with a discomfort that she could not label. She did not know if they were whistling at her, her car, or something else entirely, but she kept her head down and walked by them quickly. The young men laughed as she turned around from a distance of thirty feet to watch her Volvo's headlights flash at her as she remotely locked her car. She walked quickly on the sidewalk with her eyes straight ahead. A thin teenage girl in an oversized sweatshirt stood by a bus stop holding a bundled baby on her hip. As Kelly approached the building at 1402 North King Street, she saw an old man in a dirty winter coat turn his back and urinate on the adjacent building.

Kelly's heart quickened as she arrived at Maria's apartment building. She sighed as she realized that she stood only eight blocks from the shiny office building that housed her law firm, and only a few miles from her large home in the Highlands, with its tree-lined avenues, immaculate green lawns and luxury cars. It was inconceivable how people could dwell in such drastically different worlds that practically touched each other.

Kelly walked quickly by Maria's apartment. Her heart raced just because she was near her. She stopped in front of a building next to Maria's apartment building. The front window advertised bail bonds. She had come here to see Maria's world, just to walk on her sidewalk. But she knew she could do no more right now.

As she turned and hurried back to her car, she retrieved her cell phone and pushed the speed dial button for Sam's office.

"Hello, Sam Schultz's office," a tired woman's voice answered.

"Yes, hello, this is Kelly Malloy. Sam is working on a case with me. May I speak to him, please?"

"I'm sorry, but Mr. Schultz is not in at the moment."

"Is he at lunch?" Kelly asked. "I can try his cell."

"No, ma'am," the voice said, "Mr. Schultz is in chambers right now with Judge Silver about a matter that just came up. That's all I know. His office door opened and he flew out of here. If you know him, you know how he can be."

Kelly felt a knot form in her stomach as she unlocked her car and opened the door. This development had to concern her trial.

"I'll leave him a note to call you, Ms. Malloy."

"Thanks. He has my number," Kelly said, biting her lip.

CHAPTER 33

KELLY: OCTOBER 5, 2011

KELLY WALKED INTO her kitchen and placed two bags of groceries on the counter. She checked her phone for messages. She was expecting Sam any minute, even though she had not heard from him since he was summoned to the judge's chambers at lunchtime.

She took out a block of Gouda and a wedge of Brie and arranged them on a plate with freshly washed strawberries and green grapes. She was putting crackers in a basket when Dan entered the room.

"Is he here yet?" Dan placed his keys on the counter and took off his coat.

"Not yet. I'm glad you are, though." Kelly sidled up to Dan and kissed him on the cheek. "My mom's getting the girls and taking them to soccer practice."

Kelly had asked Dan to be present this time for her meeting with Sam. Sally Jeter had suggested it and Kelly liked the idea immediately. Dan would feel involved, instead of shut out. Kelly realized she liked having his support. He would have to hear the difficult details again, but he had assured her that he could handle it.

Dan lit a fire in the family room and nestled on the couch with an issue of *Architectural Digest*. That familiar and yet amorphous feeling of dread started to build in Kelly as she heard

Sam's knock and rose to let him in. As she approached the door, she knew she'd have to recount the details once again, and read other people's details of the horrific event. Even worse, she was preparing to go through all of this in front of a full courtroom, with Jack Barnard sitting only several feet away.

"Hey, Sam," Kelly said as she opened the door. "Come on in. I tried to reach you earlier, around lunchtime."

"I know, I got the message. I was in Judge Silver's chambers. He called us all in to have a 'Come-to-Jesus' meeting for the defense." Sam looked up at Dan sitting on the couch.

"Oh. Hi, Dan," Sam said, walking toward him and awkwardly extending his hand.

"Sam," Dan nodded and stood to shake Sam's hand.

Kelly blurted, "Sam, I called to tell you that Dan was going to sit in on this session, for moral support." Kelly looked quickly at Sam, who looked slightly wounded. "Please, Sam, sit down. Relax and have a bite."

As Sam was putting the contents of his briefcase on the coffee table, Kelly said, "Anything to drink?"

"No thanks, I'm good." Sam said.

"Dan?" Kelly asked.

"No, thanks Kel, I'm good, too." Dan responded. Then, a moment later, he proclaimed, "On second thought, I think I could use a beer." He rose and walked to the kitchen.

"Hey, this is a little unconventional, but I could really use one, too, please," Sam called as Dan opened the refrigerator door.

Kelly, laughing nervously, chimed in, "Please, babe, make that three." She started to feel the dread wash up into her throat again.

A short while later, the three of them sat in the family room with a stack of documents and three half-empty beer bottles on the coffee table.

"Apparently, Barnard's counsel filed a Motion to Exclude Testimony of Maria Hernandez and Chad McCloskey. It's a desperate attempt, but still, the judge has to consider it." Sam took a swig of his beer.

"On what grounds?" Kelly asked.

"Well, before we get to grounds, let's get to timing. The

motions won't be heard now, and so they won't affect our ability to get a probable cause finding now."

"Why did he file them now?" Kelly asked.

"They're posturing, mostly. His expensive lawyers are trying to look like they are prepared to put up a good fight. Barnard is pretty well lawyered-up. In fact, in addition to hiring Delaware's most expensive criminal defense attorney, Barnard now has retained co-counsel from a D.C. firm. He hired some woman who has done a lot more white-collar criminal defense than anything like this, so my guess is he is going for gender impact and big profile."

Sam continued. "Anyway, as far as grounds for the motions, with regard to Maria Hernandez, they are contending that she is an illegal immigrant and therefore not capable of being honest. It is offensive, really, and a clear attempt to terrorize her. Her immigration status is not grounds to exclude her testimony in any event."

Sam paused and took another swig from his beer bottle. "With respect to Chad McCloskey, they are arguing that he would not be able to testify without violating his Fifth Amendment rights, and if he waived those rights to testify, he would not be credible because he would just be saving his ass."

"Well, that makes some sense, except he is about to be released and charges against him dismissed, right?" Kelly asked.

"Well, yes." Sam said, hesitating before going on. "Today I entered a *nolle prosequi,* effectively dismissing all the charges against McCloskey. After we got the DNA match with Barnard, and with some nudging by McCloskey's counsel, I probed all the evidence regarding McCloskey. His story holds up regarding his rescue attempt and the reason he bought a ticket to fly to Arizona that day. Also, none of the evidence links him to you except the rescue part, which he admits to and which is not a crime, of course." Sam looked at Kelly and Dan and said, "He should be out of prison within hours."

"Oh, my gosh." Kelly gasped. "I don't know what to say. I feel terrible about what he went through."

"Kel, it is unfortunate, but remember, he looked pretty darn culpable when we arrested him. But it turns out he was only guilty of poor judgment and having bad luck. Today was good timing for the dismissal against McCloskey, because it simultaneously cuts out any more bullshit maneuvering by the defense, and it emphasizes the DNA match with Barnard and the rest of the rock solid case we have against him, with no other distractions. It hopefully gets us to a much quicker resolution. Now Judge Silver, Barnard's counsel, and hopefully even Barnard, know that Barnard's conviction is a no-brainer."

Dan picked up his beer and held it in his hand as he spoke. "What do you mean by 'no-brainer,' Sam? If you have a problem with witnesses or something like that, are you still confident that you'll get a conviction?"

Sam thought before speaking. "Nothing is one-hundred percent, but this one is as close as I have ever had. Just based on Kelly's testimony, police and medical reports and, most importantly, the DNA, we should get a conviction. But we also have the testimony of Chad McCloskey, Maria Hernandez, and the couple that found you and called the police."

Sam brought his hand to his forehead quickly and tapped himself there. "Oh, and I forgot to tell you! With lab analysis and another witness who's come forward, we can link Barnard to the drug that was used on you, too. It's called Anarest, and it's a mix of a sedative and an anesthetic used for what is known as chemical capture of animals. Some guy who is Barnard's occasional golfing partner called the police a few days ago, after reading about Barnard's arrest. This guy, Bill something, is a veterinarian. He told the police he put two and two together after seeing an article that recapped the details of the incident, including the use of a sedating drug dispensed through a dart. He recalled a time where Barnard was picking him up for a golf date: he got an emergency call about a dog that had part of a barbed wire fence embedded in its face and was running away from its owners and acting crazy. So Barnard went with him on the call and watched him anesthetize the dog with a dart gun so the dog could be caught and treated safely. The vet remembered that Barnard was fascinated and asked a lot of questions about the sedative mix and its use and capabilities. He also said that Barnard was with him when he went to get the Anarest, the dart and the gun before heading out on the call. It was all kept in a converted barn on his property, where he has his vet practice."

Sam paused for a moment, picked up his beer and finished it with several big gulps while Kelly and Dan waited for him to finish his story. "Well, this guy Bill does an end-of-the-month inventory check against his purchase and usage records, and after he read about Barnard's arrest, he checked and discovered that he's missing two vials of this stuff, and that there was no such discrepancy when he did his end-of-August check. He couldn't say for sure about missing darts since he doesn't inventory them, but the gun was still there. So, when he called the police he was instructed to not touch anything, so we could check for fingerprints. Sure enough, Barnard's fingerprints were on the gun, and on the glass front of the cabinet where the Anarest is kept." Sam gave a little shrug. "This Bill guy is a professional, and so he was pissed and is quite willing to testify against Barnard. He figures Barnard snuck onto his property to get the gun and the Anarest, and then came back soon afterward to return the gun before anyone knew it was missing."

Kelly's mouth fell open. Dan squeezed her hand.

"I don't want to scare you any more, Kelly, but this guy Bill told me that you are real lucky that Barnard did not use too much of those drugs on you, or you would have been a goner. He used the same dose that the vet had used on that dog. I think it was a Newfoundland, and it weighed about 135 pounds. Any more than that and it's possible that your breathing would have just shut down, and the rest of you, too."

Kelly looked up at Dan, who put his face in his hands. She knew he was trying to keep it together in front of Sam.

"So," Sam shrugged, "as you can see, he is a dangerous monster, and we have nailed his ass every way but Sunday."

Dan and Kelly laughed a little at this expression, unleashing some of their pent-up emotions. Kelly reached over and took Dan's hand. He gave her fingers a squeeze.

"I guess I should tell you that after hearing from both sides today, the judge was obviously blown away by our evidence. He made sure that Barnard was fully aware of the DNA evidence and its implications, as well as all of the other evidence. The defense will have a chance to probe our evidence, but Judge Silver was definitely helping them see that the evidence is insurmountable, and a plea agreement will save us all a lot of time and heartache."

"What would it mean if he took a plea agreement, Sam? Would he be out of prison a lot sooner than if he is convicted?" The dread feeling churned in Kelly's stomach and rose up in her throat.

"The State will not agree to any plea agreement that does not put this guy away for a very long time. He's a violent rapist, not to mention a serial misogynist with a penchant for physical violence, and we don't want him out on the streets." Sam looked at Kelly and began to speak softly. "On the other hand, we have to make some concessions, and there has to be some upside for him to plead guilty rather than fight. I'll get you a copy of the sentencing guidelines so you can see the possible range here, and of course I'll let you see any proposed plea agreement and weigh in on it, too."

Sam picked up some papers off of the coffee table. "For now, let's prepare your testimony for the preliminary hearing just in case, so we have covered all of our bases."

Kelly was surprised at how the dread that filled her seemed to diminish and then disappear entirely as she recalled the details of the day when she was attacked. Dan held her hand, squeezing it gently at times when she spoke about the man hurting her, violating her. Dan rubbed her back softly with the same hand when she talked about waking up in the woods, cold, sore and tied up. This time Kelly felt as if she was narrating someone else's story. She spoke methodically and was meticulous with the details, but she did not feel much at all. She noticed Sam kept nodding his head as she spoke, and checking off pieces of information on his notes that she assumed he had to elicit from her in the courtroom.

"Hey, Kel." Sam interrupted as Kelly started describing her rescue. "You are not going to like this, but I need you to convey the emotions, too. You know, like, your fear, your pain, and your humiliation. You sound like a robot."

"Gee thanks, Sam." Kelly said with biting sarcasm. "I am just getting to a point where I can talk about this stuff without falling apart. That's mostly because I am describing it with some form of emotional detachment. Now you want me to go back and get in touch with my pain?"

"Just doing my job to the best of my ability, Kel. I know it is not easy, but it will be helpful to convince a judge and jury, if it comes to that."

"Can't wait," Kelly said, sarcastically.

Sam leaned over the coffee table and collected his papers. He placed them in his briefcase, shut it and stood up to leave. First, he extended his hand to Dan. "Good to see you again, Dan."

Dan stood up awkwardly. "Uh, good to see you too, Sam. We can't thank you enough for helping us out like this."

"My pleasure," Sam said as he turned and started toward the door. He paused for a moment to speak. "Kel, good job. You'll be a great witness. And, with a little luck, you won't need to be."

"Amen. Thanks, Sam." Kelly said. "Hey, are you working with Chad McCloskey and Maria Hernandez on their testimony?"

"I will get on that real soon. You can see I have been busy, and access to them has been a bit tricky. I hope it gets a little easier now with McCloskey since he will be a free man. Hernandez has been a little MIA, but Sara Nuñez is reminding her that she doesn't have a choice but to answer a subpoena."

Sam saw the look of concern on Kelly's face. "I mean, we'll say that to her in a lot nicer way."

"Great," Kelly said, again with sarcasm.

Sam turned and started to walk toward the door. A high-pitched ringing emitted from his pocket. He stopped right next to the door and pulled out his cell phone. "Hello, Sam Schultz here."

Kelly and Dan stood silently, listening to his side of the conversation.

"No shit." Sam said. Then he looked up at Kelly and Dan and smiled, as he lifted his other hand and made a thumbs-up signal. "Thanks. Bye."

"What is it, Sam?" Kelly asked before he even put his phone away.

"That was my office. Barnard's counsel arranged to depose the people involved in the collection of and testing of the DNA evidence tomorrow. I'll be there to defend the depositions. Those are the only ones the defense is interested in, because really, DNA is everything. If it is sound, they know they can't beat this thing. At best, Barnard can hope for a lesser penalty and avoiding the humiliation of a trial parading all of the details of his sorry character and this horrific crime."

"Okay, thanks, Sam."

"Keep your phone with you." Sam said.

"I will." Sam closed the door behind him in a hurry, leaving Dan and Kelly staring silently at each other.

CHAPTER 34

KELLY: OCTOBER 6, 2011

KELLY STAYED BUSY all day to keep her mind occupied. She took the girls to school, went grocery shopping, caught up on laundry and even cleaned their bedroom closets. She knew that she could not call Sam while he was in depositions or if he was negotiating a plea agreement. That evening, Dan appeared equally anxious to hear from Sam, and so he made himself busy in the kitchen beside Kelly. Kelly carved a roasted chicken and took warm biscuits off of a baking sheet while Dan made a salad and set the table. Both of them had a large glass of Sancerre that they alternately sipped and placed back on the kitchen counter.

Kelly's eyes locked onto Dan's as he silently conveyed his support and shared suspense. She momentarily felt the familiar sense of dread knocking around in her stomach, pushing up into her throat and making her heart race. But oddly, tonight she felt like she had control over the dread, and with a little deep breathing, and the presence of her husband and daughters in such a warm setting, she managed to control it.

"What are you smiling at, Mom?" Anna asked, as she spun in a kitchen counter stool.

"I'm just happy," Kelly said easily.

"About what?" Anna continued the inquiry.

"About being here with you guys, and in this beautiful kitchen, and smelling Daddy's famous biscuits in the oven."

Kelly patted her stomach, causing Anna to smirk.

"And I'm happy, too, for all of those same reasons," Dan said, as he walked over to Kelly and wrapped his arms around her from behind.

The ring of the phone made them all jump. Dan dropped his hands quickly and stepped back. The girls looked up from their homework as the shrill ringing of the phone and their mother's running out of the kitchen shattered the sense of tranquility and comfort that had filled the room only moments before. Kelly ran into her office and picked up the phone on the fourth ring, breathless, trying in vain to sound normal. "Hello?"

"Hi, Kel. It's me," Sam said quickly. "We got it! We got a great deal that I think you're going to be happy about."

Kelly looked at Dan who by now was standing beside her, also desperately needing to know. "Hang on a second, Sam," Kelly said as she held the telephone against her chest to muffle it. "Dan," she pleaded, "I can't put the phone on speaker. The girls will hear." She looked frantic, "Why don't you pick up in the kitchen and listen in."

As Dan walked quickly out of the room, Kelly said, "Sam, Dan is going to get on the line in a minute, too. He needs to be part of this. Please start from the beginning. What happened with the depositions and what's the deal you're so excited about?"

"Okay, okay," Sam said. Kelly heard him take a deep breath. She pictured him ruffling his hand through his hair like he did when he was nervous or excited about something. Then she heard a click as Dan joined their conversation.

"I'm on," Dan said awkwardly.

"Hi Dan," Sam said. "Okay, here goes. First, the depositions went off without a hitch. Our guys are solid in the collection, chain-of-custody and testing of the DNA evidence. They also have impressive credentials. Barnard's counsel tried to fluster them, but at the end of the day, they got nothing helpful to the defense. So, about a half hour after depositions, they called me and said they want to talk about a deal."

"And the deal?" Dan blurted out, surprising Kelly and Sam.

"Well, we charged him initially with rape first degree, assault first degree and kidnapping first degree. Not to mention, now we can add burglary based on the crimes at the veterinary practice."

"Okay, so this is what you were threatening him with." Kelly interjected. "What is he agreeing to plead to?"

"Jeez, I'm getting to that. At first he wanted to plead *nolo contendre*, but of course we wouldn't allow that. There is no way that he was going to get off without admitting his guilt."

"Good!" Kelly chimed in. "What about the sentence?"

"As you could have predicted, Barnard has been relatively impossible. It turned out to be a good thing that he has two of the most prominent criminal defense attorneys representing him, because their influence was necessary to convince him that he better take the plea..."

"Sam!" Kelly interrupted impatiently. "What kind of time are we talking about here?"

"The sentencing guidelines for rape first degree, which is classified as a Felony, Level A offense, provides for fifteen years to life," Sam said. "And the other offenses, kidnapping and assault are, at best, Felony B which provides for two to fifteen years."

"Two to fifteen?" Kelly interrupted. "That's quite a range, Sam."

"Yeah, well, the court takes into consideration the defendant's prior record, the violence involved, and other aggravating or mitigating factors."

"So, where do you think he falls?" Kelly asked.

"There was premeditation and deliberate planning, use of a weapon—with the dart gun and the drugs—and of course, a violent act of rape. I would add the reckless disregard for your life with the use of drugs that could have been lethal. He has never been convicted of anything, but he has been arrested once for a domestic dispute allegedly resulting in his ex-wife's black eye and broken nose, but somehow he got off on that and wasn't prosecuted. He had an assault arrest record years ago when he was in high school, but that was expunged. And we have a few other women in his past that would be helpful to some degree perhaps."

"So Sam, what are you thinking? What's the bottom line here?" Kelly asked, biting her lip.

"The bottom line is, I know, and they know, we can nail him on Rape, Felony A, which is fifteen to life, and no possibility of getting out for good time served before fifteen years are up. With the violence and the premeditation involved, I think we convinced him he would certainly be looking at more than fifteen years, and we told him we were going to request life. And then of course there are the other charges he'd have to add time for. But between you and me, I am not sure we'd get much added from kidnapping, burglary, assault." Sam desperately tried to prepare Kelly for what he thought was her best option.

"Sam, I appreciate the education, but if you don't tell me right now the bottom line—what he is agreeing to serve in his plea agreement—then I am going to explode!" Kelly raised her voice to convince Sam of her desperation.

"Twenty-five years, with possibility of parole after twenty with good time served." There was nothing but silence on the other end of the conversation.

"Kel?" Sam said quietly. There was a long silence. "Kel? What are you thinking?" Sam prodded her gently.

"I don't know Sam. I absolutely hate the idea of Jack Barnard ever being a free man again. On the other hand, twenty-five years, or even twenty years, is a pretty long time."

"Kelly," Sam said. "The guy will be somewhere between sixty and sixty-five years old when he gets out and he'll age prematurely in prison. He'll look and feel much older than that. Think about it. Aside from the deterrence factor that twenty-five years in the slammer will have on him, he will be a geriatric when he gets out. He will lose his law practice, not see his kids grow up, no more fly-fishing. It is a very big deal, twenty to twenty-five years locked up."

"And you are certain this is the right way to go when we have the DNA and everything?" Kelly asked.

"I am sure we can nail him, Kel, but at what cost? And, what more do we get for it? You go through the trauma of telling your story, the lurid and painful details, in front of the man who attacked you and with the press reporting all of it. Let's not forget Chad McCloskey, who is now a free man and would much rather get on with his life than testify in court for several weeks. Of course, there is also the issue of the illegal immigrant with a newborn baby that *you* have been so concerned about." Sam paused for a moment. "You know that I'm pretty hard-nosed, and in this case I am highly motivated to crush this guy. So I would be hell-bent on trial if it made much of a worthwhile difference."

Kelly shuddered at the thought of testifying about how Barnard had humiliated her, controlled her and violated her. She was certain that she did not want to add to the burdens already borne by Maria Hernandez or Chad McCloskey.

"Dan, are you okay with this?" she asked.

"I am," Dan said, without elaboration. Kelly could tell he was choked up with emotion and afraid to say anything else.

"Okay, Sam. We are good with the plea agreement."

"Excellent! I think it really is the way to go here."

"So, how does this work now?" Kelly asked. "I mean, the court has to approve it, right?"

"Yes, but I don't think that is going to be a problem. Basically there is a process. Jack Barnard has to appear before Judge Silver so the judge can make sure that Barnard understands the nature of the charges he is pleading guilty to, and the minimum and maximum penalty imposed by law for each charge. Then he needs to make sure that Barnard is entering his plea voluntarily and that he is waiving the right to trial by entering the plea." Sam hesitated for a moment. "Then Judge Silver will actually determine the sentence: he is not bound by the agreement. But I'm not worried about that. If anything, this judge would add to, not subtract from, the sentence proposed by the parties."

"Why are you sure of that?" Kelly asked.

"He's a smart guy who has no patience for cruelty and violence. Also, it would not be good politics to reduce the sentence of an admitted violent rapist, particularly one that's a member of the Delaware Bar."

"When is this happening?" Kelly asked.

"Tomorrow morning," Sam replied. "Arraignment at ten sharp."

"Thanks Sam. You really have been a godsend."

"Well, you can buy me dinner sometime," Sam said. Then, remembering Dan was on the phone, he said, "You and Dan can buy me dinner sometime."

"That's a deal," Kelly laughed.

"Thanks for everything Sam," Dan chimed in.

Kelly pushed the "off" button on the phone and placed it on the desk. A moment later she saw Dan pop his head into her office. He was smiling.

"Twenty-five years, with no possibility of parole for at least twenty years, Dan." Kelly came to him and put her arms around his neck. She buried her head in his chest.

Dan whispered in her ear. "He'll be a sickly, impotent and bankrupt old geezer when he gets out."

CHAPTER 35

KELLY: OCTOBER 7, 2011

KELLY SAT STIFFLY in the back row of the courtroom. Dan sat next to her, in his only suit and dress shoes, holding her hand on the wooden bench between them. The door behind them opened and Sam walked in, flanked by a thin young woman who was also a Deputy Attorney General, and a stocky grey-haired woman who Kelly assumed was their paralegal. They all held briefcases and looked very serious.

As soon as Sam saw Kelly, a wide grin broke across his face. "Hey," he said as he handed his briefcase to the paralegal and sidled onto their bench. "Good to see you here." He shook Dan's hand and awkwardly gave Kelly a half-hug.

"I don't have to say anything, do I?" Kelly asked.

"No, but you might be asked questions by the press. Just stay until the proceeding is over and I'll ask the bailiff if he can get you out the back door." Sam backed out of the wooden row and strode down the aisle toward the table where the prosecution sat. Several feet away, defense counsel sat at another table.

Kelly looked over at Jack Barnard's counsel, a middle-aged woman in a black suit tapping her pencil, and a silver-haired man in a well-cut dark grey suit, who kept glancing at his thick gold watch. A court reporter came in and set up her equipment in front of the judge's bench. The routine of the courtroom started to make Kelly feel at ease for a moment. She took a deep breath and smiled at Dan as she squeezed his hand.

A side door opened and Barnard, accompanied by two men in Department of Corrections uniforms, came into the courtroom. Kelly startled at first at the shock of seeing him. But as she looked closely, she saw a broken man instead of the monster that had loomed in her mind. His shoulders were hunched over, his jowls hung loose over his collar and his hair was unkempt. He looked down at the floor as he entered and until he sat in his chair.

Kelly's eyes practically bore holes into Barnard's back once he was seated. Dan stared at the back of his head, clenching his teeth in anger. Suddenly, the door in front of the courtroom opened, sending in a beam of light. A bailiff entered and said, "Please rise for the Honorable Judge Murray Silver."

Kelly and Dan stood stiffly. As Kelly watched Judge Silver enter the room and climb the steps to the bench, she thought he looked a bit like someone's grandfather. She had appeared before Judge Silver many times, but she realized that she had never actually looked at him as a person. He was short and a little stooped. His face was weathered but kind-looking. Kelly felt sure that Judge Silver understood the gravity of this matter by his serious expression and the way he cleared his throat when he sat down. He put a pair of black reading glasses on the bridge of his nose to read the caption of the case out loud. Then he removed the glasses and held them in his right hand as he spoke directly to Barnard.

"Mr. Barnard, you are here for your arraignment. Do you understand that the Court will inform you of the substance of the charges against you, and that you will enter your plea to each of those charges?"

After a moment, Kelly heard Judge Silver clear his throat. "Mr. Barnard. I am sorry, but you'll have to speak up for the Court and the court reporter to create an accurate record." Then he added, "Surely you know that as a trial lawyer yourself."

Kelly heard a muffled giggle from one of the journalists seated in the row in front of her.

"Let's start again, Mr. Barnard." Judge Silver sounded tired.

Kelly heard impatience and something else, possibly even scorn, in Judge Silver's voice. As she heard him repeat his question about the arraignment process, Kelly looked around the room. Other than court personnel and counsel, Dan and herself, there were a dozen or so reporters in the room. They were scribbling notes and sketching drawings frantically, as laptops and cameras were forbidden. To her right she noticed an old woman, with a cardigan pulled tight over her tall, lumpy body. The woman's face was wrinkled and her eyes looked straight at Barnard's back. She had an expression of deep sorrow. Kelly tapped Dan's shoulder to get his attention and whispered, "I wonder if that's his mother over there."

Judge Silver slipped his glasses back on and began reading the charges on the documents before him. Kelly looked around the room as he did so, zoning out on the charges and losing herself in her observations of the courtroom. She noticed that the room was otherwise conspicuously absent of women. For a man who'd had many wives, girlfriends and mistresses, he certainly had little support from them. Except for the old woman, Barnard faced the consequences of his actions alone, as a solitary figure, his years of arrogant and cruel behavior resulting in isolation and loneliness.

"Mr. Barnard." Kelly's attention was refocused to Judge Silver. "You have heard the charges against you just now read in this Court. Correct?"

"Yes, Your Honor," Barnard said. He looked up to make eye contact with the judge only after his counsel surreptitiously elbowed him.

"And do you have any questions about those charges or do you understand what they mean?"

"No, Your Honor, I have no questions."

"Good, then." Judge Silver scratched his head with the hand holding the glasses. "And your counsel has informed you of the mandatory minimum and maximum penalty imposed by applicable laws, as well as any applicable sentencing guidelines, correct?"

"Yes, Your Honor."

"And do you have any questions about those mandated sentence ranges and the sentencing guidelines?" Judge Silver looked up at Jack Barnard and waited for an answer.

"Yes, I do, Your Honor." Barnard's voice got louder and he appeared to be a little indignant. "But I have an agreement for a certain sentence, a total sentence...."

"Mr. Barnard," Judge Silver cut him off mid-sentence. "We will get to that in due course. I am asking you now only if you understand the minimum and maximum penalty for each of the charges against you, and the sentencing guidelines used in Delaware."

"Uhm, yes, Your Honor, I understand that."

"Okay, Mr. Barnard, then this part is a bit of a formality, but bear with me. You understand that by entering a plea of guilty to the charges against you or to lesser charges by agreement of the Attorney General's Office, that you waive your right to a trial, and you state here today that you do so with assistance of your counsel and of your own free will and volition?"

Jack Barnard stood quietly for a moment, looking at the floor. Then he leaned over and whispered in the ear of his counsel. After his counsel whispered back, Barnard said, with a slight but noticeable hesitation, "Yes, Your Honor."

"Mr. Barnard," Judge Silver held up a stapled document as he spoke. "I have here the original plea agreement signed by you and by your counsel and signed by Deputy Attorney General Samuel D. Schultz, dated October 6, 2011."

Kelly glanced toward Sam at the judge's mention of his full name. He stood very straight, in a well-fitted dark grey suit, with a confident but alert demeanor. She noticed for the first time that his hair was turning silver around the nape of his neck and that he looked even more gaunt than usual.

Judge Silver continued, sounding almost weary with the process. "You are familiar with this written plea agreement and understand the proposed sentences?"

Again, Barnard paused a moment to quietly confer with his counsel. Kelly noticed that the female attorney at the Defense's table could merely nod her head each time, as Jack Barnard seemed to only seek advice from the man he had hired. "Yes, Your Honor, I am familiar with the terms. I have read the plea agreement."

"Fine, then." Judge Silver cleared his throat. "And you understand that your plea of guilty is given in exchange for the Attorney General's recommendation to the Court with regard to your penalty?"

Judge Silver squinted and held up the document to read the specifics, and then he changed his mind and put his glasses back on. "In this case, specifically, a total of twenty-five years of incarceration Level 1, with no possibility of parole until a minimum of twenty years served at Level 1 incarceration?" The judge put the document back on his desk, removed his glasses and turned his gaze to Jack Barnard.

"Yes, I understand that those are the terms of the plea agreement." Jack Barnard said.

"Spoken like a trial lawyer, Mr. Barnard," Judge Silver said, with a perceived hint of disdain apparent in his voice again. "Well, here is the tricky part, Mr. Barnard. You understand the deal here," the judge said as he tapped the document in front of him, "but I have to be real clear in ensuring that you understand that the Court may accept your plea of guilty—which you will be bound by—and yet the Court does not have to accept the recommended penalty that you and your counsel and the Attorney General's Office have proposed in this written plea agreement." The judge tapped the document again for emphasis. "You understand that, Mr. Barnard, correct?"

Barnard shook his head, reluctantly.

"I see you nodding your head affirmatively, Mr. Barnard, but I need you to voice your assent for the Court reporter. Is that a *yes* to my question?" The judge was growing impatient.

His defense attorneys both quickly whispered to Barnard, admonishing him to be respectful to the judge who held his fate. Barnard stood straight and looked at the judge. "Yes, Your Honor, I understand."

"Good, then. With all of that agreed to and understood, do you still stand here and ask the Court to accept your plea of guilty to the charges as they are written in the plea agreement?"

"Yes, Your Honor," Barnard said quickly and clearly this time.

"The Court will need to take a moment before sentencing. Let's recess for fifteen minutes." Judge Silver abruptly stood.

"All rise," the bailiff said, a moment too late, as the judge already turned and walked toward the door that he had used to enter the courtroom. Once the door was closed, the courtroom became a blur of motion. Reporters buzzed and chatted, and a few left for a quick bathroom or cigarette break. Jack Barnard sat at the defense table whispering with his counsel. At one point, Kelly saw him pause for a moment and look back at the old woman in the stretched cardigan. She pursed her lips and wiped a tear off of her cheek with her long, bony fingers.

"What do you think?" Sam came over to speak with Kelly and Dan. His face was back to normal, with a grin of a college boy and a little mischief in his eyes.

"I guess it's pretty much what I expected." Kelly said. Dan quietly nodded in agreement. "Except I thought there'd be someone here from Barnard's side of things, you know, family or a friend."

"He is admitting to pretty horrific crimes, Kel. No one wants to be associated with him now." He leaned in closer and whispered to Kelly and Dan. "Defense counsel told me that's his mother over there though. I feel sorry for her." Sam put his hands in his pockets as he spoke. "Well, I am going to take a quick trip to the bathroom before the judge returns." Then as he turned to leave he said, "Oh, I almost forgot. This came up so quickly. Kelly, as the victim here, you have an opportunity to speak if you want to address Jack Barnard and the Court."

Kelly looked in horror at Sam, and then turned to Dan. He instinctively put his arm around Kelly's shoulder and said, "Whatever you think, babe. You don't have to do that unless it's going to make you feel better."

"My God! Sam." Kelly said, breathless with the dread rising fast in her throat and chest. "I don't think I can do that, in front of reporters and Barnard. Even his mother is here."

"Okay, okay," Sam said. It was just an option, not a requirement."

"Would it impact the sentence?" Kelly asked, with a worried look on her face. "I mean, will he be put away for a longer period if I tell the Court about how awful it was and how I was hurt?"

"No, Kel," Sam assured her. "The judge has already made up his mind about the sentence. I am sure of that. He's very familiar with the crimes alleged and pleaded to, and he's aware of the mountain of evidence to support the charges and warrant a conviction. You don't need to tell him about it for him to get the full effect. It is more of a right of the victim, you know, being heard, getting closure or whatever you want to call it."

"I'll pass, Sam." Kelly linked her arm through Dan's as she spoke.

"All rise," the bailiff said unexpectedly.

"Oh well, there goes my pee break," Sam whispered as he quickly moved to the prosecutor's table. Kelly watched as he re-buttoned his suit jacket and straightened his back as he walked, transforming himself into his grown-up and serious courtroom persona.

Judge Silver re-entered the room and took his seat at the bench, causing everyone in the courtroom to sit down quietly in unison. Barnard's mother held her hands tightly on the back of the wooden bench in front of her, as her eyes silently pleaded with the judge for leniency.

"The Court has considered the charges as described in the plea agreement, as well as the sentence recommended therein." Judge Silver looked up for a moment, first at the throng of reporters sitting together, then at the Barnard's mother sitting alone in the back, and then at Barnard. After a long pause with his eyes on Barnard, and to Kelly's horror, the judge looked directly at Kelly. "One final consideration here before I address sentencing is, whether or not the victim would like to speak to the Court."

Kelly froze in horror, as all eyes turned to her. Barnard followed their gaze, twisting his body and then staring right at her. She heard a pounding in her head as her blood commenced fight or flight mode. She sat mute, while her face became an inferno. Dan squeezed her hand.

"No, Your Honor," Sam said as he rose in his place. "I have spoken to the victim and Ms. Malloy does not wish to address the Court."

A wave of relief flooded over Kelly as all eyes turned back to Sam as he spoke, and then back to Judge Silver. "Very well, then." Judge Silver cleared his throat. "In the matter of The State of Delaware v. Jack C. Barnard, the Court imposes a sentence of twenty-five years of incarceration at Level I, with no possibility of parole until a minimum of twenty years served."

A murmur buzzed through the courtroom as people reacted to the sentence. Barnard's counsel smiled in relief as Judge Silver accepted the sentence recommended in the plea agreement. "Quiet, please," he spoke calmly and loudly over the din. The room became silent immediately. "Except that Defendant shall satisfactorily complete a course on anger management, as well as a course regarding physical and sexual abuse."

Barnard turned to look at Kelly. She glared back at him, suddenly emboldened.

"Mr. Barnard!" Judge Silver bellowed, causing Barnard to spin around and face the bench. "Please keep your attention on the Court where it belongs. This is your life we are talking about." Barnard's male counsel quietly chastised him and then he again looked at his expensive watch, presumably so all could see that he had somewhere more important to be.

Judge Silver spoke again. "Before we close this matter, I would like to say that I was reluctant to accept the sentence recommended in the plea agreement. I did so because it was warranted by the sentencing guidelines, and because it saved the State's resources and prevented more pain and suffering by the victim. But, I would be remiss if I did not say that the misconduct that you have admitted to is abhorrent under any circumstances. And, when you consider that you are a member of the Delaware Bar, charged with upholding the law, and sworn to personally exemplify a higher standard of ethics, your admitted crimes are particularly unthinkable." The judge shook his head slowly as he spoke, looking as if he was experiencing personal pain at the thought of the horrors that had been inflicted.

Kelly felt a gentle wave of warmth as she listened to Judge Silver's words. She did not feel alone anymore in her darkness. Today, in this courtroom, and perhaps tomorrow in the newspapers, Jack Barnard would be publicly reprimanded and finally revealed to be the monster that he was. Starting today, and for many years to come, *he* would be locked up alone with nothing but his despair and regret. In contrast, Kelly's neighbors, co-workers, the moms at carpool, and the rest of the community around her would read Judge Silver's words repeated in the newspaper and they would understand, like Judge Silver understood. Jack Barnard *was the one* to be ostracized, avoided and condemned. Kelly felt herself grinning from ear to ear, and she willed Barnard to turn around just once more so she could smile to his face.

Judge Silver spoke again. "Do you want to say anything, Mr. Barnard, to the Court or to the victim?"

Kelly's heart pounded once again as Jack Barnard rose from his chair. He turned to face the back of the room. Kelly realized he was looking at the old woman.

"I'm sorry, Ma." Barnard cried as he spoke. The old woman trembled at his words, and she bit her lip and looked away from her son's face to concentrate on a string of rosary beads in her hands.

"Bastard!" Kelly heard Dan mumble.

Kelly squeezed Dan's hand and whispered, 'It's okay, babe. I don't want his apology."

"Is that all you'd like to say?" Judge Silver asked, urging Jack Barnard to apologize to his victim.

"Yes."

Barnard sat down in a heap, a defeated man.

CHAPTER 36

KELLY AND CHAD: OCTOBER 7, 2011

KELLY WIPED A light film of perspiration off of her forehead and tried to regulate her breathing as she entered the Carvel State Office Building. She remembered climbing the steps to that same building a lifetime ago, to tell Sam Schultz that Jack Barnard was her rapist. She glanced at a directory on the wall, silently reading, *Office of the Public Defender*. She pushed upon the door to the PD's office and took a breath to compose herself as she approached a woman behind a reception desk.

"Can I help you, miss?"

"I have an appointment." Kelly stammered.

"Can you be more specific?"

"My name is Kelly Malloy and I'm here to see Stuart Harlan and a client of his, Chad McCloskey."

The receptionist rose from her chair. "Please come with me. Mr. Harlan has been expecting you."

As Kelly followed the receptionist down a hallway, she passed offices where lawyers and support staff were busy defending criminal defendants in Delaware. She marveled at the fact that it was a mirror image of the other office space, in that same building, where lawyers and support staff worked to *prosecute* those same criminal defendants.

"Mr. Harlan," the receptionist poked her head in an open office door, "Ms. Malloy is here to see you."

As Kelly entered the office, she saw a young man in a grey suit sitting behind a desk, and an even younger man—*a kid*, Kelly thought—sitting opposite the desk and wearing jeans and a T-shirt. They both sprang up as she entered the room.

"Ms. Malloy," the man in the suit spoke as he hurried around the desk to shake her hand, "It's nice to meet you." Kelly noticed that his jacket cuffs were fraying from use and that he needed a haircut. Looking at his face, Kelly guessed he was in his mid-twenties. "I'm Stuart Harlan, Public Defender and counsel to Mr. McCloskey here."

"It is nice to meet you." Kelly said, shaking Stuart's hand.

Then Kelly looked over at Chad McCloskey. He had thick dark hair, a square jaw and large serious eyes. Dark circles under his eyes and hollows under his cheekbones revealed the trauma and stress of nine days in prison. She cleared her throat. "It is really nice to meet you too, Mr. McCloskey."

The young man in the jeans remained standing. "Please, you can call me Chad," he said softly.

"Thank you, Chad, you can call me Kelly." Kelly cleared her throat again, nervously. "I know you are eager to be done with all of this, so I am grateful that you agreed to see me." She noticed that Chad looked at the floor when she spoke to him. The bizarre and yet intimate nature of their first encounter in the gardener's shed in the woods hung on them both, making conversation and movements feel unnatural. "I saw you both on the evening news Wednesday when you were released from prison. It was so wonderful to see you finally vindicated."

"Yeah, that press conference was definitely the highlight of my career thus far," Stuart laughed. "Why don't we all have a seat?" He gestured to the chairs around his desk.

Kelly sat next to Chad and turned in her chair to face him. "I just wanted to meet you and thank you. I can never thank you enough for being so brave and sticking your neck out to help me, even though I know it must have been a really scary situation for you." Kelly noticed Chad looked up at her as he heard her words. "And then you were locked up in that God-awful place and slandered in the news."

"It's okay, really. It wasn't your fault." Chad folded his arms across his chest, as if he was supporting himself.

"Well, Chad. You may have saved my life. I can't just let that go. I can't live with the fact that you suffered for it so badly, too. If you don't let me do something to thank you, I think I am going to go crazy."

"Really, it is okay." Chad said. "I'm just glad it is over. I just want to move on."

"Please." Kelly pleaded, looking at Chad and then at Stuart Harlan. "I don't want to pry, or be crass, but I want to help you financially or legally, or any way I can. What do you need?"

Chad was silent for a moment, with his eyes closed. Then he opened his eyes and spoke quietly. "Ma'am, I just want to put all of this behind me. I just need to finish packing up some things and get my parents' house in order, I guess, and then I am getting out of here for good."

Stuart cleared his throat. "Well, I don't think Chad will mind if I mention that he only recently found out that his mother has moved to Eugene, Oregon. And he is flying there in a few days, after he takes care of a few things, so he can finally be with her." He stopped for a moment to look at Chad, who shrugged his shoulders. "He probably could use a little cash to get started. I am sure that he is too proud to ask." He glanced at Chad again, who was looking at the floor. "And his father recently passed away, leaving Chad or his mother with estate and real estate affairs to be sorted out, like the sale of his parents' home— assuming his mother agrees with that course of action."

"Well, that's something I can do!" Kelly said, with surprising enthusiasm. Chad looked up at her, startled. "But first, I want you to take this, please." Kelly said, as she hastily produced a blue check made out to *Chad McCloskey* for the amount of *$5,000.*

"Ma'am, I couldn't," Chad said, embarrassed.

"Please, you must. It is the last favor of you I will ask. There is no impropriety, the criminal prosecution is a done deal and I don't need anything from you. It is a gift. Please take it."

Chad took the check gently and looked at it. Then he folded it and put it back on the table in front of Kelly. "I hope you understand, ma'am, I just cannot take that. Please respect my decision." He spoke softly, "I really do appreciate your kindness, but I don't think you should feel responsible for what I have been through. You were a victim, too."

An awkward silence ensued. Kelly cleared her throat. "I hear Oregon is beautiful country. It has some vibrant little cities, too, like Portland and Eugene."

"I really will just be happy to be with my mother--and far away from here."

"Well, how are you going to deal with the issues around your father's estate, and the sale of your parents' home?"

Chad looked at Stuart again and said, "I don't know." Then, with surprising anger, he said, "We are selling that house to the first person willing to buy it. I don't ever want to set foot inside that sorry, miserable place again, and I never want my mother to have to see it or even hear of it."

Stuart looked at Kelly. "He'll need an estate attorney, and someone to handle the marketing and sale of the home. It's a tear-down home, but the property itself, right on the Brandywine and near Rockford Park, is worth a lot of money."

"It's settled then. I'll get lawyers from my firm involved in handling your father's estate, and the sale of the real estate. Please let me do that, at least." Kelly pleaded with Chad.

Chad leaned across the table. "Thank you, Kelly. I wouldn't have the first clue about what to do there, and so I can't say 'no' to that kind offer." He added, "I guess as much as I just want to get rid of that place and all those bad memories, I do need to get the best deal I can for my mother and for me."

"And, just to be clear, we're handling that *pro bono*." Kelly smiled as she handed Chad and Stuart business cards. "I wrote my home and cell number on there, too. I'm on sabbatical from the office, so this way you can reach me no matter where I am."

Chad looked up at Kelly. "Thank you again for your help with the house and everything that I am leaving behind."

Kelly shyly moved to Chad and embraced him gently. He stiffened at her touch. "It will never be enough to thank you, but it helps me clear my head about this whole ordeal, and maybe make some order of it." She backed away from him. "Please call me if you ever need help with anything. Don't lose my card."

Chad responded by pulling his wallet out of his pocket and carefully tucking her card into it.

As Kelly walked to her car she pictured Chad's face—the

face of an innocent teenager. She recalled Sam's description of Chad's childhood, tucked away in the woods with an abusive and alcoholic father and a depressed mother, a childhood filled with loneliness and turmoil. As she turned the key in her car's ignition she whispered, "Please, God, let that boy find some sense of belonging, some love, some happiness."

CHAPTER 37
KELLY: OCTOBER 7, 2011

THE EVENING AIR was sweet and warm despite the yellow and orange leaves showing in the trees. The girls threw a pink Frisbee while Dan stood over his prized Weber grill, metal tongs in hand. Kelly came out of the house with a bottle of Pinot Noir and three glasses on a tray. She set the tray down, filled two glasses with the crimson wine, and walked over to Dan. "To victory!" Kelly said, handing Dan a glass so he could join her in a toast.

Dan clinked her glass. "To us." He leaned over and kissed her warmly on the lips. The sound of a car door slamming made them both turn around.

"Celebrating without the man of the hour?" Sam asked as he strode into their back yard. He had exchanged the dark grey suit he had worn in court that day for a navy blue polo shirt and a pair of khakis.

"Maybe a little," Kelly giggled. "We toasted victory."

Sam walked over to the table and poured himself a glass of wine. He raised the glass. "I'd like to propose a toast, too. To the image of Jack Barnard in a prison jumpsuit, staring at concrete walls and attending lectures on anger management and sexual aggression."

"Hear, hear." Kelly raised her glass again.

"Yum, smells good. What are you cooking?" Sam asked Dan.

"Barbecued chicken and ribs, smothered in my own homemade bourbon sauce." Dan said, smiling.

"Oh boy! I wish I was having dinner with you guys." Sam chuckled.

"Please, join us. We both could never do enough to thank you," Dan said sincerely. He put the tongs down for a moment and looked at Sam and said, "I really mean that."

"Thank you, Dan," Sam said as he drove his hands into his pockets. "I wasn't actually mooching for a dinner invite, although that sounds like something I would do," he laughed. "But I have a dinner date tonight with a lady."

Kelly arched her eyebrows at this remark. "Wow, Sam! Please, give us the details."

"Well, let me think." Sam put his hand to his chin as he thought, as if he were addressing a jury. "She's pretty and smart and fun. Oh, and best of all, she's not a lawyer."

"Is it serious?" Kelly asked.

"I hope so," Sam said. "Her name is Mary, and she is a teacher right here in Wilmington. She loves her job and her kids; her students I mean, she doesn't have children," Sam added hastily. "She's pretty great." Sam's eyes lit up as he spoke. "We met last year at a mock trial thing for eighth graders. She was a coach, believe it or not, and I was a judge. I probably broke a few rules of mock trial ethics, but I gave her some pointers during a lunch break. She looked so sweet and earnest, but I think American History is her strength, not trial advocacy."

Sam paused and took a sip of wine. "So, we dated pretty regularly, but I kept her at arm's length for a while, always blaming my job. But recently I had an epiphany." He turned to Dan and back at Kelly. "I want what you two have. My work will never be able to share my life, and my bed, and make a family with me. So over dinner tonight, I am going to ask her to move in with me." Sam looked directly at Kelly when he spoke the next words. "Yeah, I am finally ready to go to the next level with Mary."

"Do you know if she wants that?" Kelly prodded.

"Oh, yeah. She turned thirty-two a few months ago and her friends are all having kids now, and—yes—she has made it abundantly clear she wants kids."

Kelly gave him a little hug. "We'll have you both over for dinner when you are ready. We can help acclimate her to the whole house-and-kids thing."

"And dog," Sam added.

"What?" Kelly asked, confused. "You have a dog?"

Sam put his wine glass down and held his hand up toward Kelly. "Wait. I'll be right back." A moment later, Sam returned to the yard with a tall tan dog on a leash.

"Oh, my gosh, a dog!" Gracie shrieked as she dropped the Frisbee. Both girls ran over.

"Wait!" Kelly yelled, stopping them in their tracks as they approached the dog.

"It's okay, Kel. He is completely friendly. He loves kids." Sam assured them, as he stroked the dog's head. "Look how his tail is wagging." The girls stroked the dog as he stood next to Sam, wriggling his body in joy and wagging his tail furiously.

"This is your dog?" Kelly asked.

"Not exactly." Sam said. "He's the reason I dropped in tonight. Well, in addition to wanting to have a celebratory drink." Sam looked at Dan, who was still manning the barbecue.

"Dan?" Sam asked. "Are you going to help me out here?"

Dan shrugged, leaving Sam to explain.

"I already ran this by Dan. Listen, Kel: first of all, Mary has a friend who had to move to London because of her job. She could not take Chance with her and it broke her heart. Mary agreed to take him temporarily while they looked for a good home for Chance."

"Mom, can we keep him? Please?" Anna asked.

"Please, Mommy?" Gracie wrapped her arms around him. The dog started vigorously licking Grace's chin with his large pink tongue.

"Sam," Kelly said. "He is a beautiful dog. But it is a big commitment. Do you know anything about this guy?"

"Oh, yeah. He's a Rhodesian Ridgeback. He is two years old, so the vet thinks he's done growing. He weighs about 90 pounds. He is up-to-date on his shots, very healthy, housebroken, of course, and well-socialized around people and other pets."

Kelly walked over to the dog and looked into his big brown eyes. She knelt down next to him to stroke his ear. He licked her chin with his big pink tongue.

"And, Kel," Sam said. "Here is why I thought of you." Kelly noticed Sam looked at Dan again as he spoke. "This dog is a Rhodesian Ridgeback. Do you know what that means? Despite his very sweet demeanor, his breed was created originally to keep lions away from villages and farms in Africa. So he can keep you safe, and he loves to run. His former owner was a runner and she took him out regularly for five-mile runs."

Kelly looked at Dan who smiled widely and then said, "Sam called me with this idea. I think it's a great idea all around." Then he added, "It is a big commitment. But on workdays, you can run him in the morning, and I'll come home to let him out at mid-day. And it will be a great time to get everyone acclimated, since you're on a sabbatical from work."

"What about when we go away?" Kelly asked, trying to figure out all of the details.

Sam spoke up. "Mary and I will take him when you guys travel. That much we can do."

The girls looked at their mother with pleading eyes as they continued to stroke the smooth tan coat of the dog. "What's his name again?" Kelly asked Sam as she thought it over.

"Chance," Sam said. "His owner named him that after rescuing him from a shelter as a puppy, because he was getting a second chance."

"Well, Chance," Kelly spoke directly to the dog as he looked at her. "I guess we're running buddies now."

"Yeah! We have a doggie!" Gracie shrieked.

"I have his food, leashes and bowls in my car, and some records from the vet. I'll leave all that stuff by your mudroom door." He looked at his watch. "Well, I have to go, it's a big night." Sam said, brushing a few tan hairs off his shirt.

"Good luck, Sam. And thanks for Chance." Kelly gave him a peck on the cheek.

"I should thank you guys. I'll be in Mary's good graces now. I got Chance a great home and she and I will have visitation rights." He laughed as he turned to leave.

*****

Later that night, after dinner, cleanup, and walking Chance, Kelly still felt energized by the day's events. Jack Barnard was locked up in prison and she was free, safe and, best of all, unlike Jack Barnard, she was surrounded by love. After getting the girls to bed, Dan and Kelly whispered and giggled in the hallway as they tiptoed away from their daughters' bedrooms. Chance was curled up on an old futon cushion that Kelly had found in the basement. He raised his head sleepily and wagged his tail in recognition of their presence.

"The night watchman," Dan grinned as he pointed at the sleepy dog.

Kelly smiled at this remark, knowing that she had deliberately placed Chance's bed in the middle of all of their bedrooms. Kelly whispered back, "His ancestors chased lions away. That's very comforting."

"Everyone is home safe and sleeping soundly," Dan said, gesturing with both arms toward the bedrooms and the dog on the floor.

"Yes, and Jack Barnard is tossing and turning in a cement block cell with a felon for a roommate," Kelly whispered.

She bent down over the long, tan dog and patted him on his belly. "Good night, Chance. Tomorrow, you and I are going for a run in the woods." Chance's tail wagged sleepily.

"Kel, don't kill him on the first day. Take it slow." Dan joked as he put his arms around Kelly. "I'm glad you'll be back to running, though. It agrees with you."

Kelly kissed Dan. "You know what else I feel ready to get back to?"

Dan smiled and raised his eyebrows. "Really?"

"Really." Kelly reached for Dan's hand and led him toward their bedroom door. After closing the door to their bedroom, she peeled off her shirt and bra in a fury. Dan pulled off of his clothing and fell onto the bed. Kelly climbed on top of him, reveling in the feeling of their skin touching. Their hands and mouths traveled all over each other's body, touching and tasting hungrily. Kelly felt a need and an urgency that made her crazed.

"Kel," Dan said, out of breath. He put his hands up in front of her face and made a *T* symbol with them. "Time out. Please, just lie still for one moment so I can look at you."

Kelly rolled over off of Dan with a sigh, and then quietly lay on her back, her legs stretched out in front and her hands clasped behind her head. Dan knelt next to her, gazing at her familiar body with longing. He took his right hand and gently ran his fingers over her small round breasts, sending a jolt of electricity through Kelly's body. Then he bent over her and ran his tongue down her belly, over the top of each of her thighs. He stopped there abruptly.

"What, Dan? Don't stop," Kelly panted.

"Uhm, nothing," Dan muttered as he stared at the faded remnants of bruising on Kelly's inner thighs. "Kel, are you sure about this?"

"Yes. Oh my God, yes." Kelly said, convincingly.

Dan went back to running his tongue gently over Kelly's thighs.

"That's amazing, Dan," Kelly whispered.

Heartened by Kelly's words, Dan continued down into the folds that had always given her such pleasure. Kelly ran her hands through Dan's hair. "Dan," she said breathlessly, "I need you inside of me. It's been too long."

Dan looked up at his wife from his crouch, and smiled. He lifted himself over her and entered her slowly, causing them both to shudder as he finally found his way home. They made love slowly, with Dan rocking and Kelly emitting soft sounds with her legs wrapped around his waist. They finished together, with hushed cries, and then Dan lay pressed against Kelly. "My God!" Dan said in her ear. "It is good to be back in our groove."

Kelly kissed Dan soulfully. "I know. I feel kind of right again, almost peaceful... like I am finally, really home."

CHAPTER 38

KELLY AND MARIA: OCTOBER 8, 2011

KELLY PARKED HER car and quickly grabbed her briefcase off the passenger seat. As she slammed her car door shut, she noticed the late model black Mercedes sedan with Pennsylvania license plates parked nearby. It looked even more conspicuous in the parking lot than her Volvo.

As she entered Sara Nuñez's office, she saw Mark Slattery, a partner from her firm's Philadelphia office. Kelly had called him for help every time that she had a matter that required expertise on immigration law. She felt a little uncomfortable around him, because he was the product of exclusive prep schools and Ivy League fraternities, and he associated with people who frequented polo games and yacht races. But Kelly knew that he was very smart, had good connections, and always seemed to get the desired results for his clients.

"Hi, Mark," Kelly said extending her hand to shake his. "I hope I haven't kept you long."

"Not at all." He took off his charcoal gray Armani suit jacket and held it with one hand, while he expertly loosened his Hermès tie with his other hand. "I just got here too. And I have not seen a soul yet."

"So, what's the good news?" Kelly asked. "Your message said you had good news."

Before Mark could answer, an office door opened and Sara Nuñez stepped out.

"Hello, Sara." Kelly said, shaking her hand. "This is Mark Slattery, with my firm, and as you know, he is the guy to go to for immigration issues."

"Pleasure to meet you," Mark said as he shook Sara's hand.

"Well," Sara said, rather brusquely, "my clients are in my office. Maria has been living at Juan's cousin's house with the baby, terrified because she received a subpoena regarding the Barnard prosecution."

Kelly blushed at the mention of Barnard in front of Mark Slattery. "Well, that matter has been resolved. The defendant entered a guilty plea at his arraignment yesterday, and he has been sentenced, so there will be no need for her to answer those papers."

"Yes, I know. Sam Schultz called me yesterday afternoon and told me that good news." Sara said. "I told Maria that she will not have to testify now. I also explained that today's meeting is about helping them get citizenship and avoid deportation. Just give me one more moment with them alone, and then I'll call you in."

"Wait," Mark called out, causing Sara to pause and turn back toward him. "How good is their English?"

Sara tried to conceal a smirk, but Kelly saw it. "Their English is excellent, Mr. Slattery." She turned and disappeared into her office, leaving Kelly and Mark standing uncomfortably silent.

"You're dressed up for a Saturday," Kelly joked.

"I have a thing in Philly after this," Mark said.

"Does this thing involve a country club?" Kelly regretted it as soon as the words left her mouth.

"Yes, as a matter of fact it does, and lunch, do you have a problem with that?" Mark asked, feigning anger.

"No, not at all, Mark," Kelly said quickly. "That's why you are a master rainmaker."

"It's actually a boring meeting about the Mayor's bid for a second term. God, I'd rather be hitting a tennis ball on such a beautiful Saturday."

"Well, I appreciate everything you did here. I really do. They are good, honest, hard-working people who deserve a break."

Sara's office door opened and she beckoned them forward. Juan jumped up from his chair as they entered the room, and walked toward them with his hand outstretched, to greet them. He was wearing a crisp white oxford shirt tucked into his jeans, and his black hair had been cut short. Maria remained seated with the baby sleeping in her arms. Kelly became uncomfortable as Mark's gaze lingered on Maria a little too long. Kelly noticed Maria's large expressive eyes, heart-shaped lips and long black hair. She wore the fatigue of a mother of a newborn, and yet she was still beautiful.

"Thank you. Thank you for everything." Juan said as he shook their hands.

"You're very welcome," Mark said nodding to Juan and to Maria.

"First, before Mark speaks about your immigration issues, I'd like to make sure you understand that the subpoena papers are of no concern to you anymore." Kelly paused to look at Maria. "The man who attacked me pleaded guilty, and the case is resolved. He's in prison now and will be there for a long time."

"Yes." Maria spoke softly, raising her eyes to look at Kelly as she did so. "Sara told us this same thing last night. Actually, she told my husband who was home at the time."

"I am so grateful that you took the risk and called the police that day—even though you were afraid of the attention it might bring to you. And I am sorry for the trouble it caused you."

"Now," Mark said. "If it is okay with everyone, I'd like to talk about your citizenship. Not for the little one of course—he beat you both to citizenship." Everyone in the room laughed. Juan smiled and Maria giggled softly as together they looked at their sleeping son. Mark pulled papers out of his briefcase and put them on the table. "Here's a copy of Juan's entire file at the Bureau of Citizenship and Immigration Services, which I'll call CIS." Anticipating questions from Sara and Kelly, Mark explained. "I have a friend who works there, so there was no problem in obtaining a copy."

"Anyway," he continued, "between this file and my discussions with my friend at CIS, it seems you are ready to get sworn in as a United States citizen, my good man." Kelly was grateful to see that Mark looked at Juan while talking to him.

"You came to the United States over five years ago legally, on a work visa, sponsored by relatives, right?"

"Yes," Juan answered, nodding.

"Okay," Mark continued. "So, about twelve months after you got here you received your green card, which officially means you had lawful permanent-resident status for about four more years." Mark spoke as he read notes in Juan's CIS file. "The rest of your folder tells me that you completed all of the paperwork necessary in your application for citizenship, you aced the English proficiency test, and you passed the history and civics stuff that they asked of you as well. On top of that, I see letters from a Catholic priest, a Father Delgado, who says you have been his loyal parishioner, and one from your current employer, John Stanhope of Stanhope Construction Company. Both letters state that you are of good moral character, which is a requirement for citizenship. Your boss goes so far as to say that you're his most trustworthy and dependable employee."

Kelly noticed Maria beamed with pride as she looked at Juan.

"So," Mark continued. "I asked my friend at CIS to find out what the hell was holding this thing up, and he told me they have a backlog now of anywhere from six to eighteen months. They seem to move along based on who is calling and making noise and how much influence they have. Your file was just buried somewhere. So we brought it to light and it's been deemed complete, and your citizenship qualifications have been signed off on." Mark produced a letter written on paper with the *United States Bureau of Citizenship and Immigration Services* engraved across the top. He handed it to Juan. Sara got up to read it over Juan's shoulder. "So, the only thing left for you to do is to show up at the New Castle County Courthouse on King Street Monday morning and take an oath in front of a judge."

"That's great news!" Sara said. "You'll be a full United States citizen on Monday."

Juan looked up when he finished reading the letter. His wide white smile dissolved as he caught Maria's expression of fear. "What about Maria?" Juan asked. "How do we make her a citizen? How do we protect her against deportation?"

Mark cleared his throat. "Well, Maria is a little tricky,

because she came here illegally and is still here illegally."

Maria looked like she was going to cry. Juan got up from his chair and went over to put his hand on her shoulder protectively. "She had to come illegally. We were too scared to wait for a sponsor and this whole process to work its way through. We were afraid we would lose each other."

"No one is coming after Maria." Mark said. "She will be fine. Just please let me explain." He went on, "As a citizen, you can file papers to get a K-1 Visa, which is intended to get an alien fiancée into the country for a legal marriage to a U. S. citizen." Mark paused for a second, and then looked up at Sara as he spoke. "Of course, this is intended for people who are literally living in their country, and then come here legally with the K-1 Visa. So I asked my friend at CIS, confidentially and uhm, hypothetically, what happens when the alien fiancée is here already, and he said that he is able to take care of that. There are waiver provisions for 'humanitarian purposes' and 'to assure family unity' that apply here. With the circumstances at hand, the lawyers involved, and my connections, this is going to happen and soon."

The room was very quiet for a moment. Mark cleared his throat awkwardly, and spoke again. "I hope I was correct in assuming that you do want to get married. That is what I was told by Kelly."

"Oh, yes. Definitely." Juan was still standing over Maria's shoulder and looking down at his sleeping son when he spoke. "That is our dream, of course. We were just waiting until we had this whole citizenship thing straightened out."

"Well, that's what you'll do then," Mark said, confidently. "You'll get your citizenship, Maria will get her fiancée visa status, and then you'll marry. After that, it will be even easier to get the permanent residence status for your wife, and then eventually, her citizenship."

Kelly chimed in. "Sara and I will go with you on Monday for your citizenship oath, which will be administered in private by a judge who's doing us a favor. Then, as soon as Mark has Maria's visa, we'll go with you to get the marriage license. We can help you through the paperwork and the process and we know the system. It will all be okay."

"Whew," Juan said, as he ran his hand through his close-cropped hair. "I really appreciate everything you are doing for us."

"You're welcome. I could never do enough to thank Maria for the risks she took for me."

"Okay, then," Mark said. "I must leave for an appointment in Philly."

Sara spoke up. "We really appreciate everything you've done, Mark."

"My pleasure," Mark said. He stood up and collected his suit jacket off of the back of his chair. He half-bowed toward Maria and Juan and said, "My congratulations on the baby, and your citizenship, and of course the pending nuptials. You are a very, very lucky man," he said to Juan.

Juan nodded in agreement and again put his arm around Maria protectively.

As soon as the door shut behind Mark, Sara said, "He's a bit of a stuffed shirt at first, but he seems genuinely nice. And his contacts and know-how around the CIS was really just what we needed."

"Yes, he's a good guy once you get to know him," Kelly said. "I'll see you Monday morning, nine sharp, at Magistrate Judge Kelso's chambers for the administration of your oath."

A warm feeling filled Kelly as she drove home along the rural roads of Hockessin, humming to Van Morrison's *Sweet Thing* on the radio.

CHAPTER 39

CHAD: OCTOBER 10, 2011

CHAD PULLED HIS baseball cap down over his eyes, crossed his arms in front of his chest and straightened his legs out as much as he could under the seat in front of him. He sat on the aisle with two empty seats to his right. He felt self-conscious as the other passengers entered the plane, imagining that they all recognized him as the falsely accused rapist.

After walking out of prison, exhausted and drained by the constant stress that he had endured there, Chad spent several days clearing out his parents' home. He had worked furiously, grabbing everything that was portable and stuffing it into huge trash bags, without any regard for its use or value. The only exceptions were the clothing and small items he packed in his suitcase, and his mother's few possessions which he carefully boxed and labeled with a black Sharpie, *Louisa Chadbourne*. Stuart had come through again, arranging for a trash removal company to remove all the bags, and Kelly Malloy had insisted on paying for their services. Kelly was going to ship the boxes to Louisa's home in Eugene a week later.

Chad paged through a worn copy of the airline's SkyMall catalogue. As he tried to focus on the merchandise pictured, he saw instead the doors of the prison closing behind him. He smelled his musty old bedroom as he tossed and turned during his last few nights there, alone in the little farmhouse and haunted by the memories it held. He recalled how he stuffed his father's old terrycloth robe and his empty beer bottles into the same garbage bag, hating him with a fury as he worked. He remembered the eerie silence and loneliness of his old house as he ran back inside one last time to retrieve the remaining cash out of the coffee can in the kitchen.

As passengers continued to settle into the plane, Chad felt fatigued. The soft amber glow of the sunset spilled through the tiny glass window, making him even drowsier. He slumped down in his seat but could not fall asleep. The maelstrom of emotions inside of him raged; relief, grief, anger, fear, anticipation and longing.

"Excuse me," Chad heard a voice.

He looked up and saw a slim young woman with big green eyes, an easy smile and yellow curly hair that framed her face and cascaded over her shoulders and back. She wore a green-and-yellow University of Oregon Ducks football sweatshirt. Chad was so startled that he did not hear her words.

"Uhm, excuse me, but, I think you're in my seat," she said while glancing at her boarding pass.

"I'm sorry," Chad said, as he got up and moved over to the window seat. "I've never done this before," he blurted awkwardly—instantly regretting the comment. He blushed. Once again, he was the weird kid who couldn't talk to girls.

"You mean you've never flown before?"

"No. I haven't." Chad tipped his baseball cap further down, and pretended to try to sleep.

"Why is that?"

"I never got the chance, I guess," he responded. "My childhood was not exactly the kind where your parents take you to Disney World for spring break."

"Wow," the girl said. "I've been on a plane probably twenty times. But if it makes you feel better, I've never been to Disney World, either." The girl gave a little laugh then she reached her hand out to Chad and said, "I'm Lisa Hughes, by the way."

Chad awkwardly took her hand and shook it over the still-empty middle seat. He thought about "Sad Chad" and the kids mocking him on the school bus. After a moment, he said confidently, "Chad McCloskey. My real name is Chadbourne, but I go by Chad."

"Chad, huh? That's a cool name," Lisa said. "Why are you going to Seattle?"

"I'm going to Oregon actually, connecting in Seattle."

"Awesome!" Lisa exclaimed. "I'm going to Eugene, too!" She pointed to the lettering on her sweatshirt to corroborate her claim. "Are you a student there?"

"No, I'm not a student. It's a long story."

"I'd like to hear your long story if you don't mind telling it. We have about nine hours of travel time together, with our stop in Seattle. And that's after we manage to get off of this runway... Philly is notorious for delayed takeoffs." Lisa laughed again.

Chad felt a flutter in his stomach. He liked how comfortably she said the words, "nine hours of travel time *together*." He had never had a conversation with a girl his age—yet she seemed warm and easy to talk to. He started to speak slowly, cautiously. "My mother moved to Eugene, so I'm going to see her."

"Oh, you mean your parents are divorced?" Lisa asked.

Chad sat quietly in response to Lisa's question. He knew he could not tell her what his circumstances really were. It seemed creepy even to him and he did not want to be the creepy kid. Before he could open his mouth however, Lisa moved over to the empty seat between them and she began speaking again.

"My parents are divorced. They have been since I was twelve years old. I was just visiting my dad in Philadelphia, for his birthday. He is a professor at Penn. My mom is a professor too, she is at University of Oregon," Lisa pointed to the *O* on her sweatshirt again.

"Wow, so that's why you're a veteran air traveler. Where do you live?"

Before Lisa could answer, a man's voice boomed out of the speaker above them. "Air traffic control just told us we are twelfth in line for take-off, so we are looking at a delay here on the ground and I will keep you posted as we go."

In the midst of the collective groan of the passengers, Chad heard Lisa say, "I could have predicted that. Philly is always such a mess." She reached into a blue knapsack and pulled out two Powerbars, offering one to Chad. "Want one?"

"No thanks, I'm good," Chad said, waving his hand.

Lisa leaned slightly toward Chad and resumed her lively conversation as if he were an old friend. "I grew up in Eugene. My parents were grad students there and they both became professors at UO. My dad took a job in Philadelphia when I was thirteen. He said it was a tremendous opportunity, that I could visit him on holidays and summers, and that I'd be in college before I knew it." Chad thought that Lisa looked less cheerful than her tone suggested. "Now I'm in college, but still in Eugene."

"So, you live with your mother?"

"Now I live at OSU. I'm in a crummy freshman dorm right now, but I'm going to rent a house near campus next year with a few friends." Lisa said.

Chad was still quiet. He was afraid he would say something he'd regret and he was quite content to just stare at this beautiful girl sitting with him.

"Do you go to school anywhere?" Lisa asked.

"No. I mean, not now," Chad stammered. He sat up straighter in his chair and said, "I finished high school last June and had a bunch of stuff happen that sort of delayed my college plan."

"Oh, I see." Lisa asked. Something about Chad's pained expression caused her to stop there. She opened a magazine and started to casually flip through the pages. After about five minutes of silence, she spoke again.

"I know it's not my business. I'll shut up if you want me to, but, are you okay?" Lisa asked softly. Her voice stirred something inside of Chad, literally taking his breath away. Chad sat silent.

"Oh, my God, did I offend you? I am so sorry, Chad," Lisa said. She lifted her arm and briefly touched Chad's hand resting on the armrest between them. "I'm sorry I asked if your parents are divorced. I always say the wrong thing. I am so sorry." Lisa stammered. "Damn, I always say the dumbest things."

Chad took off his cap, and ran his fingers through his thick hair. Lisa watched the ripples of his bicep and forearm. "I'm really sorry, Chad." Lisa repeated. "I don't know why I asked such a personal question."

He cleared his throat and spoke slowly, carefully. "No, I'm sorry. It's a lot weirder than a divorce." He paused. "But I also feel this strange need to tell you." Chad smiled a little at this last statement, causing Lisa to smile back.

"Try me," Lisa said. She raised her hand and placed it briefly on Chad's shoulder, trying to reassure him. A loud voice over the speaker caused him to jump. "We have been cleared for take-off. Please remain seated with your seat belts on and your tray tables in the upright position."

Chad braced himself as he felt the plane accelerate down the runway. His hands tensed on the armrest of his chair as the runway and the lights of the Philadelphia airport became a blur of motion outside the window next to him. His heart raced. The five slender fingers that gently covered his hand sent a tingle through his whole body.

"It's okay, Chad." Lisa said. "This is normal: we're going to be up in the air in one second and it will be a piece of cake."

So, this is what it feels like to connect with someone, he thought.

Once the plane leveled off, Chad began to tell Lisa his story, starting with his childhood. He told her about the harsh and lonely life his mother had endured in their little ramshackle house in the woods. He told her that Louisa had been an orphan, and that his father was both her rescuer and her captor. He described his father's mean words, his cold, harsh manner and his drunken binges. He explained how his beautiful and loving mother withered away before his eyes and he could do little to help her. Chad left out the part about his having no friends and the years that he went to and from school just trying to be invisible. When he told Lisa about his mother's sudden disappearance, Lisa gasped and put her hand to her mouth.

"It's okay," Chad said softly. "I know now that she's living in Eugene and I know things are about to get better." He liked the way Lisa looked at him. He would no longer play the part of the shy outcast or lonely loser that his father had cast him in before.

"What did your dad say about you going to Oregon?" Lisa asked.

"My father died twelve days ago." Chad said without any emotion.

"Oh, my gosh!" Lisa squeezed his hand. "I am really, really sorry! That is too much to deal with."

Chad nodded his head. *You have no idea,* he thought. "I am sorry for my dad, you know, because he is dead. But he was the meanest person I ever knew, and all he ever did was hurt my mom and try hard to keep me under his control by scaring me and putting me down. He didn't really act like a father or a husband, if you know what I mean."

Lisa shook her head slowly in understanding, as she recalled the warm embrace her father had given her only two hours earlier as they said goodbye in the airport. "Wow, you must have been really strong." Lisa said. "I never could have gotten through that."

Chad had not looked at it that way. Someone was admiring him for his strength and his maturity. "Thanks, I'm okay. I am going to see my mother in Oregon, and hopefully stay there, maybe with her. I might even go to UO, who knows." Chad tipped his hat brim down and settled into his seat a little, as if he was finally able to relax. He turned his overhead light out, crossed his arms across his chest and put his head against the window of the plane.

"I'm really wiped out, too," Lisa said, quietly. "I really feel good talking to you....and I'd love to see you in Eugene. I could show you around the place, introduce you to my friends. Do you bike? There are incredible trails there where we could ride."

Chad turned to look at Lisa. "You're unbelievable." He said with a smile. "You don't quit, do you?"

She smiled back. "Too much?"

"No, not at all," Chad said. He had an overwhelming gratefulness for her, and a need to be with her at that moment and thereafter. He felt comfort, strength and possibility. He summoned up his courage, pushed up the seat armrest separating them, put his arm around her shoulders and drew her close to him. "You are already the best thing that's happened to me in a long, long time."

They sat like that, quietly, in the darkness of the plane for a long time. A movie flickered and droned on, a beverage cart rattled up the aisle, and Chad dozed off to sleep with the warmth of Lisa's breath on his neck.

During their connecting flight from Seattle to Eugene, Chad gazed at Lisa as she slept with her head on his shoulder. He would be eternally grateful that, as they entered the plane to Eugene, she had been bold enough to ask the man seated next to

Chad to switch seats with her. He didn't want their closeness to end and he did not want to walk out of the Eugene airport alone.

As the plane had taxied toward blinking lights of the Eugene airport, Lisa pulled out her cell phone and turned it on. "Let me give you my number and email address, and you can give me yours."

Embarrassed, Chad pulled out a cell phone he had purchased the day before. It had no numbers on it—he'd had no one to call. He wasn't even sure how to use it. He turned it over surreptitiously, grateful that he had scribbled its number on the back with a Sharpie.

"Give me that," Lisa said as she put out her hand. Chad gave her the phone and watched her enter her name and phone number. "Here is how you call me," she said, showing him the buttons to push. "I really doubt that I have ever been the first phone number in any cell phone before. I'm honored," she said, handing him back the phone.

Passengers were getting up now, starting to move up the aisle and disembark from the plane. Chad helped Lisa get a bulky bag out of the overhead. Lisa asked, "How are you getting to your mother's from the airport?"

"I guess I was going to get a cab."

"You can ride with me. My roommate Janine is meeting me. She won't mind at all."

*****

As they approached the exit doors near baggage pickup, where Lisa said her ride would be waiting, Chad reached out and grabbed her elbow. "Wait, Lisa."

"What?" She looked startled.

"I really appreciate everything, but I'm going to see my mother."

"Yeah, I know," Lisa said. "I think that's awesome."

"But I haven't seen her in almost five months....and I told you how she left, abruptly, just disappeared. I don't know if she'll be home or how she'll react, or what this even means." Chad nervously ran his hand through his hair.

"Oh, I hadn't really thought about all of that. It's pretty scary, huh?" Lisa touched his elbow gently again. "Janine and

I will take you straight to her address. If she's not there, we can wait a while, and after that, you can crash with us tonight and try again tomorrow."

Chad briefly considered the thought of spending the night near Lisa. But his urgent desire to see his mother was too much. "Thank you. You are amazing."

Lisa laughed. "Well, don't think I meet strange men on airplanes all the time. You're my first." The double exit doors slid open and the two young travelers walked out into the crisp Oregon air.

Twenty-five minutes later, Chad sat in the back seat of an old Volkswagen Jetta, as Lisa's friend Janine chatted and drove along Route 99, toward downtown Eugene. He fingered the scrap of paper with his mother's address typed on it. They pulled off the busy road and made a few turns on quiet neighborhood streets. Lisa interrupted his thoughts. "Chad, this is the address."

Chad looked up, seized with fear. A small yellow Cape Cod-style home with overgrown flower boxes in its windows sat back from the road. A thick green hedge formed a fence in front of the lawn. He noticed a porch light shining by the front door, and soft light coming through the windows. He got out of the car with great difficulty: his legs felt wooden. "Well, I guess this is it." He took a deep breath and steadied himself, as he swung his bag over his shoulder. "I can never thank you enough, Lisa. And you too, Janine, thank you for the ride."

"We'll hang out to make sure she's home."

"I'll be okay, really. I'll figure it out. It's late. I don't want you to be inconvenienced any more."

Lisa got out of the car and walked around to the side where Chad stood. She wrapped her arms around him. He hugged her back for a moment and then said, "I'll call you soon. I mean it."

Lisa got back in the car and directed Janine to pull up a little so she could watch from a distance. She saw Chad walk slowly up the lawn toward the front door of the house, his bag slung over his back. She thought that he looked vulnerable as he rang the bell and stood motionless. The door opened and she saw a petite woman with long, wavy raven hair shriek joyfully as she embraced Chad and then brought him into his home and shut the door.

CHAPTER 40

MARIA: NOVEMBER 19, 2011

MARIA TREMBLED AS she entered the center aisle of the church. She smoothed the front of her gown and took a deep breath to calm herself as the beginning chords of *Ave Maria* filled the air. As Juan's Uncle Miguel took her arm gently to walk her down the aisle, she felt a pang of regret that it was not her father's arm that she was holding. She focused straight ahead, on her family. Juan looked handsome and almost regal in a rented black tuxedo. Only steps away, Baby Miguel slept in the arms of Juan's Aunt Sabrina, their maid of honor. Maria quickened her pace as she got closer to her family, feeling their pull.

As Maria knelt and stood and sat through the long Catholic mass, she took a moment to peek out into the faces in the church. Many of the faces were familiar; mostly cousins and relatives of Juan's, first- and second-generation Mexican-Americans. Toward the back of the church, Maria spotted a few men that Juan worked with and a couple of Maria's co-workers from Cleaning Angels. In the second-to-last row on the right hand side, sitting near the center aisle, was Kelly Malloy and her husband and two daughters. Maria remembered the fateful day that brought Kelly into her life, and the events it set into motion, culminating in this day.

Maria woke from her thoughts as Juan reached out to hold her hand. "It's time to get married." Maria and Juan rose from the bench they shared on the side of the altar during the mass, and moved together to stand directly in front of the altar, with Father Delgado at their side.

"Maria Anna Hernandez, do you promise to love Juan for the rest of your life, in sickness and in health, whether rich or poor, through good times and in bad?"

Maria looked into Juan's eyes and wiped a tear from her eye as she spoke softly, "I do."

A moment later, after Juan was asked the same question, he enthusiastically wrapped his arms around Maria as he declared, "Yes, I do," and then kissed Maria hard.

Father Delgado spoke while Juan was still embracing his wife. "Well, ladies and gentlemen, this is the part where I usually say you may kiss the bride, but I see that is not necessary for the newlywed Mr. and Mrs. Reyes." Laughter rose from the wedding guests.

Later, at the Hockessin Fire Hall, a band played lively music and people danced. Little white Christmas lights had been strung up and a few potted trees had been brought in to make the hall look festive. Juan's Aunt and Uncle had provided matching white tablecloths and floral centerpieces for the ten round tables in the hall. Long tables around the sides of the hall held an abundant array of food and drinks to serve the guests. A three-tiered wedding cake with white frosting stood as the centerpiece to the buffet, courtesy of Juan's employer, and a large empty area in the middle of the hall served as the dance floor.

Maria was still greeting guests when the band had stopped playing abruptly and she saw Juan speaking into a microphone on the dance floor, holding a champagne flute in his hand. "Maria," Juan said, gesturing for her to join him. She hurried through the crowd toward Juan.

"Maria," Juan said as he took her hand and faced their guests. "I want to thank you for your love and for our beautiful son, Miguel. And I will be forever grateful that you took risks, and you struggled and worked very hard to follow me here to begin our life together. So first, we raise our glasses to toast my beautiful wife, Maria." He raised his glass and then took a small sip.

"Second, I want to thank my Uncle Miguel and Aunt Sabrina for bringing me to this country and loving me like a son. I also want to thank them for welcoming Maria as their own daughter, and for making this wedding party so perfect."

The guests raised their drinks again, to join Juan in the toast.

After a moment Juan spoke again. "And third, to new friends, friends who we may not have met if it were not for some hard times, but friends who immediately jumped in and helped us without hesitation, and who by doing so ensured our bright future here in this country, Sara Nuñez and Kelly Malloy."

Maria looked beyond the throng of guests standing by the dance floor. She spotted Kelly and Sara seated at a table, both looking up in surprise at the mention of their names. Both of them smiled, and held their wine glasses up to meet Juan's toast.

"And finally," Juan spoke yet again. "Our wedding ceremony and this party are being recorded as a gift from a friend." Juan looked at Kelly when he said these words. "And now we can share it with Maria's parents, who could not be here. To Maria's mother and father, I raise my glass to you and tell you I cannot wait to share this video with you, in sunny Baja, yes, but also here in our new home, with our children circled around you." As Juan raised his glass toward the videographer, Maria wiped tears from her eyes and then wrapped her arms around Juan tightly, causing his glass to spill. They laughed and hugged each other as if to never let go.

"I love you so much, Juan." Maria whispered to her new husband. "I am happier than I ever dreamed, with you, Miguel, everything here in a place we can all finally call home."

CHAPTER 41

KELLY: NOVEMBER 20, 2011

KELLY'S FEET HIT the soft mossy trail along the river and her breathing was slow and steady. Despite her hangover from too much tequila at Maria's wedding, it felt great to be running. Chance bounded ahead, chasing an occasional squirrel. It was a cool, dry November day, and the absence of the leaves on the trees made the view of the river that much more spectacular. The steady sound of the waterfall near Breck's Mill was punctuated by the calls of the waterfowl.

She stopped short for a moment when she saw the "Sold" sign where Chad McCloskey's house once stood. The little farmhouse had been reduced to piles of splintered wood, shingles, and crumbled bricks. A large dumpster was filled with other remnants of the home. The demolition work had been halted for that Sunday morning, but Kelly knew that soon there would be no trace of the building that had stood as a reminder of loneliness, anguish and despair.

Chance trotted back to Kelly and started nosing her with his big tan head.

"Okay, boy, I know you want to go. Pace yourself: we still have to climb this long hill home."

ACKNOWLEDGMENTS

I am deeply grateful to John Koëhler for giving me a shot and for taking a risk on a debut novelist, and to Joe Coccaro for his time and wisdom in editing my manuscript. I am also grateful to Marshall McClure, for her careful proofreading and for polishing up my punctuation and grammar.

I'd like to thank Danielle at Dalitopia Media for creating the perfect book cover for Long Hill Home, and for her artistic and technical genius in helping me with social media.

I'd like to thank Steve Wood for letting me pick his brain on Delaware criminal law and procedure, and Cynthia Pruitt, for providing insight into legal advocacy in association with the LACC.

I am grateful for my parents, who taught me that it's OK to dream, as long as I am prepared to roll up my sleeves and get to work to realize the dream.

Finally, I am eternally grateful for my family. They are the reason I know the true meaning of the word *home*.

QUESTIONS AND TOPICS FOR DISCUSSION

1. TOPIC: The concept of *home* is woven throughout this novel. Kelly looks through her office window and toward her home in the Highlands as she has an uncomfortable conversation with Jack Barnard. During her morning run, she likes to climb a steep hill that is physically challenging, *because* it takes her home. Maria feels unmoored in her life with Juan in their modest one bedroom apartment in a poor section of the city. She reminisces about her home in the Baja Peninsula and she struggles to share Juan's optimism about the wonderful home that will someday be theirs. Chad runs into the woods filled with rage and despair when his mother leaves him, but as he walks back toward his sad little farmhouse, it "no longer felt like home." Later, when Chad believes his mother is living in Arizona and then discovers that she is in Oregon, his sole desire is to be with her wherever she is, because she is his home.

Questions: What is the author saying about the concept of home?

Is it different for Kelly, Maria or Chad—or do they all have similar feelings about what the word home means?

Is this concept of home a universal concept?

2. TOPIC: Throughout the novel the reader is reminded that Kelly, Maria and Chad live and work in locations proximate to each other. Kelly reflects on this when she drives home from work and when she stands in front of Maria's apartment, "only eight blocks" from Kelly's "shiny office building" and "only a few miles from her large home in the Highlands." Chad has childhood memories of standing at the top of Rockford Tower, at the edge of "his woods," and seeing the Highlands neighborhood below him and the buildings of downtown Wilmington just beyond the Highlands. Maria cleans the big houses in the Highlands and the "shiny office buildings" of Wilmington, and yet she travels only a short distance to return home to an apartment in a poor section of Wilmington.

Questions: Why do you think the author emphasizes how Chad, Maria and Kelly geographically live in the same small world?

Do their vastly different economic or social circumstances factor into this discussion point?

Does their physical proximity make it more interesting that they are complete strangers when they meet as a result of Kelly's attack?

3. TOPIC: Chad discovers Kelly's unconscious body only moments after waking and deciding, "he could not wait any longer.....he was leaving, he could bear it no longer."

Questions: Do you think Chad's state of mind that morning before he found Kelly had any bearing on his decision to move Kelly's body to the trail—and let "someone else" rescue her?

Can you identify other experiences that Chad endured that may have affected him and would cause him to make such a poor decision about Kelly's rescue?

4. TOPIC: In the aftermath of her attack, Kelly expresses anger toward her husband Dan, despite the fact that he cares for her in such a loving and loyal way.

Question: Why is Kelly angry with Dan?

5. TOPIC: Stuart Harlan, the Public Defender assigned to represent Chad, explains that he "just graduated from law school last year," and that Chad's case is his "first felony."

Questions: Does Stuart's youth and inexperience help Chad relate to him more and open up to him easier?

Does the fact that both Chad and his attorney are young and inexperienced cause the reader to empathize with them more and care more about the result of Chad's prosecution?

6. TOPIC: When introducing their baby boy to the doctor and nurse in the delivery room, Juan declares that Miguel "will be his name on his birth certificate," and that they, "will call him Michael mostly."

Questions: Why does Juan say this?

Do you think Maria and Juan will feel more comfortable calling their baby by his real name, Miguel, at some point in the future?

7. TOPIC: Sam Schultz tells Kelly in very clear terms that she'll "have no contact at all" with Maria before the proceedings involving her attack are completely over.

Questions: Why does Kelly feel compelled to stand in front of Maria's apartment and walk on her sidewalk?

Does Kelly truly believe that she is not violating Sam's rules when she visits Maria's lawyer-- Sara Nuñez-- to offer her partner's legal assistance in obtaining Juan's citizenship? Or does Kelly's rationalization as to why that brief meeting was appropriate ring hollow?

Is it difficult to get angry with Kelly in any event, since she is motivated solely by her need to help Maria?

8. TOPIC: Sam Schultz is described as having an unrequited love for Kelly, in the past when they were law students, and in the present while he prosecutes her rapist.

Question: Does Sam's strong feelings for Kelly enhance or diminish his ability to do his job in prosecuting Jack Barnard? How?

9. TOPIC: On the eve of his release from prison, Chad is the victim of a terribly traumatic rape attempt. He experiences terror and pain, and is saved just seconds before he is a rape victim.

Questions: Was this experience in the novel to help you sympathize with Chad, with Kelly, or with both?

Does it affect Chad's understanding of Kelly—or his interaction with her when they finally meet?

10. TOPIC: When Chad is on the airplane, waiting to take off on the journey to his mother, he meets a beautiful and talkative girl his age, Lisa. He tries hard to not "be the creepy kid" any more. In stead, he finds Lisa to be warm, relatable, and genuinely interested in connecting with him. She forges an easy relationship with Chad at a time when he needs it most.

Questions: Is Lisa's personality and genuine interest in Chad the reason that Chad can finally make a positive and natural connection with another person? OR

Is Chad a different person when he meets Lisa, and therefore finally able to see this possibility in her and respond to it appropriately?

If you believe Chad is a different person when he meets Lisa, explain how he has changed and why.

CPSIA information can be obtained at www.ICGtesting.com
Printed in the USA
BVOW07s1605231214

380610BV00001B/1/P